Osmun Johnson

Johnson's Journey Around the World

Fifty Thousand Miles of Travel, from the Golden Gate to the Golden Gate - Vol. 1

Osmun Johnson

Johnson's Journey Around the World
Fifty Thousand Miles of Travel, from the Golden Gate to the Golden Gate - Vol. 1

ISBN/EAN: 9783337127879

Printed in Europe, USA, Canada, Australia, Japan

Cover: Foto ©Andreas Hilbeck / pixelio.de

More available books at **www.hansebooks.com**

JOHNSON'S

Journey Around the World.

FIFTY THOUSAND MILES OF TRAVEL, FROM THE GOLDEN GATE TO
THE GOLDEN GATE. INTERESTING OBSERVATIONS IN
VARIOUS COUNTRIES OF EUROPE.

TWICE ACROSS THE ALPS.

SIGHTS IN EGYPT, INDIA, AFRICA, NEW ZEALAND AND THE
SANDWICH ISLANDS.

SIX THOUSAND MILES THROUGH AUSTRALIA.

DARING ADVENTURES OF A LONE WHITE MAN AMONG THE NATIVES IN
THE INTERIOR OF CEYLON, CHINA AND JAPAN. TWELVE
TIMES ACROSS THE WESTERN CONTINENT, WITH
A DESCRIPTION OF ALL THE VARIOUS
ROUTES AND SIGHTS OF
INTEREST.

BY OSMUN JOHNSON.

SOLD BY SUBSCRIPTION.

CHICAGO.
1887.

Printers, Publishers and Engravers,
Chicago.

PREFACE.

During thirty years' residence in California, I have led a busy life, enduring much hard toil and the many privations incident to life in the gold mines in early days. I have pursued many different avocations: mind and body have been in constant motion. After such an exciting career I resolved to take a rest, and have a change of scene ; to travel abroad, and visit all of the principal places of note ; to traverse the ocean, and to feast my eyes and mind upon the wonders of the Old World. For the last twenty years I have had an increasing desire to take a spin around the ball. I felt it to be the greatest gift and treat that I could bestow upon myself, and finally determined to put my ambitious desire into execution. So I hastily prepared to go, and made arrangements to remain as long as I should find enjoyment among an unknown people in unknown lands. Now, what I rely on to make this simple narrative interesting is not the talent or literary training that I have had, but my ability to present, in an original manner, the information obtained, not only from guides and interpreters, but from my own observation.

During my travels I kept a daily record of events and incidents connected with my tour around the world. And in writing an account of this extended tour, brief mention will be made of my adventures on this continent, across which I have made twelve different trips during the last thirty years; I shall state the years the journeys were made in, the different routes traveled, the distance, and the principal points of interest on each one. As this narrative is to be filled up with mixed material, and possibly presented in a somewhat rambling manner, the writer asks the indulgence of the reader, as he makes this his first venture in the new and untried field of literature, remembering always that a wide difference frequently exists between the farmer and the educated traveler, the plowshare and the pen.

OSMUN JOHNSON.

MODESTO, CAL., August 5, 1887.

CONTENTS.

(5)

ILLUSTRATIONS.

CHAPTER I.

THE UNITED STATES.

BEFORE starting on such a long and perilous journey, it became a matter of great importance to select to advantage the best routes of travel o'er land and sea; to visit the frigid regions in Europe during the warmest season of the year, so as to avoid the oppressive cold; to travel in the tropical climes of Asia and Africa during that portion of the year when the terrific heat of the sun's rays would be the least oppressive, and to avoid the dangerous monsoons and typhoons that prevail at certain seasons of the year. Many travelers had gone before me, and many had never returned, and, keeping this fact in view, I endeavored to so shape my journey as to avoid all of the dangers incident to such a trip. I had traveled over the various routes on this continent before starting on this tour, except by way of the Northern Pacific Railway; and, as this route traversed a country which I had never seen, I decided to take it, and thus avail myself of an opportunity to view the grand and picturesque scenery on the Columbia River, the Cascade Mountains in Oregon, the Yellowstone, the great National Park, the Geysers, etc. So I left instructions in regard to my business affairs, and started out on my rambles, promising myself to take in all that was worth seeing in Europe and the Orient.

Before beginning to give a description of the varied scenes I witnessed in my travels, the panorama of faces, skies, cities, mountain, valley and desert, I am going to give a brief description of my home in the once far-off West. I started from Modesto, a thriving, enterprising little city situated in the San Joaquin Valley, the great wheat region of California. This beautiful little place of between three and four thousand inhabitants is exceedingly well located in the centre of a grain-growing country. It is the county seat of Stanislaus County,—has many fine and substantial buildings, both business and private; has the advantages of a healthful climate, and nearness to all the large commercial centres of the State; has splendid schools and many churches. So, after bidding adieu to my many friends at this place, I boarded the train, and was soon speeding away over the plains. The chief attraction on this line was the wheat fields dotted with bags filled with grain awaiting transportation,—for we of this valley can raise grain enough to feed the hungry at home and abroad and have an abundance to spare. Everywhere could be seen the indications of a bountiful harvest, the reward which always rejoices the heart of the tiller of the soil.

The first point of interest on this route is Port Costa, on San Francisco Bay. It is one of the greatest wheat depots in the State, and has an immense warehouse capacity. Here the farmer of a speculating turn of mind stores his wheat, and takes chances on the rise and fall of the market. The Star Mills, the largest flouring mills in California, are located near here, and some of the largest ocean vessels afloat can always be seen at the wharves loading the precious cargo. At Port Costa there is also a railway ferry boat of enormous size which is used in transporting overland passenger trains across the straits to the Benicia side.

From here I journeyed on to Oakland, the city of churches, seminaries, and colleges of learning, and, so far as piety and good morals are concerned, considered the model city in the State, not excepting San José. Oakland is noted for its elegant private residences, its parks and gardens, its profusion of majestic live oaks, and the picturesque beauty and variety of scenery by which it is surrounded. Many of the wealthy citizens of San Francisco and a large number of retired farmers have their homes here, where they and their families can enjoy the many educational and other advantages of this quiet city.

Five miles from Oakland, on the opposite side of

San Francisco Bay, I found myself in the bustling city of San Francisco. This city is famous for its magnificent harbor and its exports of gold and wheat,—it is the largest city of the Pacific coast, and is the fourth city of the United States in foreign commerce ; it has a population of 350,000. San Francisco is lined with costly edifices, from Golden Gate Park to the home of the lucky millionaire on Nob Hill. A few of the many attractions this city contains are Golden Gate Park, the Cliff House, the Presidio; Telegraph Hill, from which you obtain a fine view of the bay, Oakland, Saucelito, and, in fact, of all the surrounding country; Woodward's Gardens, Sutro Heights, the Panorama, Theatres, Operas and Museums. It has a goodly number of fine hotels, the most extensive of which is the Palace. This hotel was erected at a cost of four millions of dollars, and is the largest caravansary in the world. In my estimation, the Southern in St. Louis, the Palmer House in Chicago, or the Windsor in New York are inferior in comparison with the Palace. The city contains many magnificent cathedrals and imposing structures, and possesses every facility and advantage to enable it to maintain its position as the metropolis of the Pacific coast.

On the 25th day of July, 1885, I embarked on the coast steamer State of California for Portland, Oregon,—a distance of 800 miles from

CALIFORNIA STREET, SAN FRANCISCO.

(13)

San Francisco.   As we moved out from the dock,
we waved a last adieu with our hats and handker-
chiefs to the friends we left behind us.   This last
parting will long be remembered.   Soon the faces
of those we loved were left in the dim distance; and,
as we sailed out of the Golden Gate into the broad
Pacific, I felt this to be the practical beginning of
a long and perilous journey, and it led to queries
in my own mind as to whether I should ever return
to my home in sunny California, or whether I
should meet the fate of many an adventurous
traveler who has found a last resting place in some
distant clime or been consigned to the tender mercies of the restless deep.   This portion of the
Pacific was not pacific, a fact soon determined by
many of the passengers, who were decidedly sea-
sick.   At sea this most disagreeable of sickness is
called "feeding the fishes."   The swell of the sea
and the roll of the vessel soon proved too much
for a landsman like myself, and I joined the number of *sea-sick* passengers.   But in my case the
sea-sickness lasted only two days, and I found myself with better health and a better appetite, so
concluded there was much truth in the old adage
that "it is an ill wind that blows no one any good."
After recovering my equilibrium I made new
friends and some interesting acquaintances, who
helped to make the days pass swiftly by.   On this
coast there is no object worthy of note after leav-

ing Cape Mendocino; and no incident worthy of mention occurred. We could see nothing but the fish, the broad expanse of water, and the blue sky overhead.

On the third day at sea we steamed into Astoria, at the mouth of the Columbia River. This place has the largest salmon fisheries in the world, and is about 650 miles from San Francisco. The bay in the vicinity of Astoria is dotted with fishing boats whose occupants are engaged in catching fish for the canning establishments. These unfortunate fishermen often meet with accident, and wrecks and loss of life are of frequent occurrence, as this is a stormy shore. Astoria is an old, flat, rusty-looking town, with wooded bluffs in the background. The surrounding country is well timbered. A large number of sailing craft can be seen from Astoria plying up and down the coast between Puget Sound and San Francisco; they are principally engaged in the lumber trade. The northern coast of California exports a large amount of choice lumber, such as sugar pine, spruce and redwood to Australia, Japan and the East.

After leaving Astoria we entered the famous Columbia River. On either side of this stream is a succession of elevated ranges thickly dressed in spruce and pine. When the powerful engine of our steamer had forced its way through the foaming current for 100 miles, we found ourselves at Portland, which is situated on the western bank of the Willamette River, a tributary of the Columbia. Portland is the metropolis of Oregon, and has a population of 40,000. It is said to be one of the richest cities in proportion to its size in the United States. It is well laid out, with many beautiful residences, and is destined, by reason of its natural advantages, to become a large city within the next twenty years. Several large ocean vessels were anchored at her wharves loading wheat for Europe. Oregon is blessed with a very rich soil, an abundance of rain, and an almost inexhaustible supply of timber; her many valleys are fertile and picturesque. The lofty eminence which girts the city of Portland seems to prove the greatest attraction for tourists. Here they can overlook the shipping, and the life and bustle in the city below. Here, also, can be seen the farms and groves of the broad Willamette Valley, and a distant view can be had of five of the largest mountains in the United States: Mount Hood, Mount Jefferson, Mount Tacoma, Mount Adams and Mount St. Helens. The peaks of these mountains are covered with perpetual snow.

After leaving Portland, I resumed my journey by rail for St. Paul, a distance of about 1,950 miles, which we made in less than four days. It seemed but a short space of time before we were over the Cascade Mountains and into Eastern

Oregon. Along this route, on the Columbia River, can be seen some of the finest railway engineering and wildest mountain scenery in the West; the further you follow the winding, foaming stream, the more the scenery increases in grandeur and interest. At Wallula Station we found that we had left the Web-foot State. Here I resumed my journey in the direction of Walla Walla. The country, as seen from the cars, presented a variety of scene and soil. At times fertile fields presented themselves to our view, again we were treated to a succession of hills covered with bunch grass, and at other times stretches of country which boasted of no vegetation but sage-brush met our view. As the eastern portion of Washington Territory is remote from the market, and has no extensive railway system to transport its products, wheat-raising is indulged in to but a limited extent. The principal industry is stock-raising ; vast herds of cattle can be seen grazing on the hills. At Ainsworth the cars crossed the Snake River on one of the largest iron bridges on the Northern Pacific. Spokane Falls is the last and one of the most important towns in Washington Territory. It is surrounded by timber, and contains several sights of interest, including the most imposing water-falls east of the Cascade Mountains. From here on to the Idaho line the land is uncultivated, and barren of vegetation. We crossed over into

2

Idaho, and journeyed along the shores of Lake Pend d'Orielle. This beautiful body of water is fed by snow from the surrounding peaks. Our road wound its way around these lofty mountains, until at last we found ourselves in the gateway of the Rocky Mountains. Here a grand sight met our eyes: the snow-covered peaks glistening in the sun, the streams and cataracts tearing their way down the mountain's side, all proclaimed this to be one of Nature's masterpieces. Idaho produces large amounts of gold and silver. We found the country to be thickly timbered, but poorly improved. The principal resources of this Territory are stock-raising and mining. Boise City, its capital, is the centre of a large mining district, and many extensive mines are in operation in its vicinity.

Speeding along at a rapid rate, we soon reached Montana, the finest stock-raising country on the Northern Pacific road. Vast herds of cattle could be seen all through this country: the land is mostly owned by the government, and these Montana stockmen have extensive ranges now, where probably, in a few years, when the tide of emigration turns that way, there will be many farms and the land will be extensively cultivated. Much of the beef is exported to Europe. In addition to her stock-raising interests, Montana has a fine climate, much rich soil, and great mineral wealth. At Mullen's Pass we crossed the main chain of the Rocky

Mountains, passing through a tunnel nearly 4,000 feet in length, and at an altitude of 5,500 above the level of the sea. The road eastward runs through a level valley which is well timbered. We found the scenery very picturesque. The next place of interest was Helena, the capital and largest city. It is situated on the eastern slope of the Rocky Mountains, and also near the headwaters of the Missouri River. The country on the northern side of the city has a panoramic appearance,—lofty mountain peaks loom up in the distance, and add much to the grandeur of the scene. Helena is the centre of one of the largest mining districts on the continent. In the last few years many million dollars have been taken from the soil, and there are a large number of extensive paying mines at present in operation. Montana, however, seems to have been designed by nature for a great pastoral country, and reaps larger returns from her stock-raising interests than from her mineral wealth.

As we journeyed eastward from Helena, I was much impressed by the extensive valleys : always could be seen in every direction the vast herds of cattle grazing on the seemingly abundant feed. To my mind, it was a perpetual reminder of beefsteak. At Livingston, 125 miles east of Helena, there is a branch road to the National Yellowstone Park, a distance of sixty miles. This famous resort I decided to visit, and while here I met tourists from home and abroad, who, like myself, had been impressed with a desire to witness one of nature's greatest wonders. This valley is enclosed by mountains, many over 10,000 feet in height. Its deep canyons, lofty falls and numerous bathing pools, geysers and lakes, make it in many respects the most wonderful portion of the continent, and even of the world. It has been set aside by Congress as a "perpetual reservation for the benefit and instruction of mankind." Some of the hot springs and geysers throw boiling water hundreds of feet into the air. Yellowstone Lake is seventeen miles wide by twenty miles long. Several small steamers on this lake convey the tourist to various points of interest. It strikes me it would be well to call this park the playground of America, as Switzerland is termed the playground of Europe.

Well, as the writer is a traveler on the wing, he resumes his journey on the main line. Journeying eastward from Livingston, we arrived at Glendive, an important trading post. We had now traveled 800 miles, the extreme length of Montana. While penciling these last notes in my memorandum book the iron horse has whirled us over the boundary line into Dakota. Medora is the first station on the Little Missouri. It is surrounded by many odd and curious hills, in all shapes and sizes, called "The Bad Lands," and I was fully convinced that these lands did not

belie their name; the soil seemed to be of every
kind and color ; great numbers of cattle were seen
grazing on every hill. Here, also, are extensive
hunting grounds; wolves, buffalo, deer and elk can
be found on the prairies. This must be a paradise for hunters. The next station we arrived at
was Dickenson, which is located in a fertile valley. It had the appearance of being a hunting
ground also, if one could judge from the variety
of stuffed deer, wolves, and the skins of wild animals which were hanging in sight and were for
sale at the depot. After passing New Salem, we
began to see new settlements, the first we had
seen in this remote region. Western Dakota has
a fertile soil, and vegetation grows luxuriantly.
It is, however, destitute of timber: this creates a
scarcity of fuel, which is a great drawback to the
prosperity of this section, where the winters are
long and severe. The coal which is used here
has to be brought a long distance, and at great
expense for transportation. Mandan is a thrifty
city of 3,000 inhabitants, situated on the west bank
of the Missouri River, about half way between the
Montana and Minnesota line, and is the terminal
point of the Dakota and Minnesota division of
the road.

The whole country west of Mandan is dotted
with rude farm houses. All of these farms are
scantily improved, and everything bears evidence

of newness and want of means. But the tiller of
the soil in Dakota has a fine prospect before him,
and in a few years will reap the reward of his
labors, and independence and comfort will take
the place of the inconveniences and discomforts attending the life of the pioneer. On the east bank
of the Missouri stands the thriving city of Bismarck, a place of about 10,000 inhabitants, a
large proportion of whom are Europeans. The
Missouri here is spanned by an enormous iron
bridge, the largest structure of the kind on the
Northern Pacific between Portland and St. Paul.
Between Bismarck and the Minnesota line the
aspect of the country changes most favorably; it
is level and fertile, covered with fields of waving
grain. The main attraction to farmers in this
section of Dakota is the farms of Dalrymple.
These farms consist of 75,000 acres, all under
cultivation. It was harvest time when I saw
them, and the vast prairie, covered with its wealth
of golden grain, presented a brilliant sight.
The Dalrymple farms are situated in the valley
of the Red River of the North, the banner farming belt of Dakota. I was now reminded of our
extensive farms in California, to me the garden
spot of the earth. I could not but think how her
farmers were favored with the mild, even climate
and the long, dry summers that afford such ample
time to harvest the grain.

After 350 miles of rapid riding in Dakota, we arrived at Fargo, on the western bank of the Red River of the North. This stream is the division line between Dakota and Minnesota. On the east side of the river we found the enterprising town of Moorhead, and had our first glimpse of Minnesota, the fourth greatest grain State in the American Union. Were it not for the high latitude and the long and severe winters, she would lead the van as a great grain-growing State. All along the line of the railroad could be seen signs of wealth and prosperity, especially in the Red River Valley. Brainerd, an attractive and flourishing city of 10,000 inhabitants, is situated on the Mississippi River 140 miles northwest of St. Paul. It is surrounded by a vast and fertile prairie that is dotted with beautiful farms. Pursuing my journey eastward, the next place of importance reached was Little Falls, situated among and surrounded by forest trees, and boasting of having the largest hotel on the Northern Pacific Railroad. It also has a branch railroad running to Minnewaska Lake, one of the loveliest summer resorts in Minnesota.

One hundred miles more and we entered Minneapolis, the queen city of the Northwest. This city has a population of 125,000, and is one of the greatest milling points in the world. It is situated on a level plain on the western bank of the Mississippi.

Many of the streets are lined with imposing buildings which would do justice to either London or
Paris.   Aside from being a great railroad centre,
this city is backed by a densely settled farming
country, extending over the fertile plains to the Red
River Valley.   One of the chief points of interest
is St. Anthony's Falls.   It is a magnificent sight to
watch the foaming torrent as it tears its way over
rocks and precipices until it reaches the Mississippi.   This fall is often called the Niagara of
the West.   It has an estimated capacity of 135,000
horse-power at the lowest stage of water.   This
water-power is utilized in the various mills, some
of which I visited.   The Washburn and Pillsbury
Mills are said to have the greatest grinding
capacity of any mills in the world.   Long trains
of cars can always be seen here loading flour,
which is shipped to Chicago, and from thence to
various points on both continents, and this flour is
converted into bread to feed the hungry millions
with.   While here I also visited several woolen
factories, where hundreds of men and women are
constantly employed in the manufacture of woolen
goods.

Twelve miles from Minneapolis lies St. Paul,
the capital of the State.   It is a thriving, enterprising commercial city, situated at the head of
navigation on the Mississippi River.   This city is
built on an elevation, and one can have a magnifi-

cent view of the river, upon which boats can be
seen during most of the year plying up and down
the stream. While St. Paul has not the water-
power that Minneapolis has, she has the advantage
of being the capital of a growing and prosperous
State, and this advantage she intends to retain. A
great rivalry exists between these two cities, each
trying to control the great growing Northwestern
trade; but the suburbs of each are growing out in
the direction of the other, and it seems as if the
two must soon become one great city, with interests in common and a common destiny. The
growth they have made within the last score of
years has been marvelous. When I first visited
Minnesota, twenty-five years ago, each of these
places had less than 7,000 inhabitants. In 1886
they had a combined population of over a quarter
of a million.

St. Paul has various means of egress. One
can have their choice of a number of routes by
rail, or they can travel by water on the river
steamers until that becomes monotonous, and then
can return to the swifter method of transit. But
at this juncture I concluded to stay with the
rail, so took the train at the Union Depot, on
the line known as the Chicago, Milwaukee &
St. Paul. The first city of importance that I
arrived at in the Badger State was La Crosse,
situated on the Mississippi River, and also at

the mouth of the Black River. It is the centre
of a large lumber industry. From here I resumed my journey to Kilbourn City, on the
Wisconsin River, a distance of eighty miles.
The chief attractions on this route were the
numerous bluffs and thickly wooded valleys, until
we arrived at the Dells. This place is quite a
summer resort for Milwaukee and Chicago people, who come here during the warmest part of
the summer to enjoy a change of scene and of
air. The Dells are a narrow, rocky gorge, only
a few feet wide, and miles long, where the Wisconsin River penetrates through bluffs whose
high and curious walls extend perpendicularly in
the air. It is an interesting sight to stand on
one of these high elevations during a freshet in
the spring, and watch the foaming torrent of
water pouring into this narrow passage. Thirty
years ago, before I became a pioneer to the
then far West, my home was near Kilbourn
City. Here my parents first made their home
after emigrating from Europe. Here my boyhood
days were spent among the tamaracks and oaks
in the green meadows. In the winter we were
surrounded by snow-clad hills, and near us were
beautiful lakes. I enjoyed a brief and pleasant
sojourn among my many old and almost forgotten friends. Time had wrought many changes;
but memory, busy with the past, brought many

pleasant recollections to my mind. Old-time scenes and incidents were recalled.

After bidding my friends adieu, I again resumed my journey. I took the cars at Kilbourn City, and was soon swiftly speeding away over marshes, swamps, tree-clad hills and rolling prairie. On this route the towns worthy of note were Portage and Watertown ; ere long we arrived at Milwaukee, the largest city in Wisconsin. It is one of the five great lake ports, and has a large commerce in breadstuffs, provisions and lumber. The next city of importance was Racine, which is not far from the boundary line of Illinois, and we soon arrived at Chicago, which is a great railway centre, and I again have my choice of a variety of routes. It is not the intention of the writer to make extended mention of these large cities which lie on the beaten line of travel and are so well known to us all, but rather to give a brief *résumé* of the places of importance he passed on his journey over the continent.

Chicago is a city of recent and remarkable growth, its population having increased nearly 70 per cent. in the last ten years. Originally built on low ground, it has become, in its grading, drainage and water supply, a monument to the energy, sagacity and public spirit of its citizens. In October, 1871, a fire, one of the most destructive in modern times, swept away three and a quarter miles of its most valuable storehouses and resi-

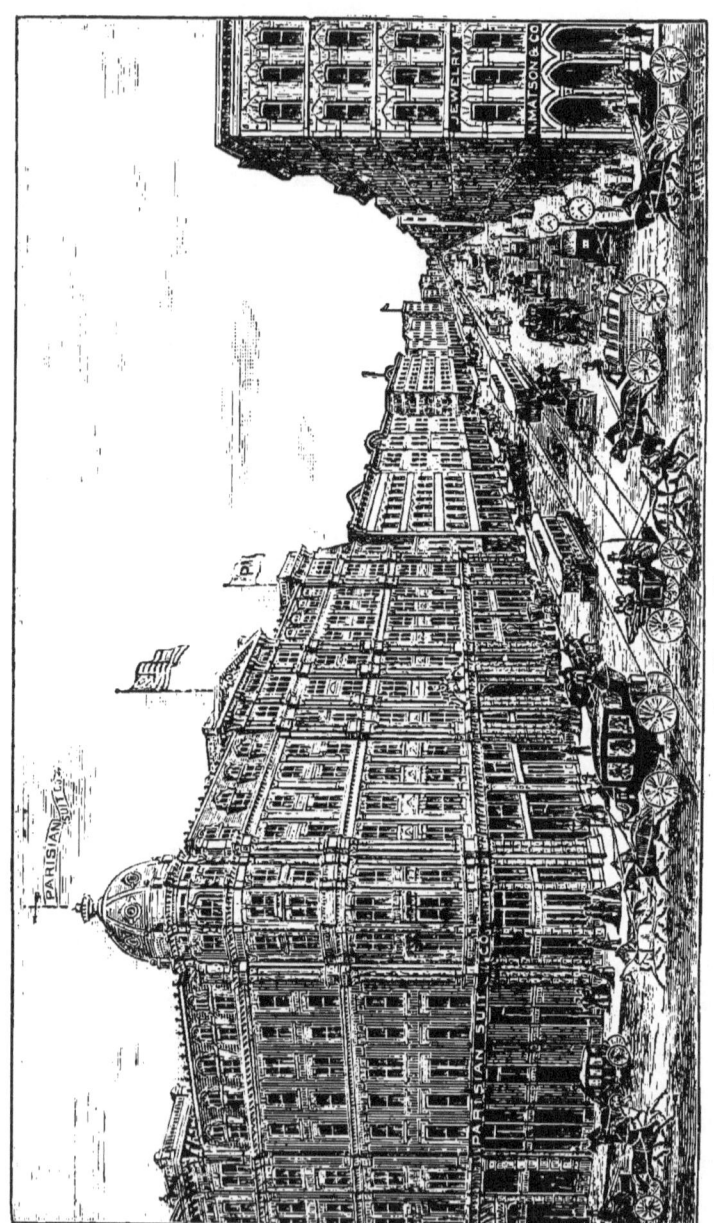

The Palmer House.

(28)

dences. Notwithstanding this sudden calamity, the most extensive and disastrous that ever befell an American community, the new Chicago that has already sprung from the old is, in every respect, a grander city. It is the commercial metropolis of the St. Lawrence basin, the chief lumber and pork market in America, and, next to London, the greatest grain market in the world.

On leaving Chicago, I decided to travel by way of the Fort Wayne & Pennsylvania Railroad, and, by so doing, I passed many of the largest iron mines, viewed some of the rolling mills, and visited all of the principal cities in Pennsylvania, including Pittsburg, Harrisburg and Philadelphia. I also crossed the largest rivers in the State, and made the climb over the Alleghany Mountains. I here saw some of the grandest mountain scenery and most difficult railway engineering in the Union. Arriving at Philadelphia, I proceeded to view the points of interest. I visited the U. S. Mint, and had a fine view of the city from the elevated railway. The most famous public building is the old State House, where the Declaration of Independence was adopted, July 4th, 1776. Philadelphia is the second city in the United States in manufactures and population, and the fifth in the amount of its foreign commerce ; it also has an extensive domestic commerce, and is the greatest coal depot in America. It is noted for its Fairmount Park, its well supplied markets, and its abundance of cheap and comfortable dwellings; it is sometimes called the "City of Homes."

After leaving Philadelphia, my next stopping place was New York City. All along the line of the railroad between Philadelphia and New York can be seen busy cities, bearing the marks of age, enterprise and prosperity. New York City is the richest and most populous city in America. It is noted for its extensive commerce, the number of its magnificent hotels, banks, churches and private dwellings. I visited Central Park and the Brooklyn Bridge, saw the Vanderbilt and Gould mansions, and gazed upon the busy, bustling throng in Broadway and Wall street. The elevated railway extends twelve miles, from Harlem River to Castle Garden. In 1880, only two cities in Europe, London and Paris, exceeded New York in population. Brooklyn, the third city of the United States, and Jersey City, in New Jersey, are so closely connected with it that they really constitute one great city. Besides these are many *residential towns* connected with New York by rivers and railroads. So numerous are these towns that the total number of inhabitants within a radius of thirty miles around New York City is not less than 2,500,000. While in New York I attended the funeral of General Grant, the most imposing pageant ever witnessed in America.

THE BROOKLYN BRIDGE.

(81)

Now that my journey from San Francisco to New York over the Northern Pacific road has been described, before I cross the Atlantic, and enter upon my tour of the Old World, I will make brief mention of my other transcontinental trips. Perchance, some other traveler may follow in my footsteps, and, finding himself in San Francisco undecided which route to travel by, would be glad to know what the various points of interest are on each route. Not that these few pages are intended as a guide book, for they are not, but simply a narrative of the experience of a traveler.

When I made my first journey overland, in 1870, I traveled by way of the Central and Union Pacific. San Francisco was my starting point; at Port Costa we crossed, on the large railway ferry heretofore mentioned, to Benicia, and were soon speeding away toward Sacramento, the capital of our Golden State. A few miles from Sacramento the character of the country changes, we leave the fertile valleys behind, and find ourselves in the foot-hills of the Sierra Nevadas. The climate and soil of these foot-hills are peculiarly adapted to fruit-raising. All varieties of grapes grow to perfection, small fruit trees of every kind are cultivated here, and even tropical and citrus fruits are raised successfully. This portion of California has also been a great mining region, and there are still a number of rich mines in successful operation. One of the grandest sights in the Sierras is Cape Horn, where some marvelous engineering can be seen. Here the track is cut on a narrow ledge around the peak, from which there is a perpendicular descent of almost 2,000 feet. The scenery along here will compare favorably with that of the Alps, the Alleghanies, the Kandy Mountains in Ceylon, or even that seen from the zigzag railway in the Blue Mountains in Australia.

The Sierra Nevadas constitute one of the grandest mountain chains in the world. Their loftiest peaks reach an elevation of about 15,000 feet, and are the highest in the United States. Their forest-clad western slope has its foot in the low valleys almost at the level of the sea ; and, with their long line of peaks covered with perpetual snow, their gigantic spurs and numerous foot-hills rich with gold, their deep canyons, foaming torrents, and giant trees, they present landscapes famous throughout the world for variety, beauty and sublimity. Their eastern slope, though bold and rugged, is much narrower and less imposing. Truckee, situated on the eastern slope of this range of mountains, is surrounded by a country that is grand, romantic and heavily timbered. Near here are the famous snow-sheds, which are about thirty miles in length. A few miles distant are Donner Lake and Lake Tahoe, both noted summer resorts These beautiful

3

sheets of water will compare favorably with Lake Lucerne, in Switzerland, or Lake Como, in Italy. Lake Tahoe is about twenty-two miles long by fourteen wide. It is 1,500 feet deep, and its surface is about 6,000 feet above the level of the sea.

Thirty miles east of Truckee, we arrived at Reno, the first town of note in Nevada. Here are two railway lines, one running to Carson City, the capital of the State; the other for Virginia City, which lies in one of the richest silver regions in the world. A peculiar feature of the latter road is that it is about as crooked as a corkscrew. Nevada is called the Silver State, and with equal truth might be called the Sage-Brush State, as sage-brush abounds so plentifully. It is, however, pre-eminently a mineral State, its resources of this nature being extraordinary in variety and value, and inexhaustible in quantity. Prominent among the hundreds of rich mines are those of the famous Comstock ledge, from which many millionaires have evolved. From Reno eastward, we soon strike the Humboldt River, which is the largest river in the State. After a winding course of about 350 miles, it is lost in the Humboldt and Carson sink, a shallow lake or marsh of vast extent, its waters being brackish with salt and soda. As we go eastward, we travel through a country which is for the most part level and covered with sage-brush. We pass Wadsworth, Winnemucca, Battle Mountain, Palisade, Carlin and Elko, occasionally catching a glimpse of some beautiful bits of scenery.

We next reach Utah, the land of the honey bee, as the Mormons style it. These Mormons constitute four-fifths of the population of this Territory. One could not but note the great contrast between the dry sage-brush country of Nevada and the fertile valleys occupied by the Mormons, or Latter-Day Saints, as they style themselves. Salt Lake City, the capital of Utah, is situated on the east bank of the Jordan River, the stream which connects Great Salt Lake and Lake Utah. It is 4,350 feet above the level of the sea, and is picturesquely located. Its streets are lined with shade trees, which, when in leaf, conceal many of the buildings from view, which gives a large portion of the city the appearance of a garden. These streets are 128 feet wide, and a stream of water flows through each, from which the gardens are irrigated. The climate is considered very healthful. One of the chief attractions and points of interest is the sacred square, or temple block. Here the new temple, which has been years in the course of construction, is now nearing completion. I last visited this enormous granite structure in April, 1885, on my return from the New Orleans Exposition. I also visited the Tabernacle, which is a spacious wooden structure 250 feet long by 150 feet wide, is seventy feet in height, and has an oval

TEMPLE AND TABERNACLE, SALT LAKE CITY.

(36)

roof. It has a seating capacity of 10,000 people; its twenty doors all open outward. In the west end stands the organ, which the Mormon attendant who guided me around, informed me was the largest organ in the United States. It is thirty feet wide, thirty-three feet long, and has 3,000 pipes. On leaving the church, I was requested to register my name in the great church register. I also visited the Zion Co-Operative Mercantile Institution. The head manager of this institution informed me that this was the largest mercantile house west of Chicago, that the capital invested in merchandise was $1,000,000, and that they constantly employed 160 clerks. There is a museum containing a good collection of specimens. Another point of interest is the Black Rock bathing resort. The residence of the late Brigham Young, the Salt Lake Assembly Hall, and the Walker House, the leading hotel, are magnificent structures that would do credit to a city twice the size of Salt Lake. The Mormons occupy fertile valleys at the western base of the Wahsatch Mountains, and carry on extensive agriculture by means of irrigation. These mountains are 10,000 feet high, and are covered with perpetual snow. A great many travelers and tourists visit Salt Lake City.

On leaving here we have the choice of two routes. One can return to Ogden, and there take the Union Pacific Railroad, the straight line to

Omaha, or he can take the Denver & Rio Grande road. The latter is the route I traveled in the spring of 1886, and by so doing saw some of the grandest mountain scenery in the State of Colorado. Denver, the capital of this State, is a thriving city of about seventy-one thousand inhabitants. Thirty years ago it was a mining camp, numbering less than two thousand souls. It is said to be the most rapidly growing city in America. From Capitol Hill we had a fine view of the city, which is well laid out. The streets contain many substantial buildings and many beautiful private residences. The St. James Hotel and the new Opera House are costly and elegant structures. Mr. Tabor, an enterprising millionaire, has erected several buildings, at a cost of a million dollars each. Denver is situated at an altitude of 5,000 feet above the sea-level; the climate is peculiarly dry and healthful. It is surrounded by a country which is rich in mines of gold, silver, coal, iron and salt. It is by nature a railway centre. At the present time there are eight tracks running in different directions, and there are more railroads being built, which will pass through Denver, and consequently help to swell the traffic of an already busy city. Much of her prosperity is due to the sagacity of her business men. Journeying eastward from Denver, we find ourselves in a well improved and thickly settled farm-

VIEW IN DENVER.

(39)

ing country. All along the line of the railroad are numerous cities and towns, until we reach Topeka, the capital of Kansas. The next place of importance after leaving Topeka is Kansas City, in Missouri, which is also a great railway centre, and is situated on the boundary line between Kansas and Missouri.

Before going farther east, I will betake myself to Ogden, and give a brief description of what can be seen on this route, over which I have traveled three different times. After two hours' run from Ogden, we enter the Weber Canyon. Here the scenery is varied, and grand to behold. To the left of the road is a peculiar wall or overhanging red bluff. Lofty peaks which extend heavenward arrest the eye. But these are soon left behind, and we come upon new sights and scenes. We pass Echo Canyon, Devil's Gate and Devil's Slide in swift succession, and I soon found myself at Granger's Station, on the boundary line of Wyoming Territory. This station is the terminus of the Oregon Short Line. Here a traveler for the Pacific coast can connect with the Northern Pacific, and see the magnificent scenery in Idaho and Washington Territory. He can go over the Cascade Mountains, and travel along the Columbia River to Portland, or he can reverse his journey and travel eastward and visit the National Yellowstone Park, and thus, by zigzagging around a few hundred miles, can see some of the grandest and most wonderful scenery in the world.

Traveling from Granger's Station along the main line of the Union Pacific, we arrive in a short time at Sherman, the most elevated railroad station on the continent, having an altitude of 8,235 feet. East of Sherman, we are continually passing towns, cities and sheds, rocky cliffs and precipices, until at last we leave them all behind, and descend the eastern slope of the Rocky Mountains. Arriving at Cheyenne, one of the most important cities of the Union Pacific, and the capital of Wyoming, we find that we have traveled half the distance between Ogden and Omaha. Cheyenne is situated on a level prairie, and is quite a railway terminus. Here, again, the tourist can make a break in the journey if he desires, and visit Denver, a distance of 106 miles, by taking the Julesburg short line. This, however, I consider a rather uninteresting route, as it runs through an open country, destitute of scenery, or any particular point of interest. The ride through Nebraska to Omaha, on the Union Pacific, is a very pleasant one. We traverse a vast prairie, watered by the Platte River; an apparently endless number of horses and cattle can be seen roaming at will, and grazing on the plains; in the far distance, one could occasionally catch glimpses of herds of antelope or buffalo. As we travel eastward, the towns become more numerous, the country more thickly settled, and better improved.

Omaha, a busy, bustling railroad centre, is situated on the Missouri River. This city has grown like magic in the last twenty-six years; in 1860, it had only 4,000 inhabitants; now it has a population of 60,000. In 1860, I crossed the plains from the Missouri River to the Pacific coast in an ox team. This was my second journey over the continent. What a contrast between then and now! On these broad plains roamed herds of wild buffalo, and travelers were always more or less at the mercy of the Indians, who attacked the trains of emigrants and were always making raids on frontier settlements. Our train was called Captain Hereman's, of St. Louis, and consisted of about one hundred emigrants. We were attacked by Indians while camping near Salt Lake City; the night was dark, and, after a severe conflict and with the loss of two of our number, we drove them off, but not until they had stolen our stock and left us destitute of teams. We were obliged to take our choice between traveling on foot or remaining in our wagons and starving. I was shortly afterward attacked by a grizzly bear in the Sierra Nevada Mountains, and had a narrow escape. These are but incidents of the many hardships endured by the pioneers of early days in their endeavors to reach the golden shores of California. Contrast the difference! Then it required five months to make such a journey, and the weary, forlorn and footsore traveler endured many hardships and much privation. Danger was always staring him in the face. Now the traveler over the same route can sit in a palace car surrounded by many comforts and luxuries, and in five days reach his journey's end. The hostile savage has fled from civilization, and the vast wilderness is filled with new life,—towns and cities are springing up everywhere, the old hunting grounds have been converted into well-tilled farms, and the whole country bears evidence of that change which can only be effected by the indomitable will and energy of a free people.

I will now take the reader over the Southern Pacific Railroad, and, when at my journey's end, will have completed a description of all the various routes that I have traveled across the continent.

This takes me back to San Francisco again as the starting point, and here let me remark, that the Eastern tourist in San Francisco will find many points of interest to visit within a few hours' ride from that city ; he will find much to see and admire at Monterey and Santa Cruz, both noted watering places. The Hotel del Monte, at Monterey, is one of the finest hotels on the coast ; it is built in a beautiful grove of live oaks. The grounds are handsomely laid out, and the climate is unsurpassed for mildness and evenness. Many tourists from all over the world delight in wintering at this famous resort. The Geysers, in Sonoma County, are a great natural wonder, and are visited by all travelers. The Big Trees and Yosemite Valley are two of the greatest wonders of the world. The Big Trees are gigantic evergreens, a species of redwood, some of which are more than 100 feet in circumference and 400 feet high. In the Calaveras grove one was cut down which measured ninety-six feet in circumference and over 300 feet high; its concentric rings showing its age to be about 3,000 years. The Mariposa grove contains many large trees. The Yosemite Valley is a remarkable chasm, ten miles long, and three miles wide in its greatest width, with perpendicular walls of granite from 3,000 to 5,000 feet high. It is one of the many wonders sought out by tourists who visit California.

We start now on the Southern Overland for New Orleans. The first part of the journey takes us through the great San Joaquin Valley. In the spring-time it is covered with fields of waving grain; in the "fall," or autumn, the broad expanse of yellow stubble shows that the husbandman has reaped the reward of his toil. All along this valley are numerous small towns and cities where fifteen or twenty years ago there were no signs of civilization. The broad plains and fertile valleys were uncultivated and unappreciated. The California farmer often counts his acres by the thousand, and sometimes by tens of thousands. Leaving this fertile valley behind, we enter a spur of the Sierra Nevadas, and cross the summit at Tchachapi, where there is some wonderful railway engineering in what is called "The Loop." We soon pass over the Loop, and reach Mojave, where we connect with the Atlantic & Pacific Railroad. This road runs along the southern slopes of the Sierra Nevada Mountains, and crosses the Colorado River at a point called the "Needles," which are a peculiar formation of rock extending high in the air above every other object, and are visible for a great many miles. This route is highly praised by tourists on account of the scenery.

At Mojave the tourist can take the Atlantic & Pacific, or continue on with the Southern Pacific via Los Angeles, the garden city of Southern California. This city is beautiful, with its gardens and orchards, which contain a remarkable variety of tropical and semi-tropical fruits and trees. Among them are hundreds of thousands of orange, lemon, lime and fig trees, and an endless number of grape-vines. Besides these are the pomegranate, the palm, the cypress, and many others too numerous to mention. The public buildings and the educational and religious institutions are among the best in the State. Five lines of railroad have here a common centre. The Southern Pacific connects the city with the general railway system of the State and Union. The lines to Santa Monica and Wilmington give ready access to the ocean. The facilities for transporting, together with the extraordinary fertility of the soil and salubrious clime, make it a favorite resort, and the chief centre of trade for Southern California. This city has grown rapidly within the last few years, and now contains nearly 50,000 inhabitants.

From here we continue our journey southward, through a beautiful, fertile valley, until Colton, another railway junction, is reached. Shortly after leaving here, we begin to travel over the desolate plains of Southern California. As far as the eye can reach, nothing can be seen but sage-brush and hills and cactus until we arrive at Fort Yuma, on the Colorado River. Near this river we crossed a barren desert, the surface of which is below the level of the sea, and through which the railroad extends a distance of sixty-five miles. Fort Yuma is one of the hottest places in the United States. The Yuma Indians, however, do not seem to mind the heat; they ramble over the hot sands in a costume as scanty as that ascribed to Adam. These indolent fellows exist without industry, and appear to be born only to roam and die in the wilderness. I visited, while here, the United States Fort and the Territorial prison. The latter I found well filled with Arizona criminals. I was informed that very few of these culprits live to serve out their sentence, on account of the extreme heat.

On our journey eastward, we cross desert after desert, the route over which many immigrants came to California in 1849, and the years following the gold excitement.

The first town of importance we arrive at after leaving Fort Yuma is Tucson, the largest town in Arizona, and one of the oldest in the United States. It lies in the fertile Santa Cruz Valley, is the centre of many stage routes, and has an extensive trade with the Territory and Northern Mexico. The population numbers about 7,000. Many of the buildings are of adobe, and bear the marks of age. In a short time after leaving Tucson, we reach Benson, where there is a branch railway for Tombstone. This city has a population of about 7,000, and is surrounded by rich silver mines. In a few hours after leaving Benson, we found ourselves in Lordsburg, New Mexico, also situated among rich silver mines. Continuing our journey, we soon arrive at Deming, a general railway terminus, where the traveler again has an opportunity of choosing routes for the East. The Atchison, Topeka & Santa Fé runs through an extensive pastoral region, and intersects the Atlantic & Pacific at Albuquerque. This route I have been over once, seeing a diversity of country, but no particular point of interest.

The Southern Pacific, however, is the route I intend to follow on this particular journey. After leaving Deming, we travel for a hundred miles over a parched and desolate region in the southern portion of New Mexico. Arriving at El Paso, we catch our first glimpse of Texas. This is the largest city and greatest railway centre between Los Angeles and San Antonio. At El Paso, by slightly turning your eyes, you can view a State, a Territory and another country. The Rio Grande River divides El Paso, in Texas, from Paso del Norte, in Old Mexico. Here the traveler who is not pressed for time has a fine opportunity to take a trip across the line and inspect Mexico and Mexican customs. By taking the Mexican Central Railroad, one can travel through this country for several hundred miles, and form something of an estimate of its resources. After leaving the thriving, enterprising American city of El Paso, and crossing the river to the Mexican side, one can not but be impressed with the contrast. Everything bears the impress of age : the buildings are old and of rude construction, and the implements used in tilling the soil must have been patterned after those of the time of Moses. Notwithstanding the rich soil and fine climate, this slow-going country seems a hundred years behind the times. Ninety miles eastward from El Paso, we arrive at Sierra Blanca, where the Southern

Pacific, or Sunset Route, diverges from the Texas Pacific, and the tourist again has the choice of several routes.

Should the traveler decide to continue on the extreme southern route, he will travel the entire breadth of Texas, see many of the principal cities and towns, and pass over the most cultivated and fertile portion of the State. On tiring of travel by rail, he can take a steamer, and go to New Orleans by way of the Gulf of Mexico, taking in Louisiana, the land of cotton and cane ; and thence up the Mississippi to St. Louis, and in this way have a fine view of the numerous plantations that border this great river. I have journeyed up the Mississippi twice during the last ten years, and, after a 2,000-mile ride by rail, found the change in scene and motion quite refreshing. At one time I happened to strike one of those exciting steamboat races so often pictured on the Mississippi, and which are now a thing of the past. The excitement ran so high that one immediately forgot the danger of explosion, etc. The two boats would travel for miles at the top of their speed, side by side, each, of course, bent on victory. I have seen, when the excitement was at its height, boxes of bacon thrown into the furnace for fuel.

Should the traveler decide in favor of the Texas Pacific and Missouri Pacific, he will also travel the entire breadth of the State, but further north

4

than on the other road. This road I have been over several times on account of my landed interests in Central Texas. For the first three hundred miles after leaving El Paso, the road traverses a barren country destitute of any object of interest save the prairie dogs and antelopes. For miles along the road the plains are dotted with cattle, and here can be seen, in all his glory, the somewhat famous cow-boy, as he rides over the plains on his prancing pony, sheltered by a broad-brimmed hat which seems to have been constructed with a view of defying the elements, as it serves not only as a protection from the burning sun, but, as the seasons change, is equally service-able in wind or rain. For hundreds of miles along this road can be seen neither church nor school-house. The *Police Gazette* and *Texas Siftings* seem to be the cow-boy's substitute for the Bible. Arriving at Abilene, one of the largest wool centres in the United States, we leave the wilderness behind, and find ourselves once more in civiliza-tion, and from here eastward prosperity and enter-prise seem the rule all along the line of the road. The next point of importance reached was Fort Worth, where the road again diverges, and one can take the Missouri Pacific, running up through the Indian Territory, and from thence into Southern Kansas, and on to Kansas City; but it is our inten-tion to journey more directly eastward, and we

continue our route in that direction until we reach
Dallas, a growing town thirty miles from Fort
Worth. We pass on, and soon reach Texarkana,
situated on the boundary line between Texas and
Arkansas, and here take our last glance at Texas,
a State larger than several kingdoms in Europe.

Traveling through Arkansas by way of the Iron
Mountain Railroad, we pass through a region of
swamps, cross the Red River at Shreveport, and also
pass through Little Rock, the capital of the State.
The main attractions along the line of this road
were the negro cabins, corn fields and cotton plantations. Journeying through the southern portion
of Missouri, we pass through a low, swampy region
which is heavily timbered. Here I noticed several
saw mills. One of the principal points of interest is the famous Iron Mountain mines. These
mines, when in operation, employ several hundred
men. In this vicinity are several noted mineral
springs, which are great resorts for the health and
pleasure seeker. In the direction of St. Louis our
road runs along the Mississippi for some distance.
I passed over this route in the winter of 1884,
which was a winter of floods, and the train appeared
to be traveling in water half the time ; but, in a
less stormy winter, I should imagine this to be a
very pleasant route, as the climate is so much
milder than that of the sections traversed by the
roads running farther north.

The New Bridge at Niagara, with the Falls in the Distance.

If one remains over at St. Louis, he will, in all probability, seek the best accommodations, which I found at the Southern Hotel, the largest and most magnificent hotel in the Southwest. As a guest I have found it to be as good as it looks. In journeying from St. Louis to New York, the traveler may, with a slight loss of time and a little roundabout travel, visit all of the principal cities in the central States. He can take in Louisville, Indianapolis, Cincinnati and Chicago. If he should become wearied with mountain scenery, and care nothing for the attractions in the Alleghanies, New York or Saratoga, he can visit the cataract of Niagara, the grandest waterfall in the world. The water from the broad basin of four of the Great Lakes here falls over a precipice 164 feet in height. One can pass on through Canada, and visit Montreal, the chief city of the Dominion, and, after Chicago and Buffalo, the largest in the St. Lawrence basin. On leaving here, a few hours' journey either by water or rail will bring us to the busy city of Quebec, the capital of the Province of Quebec, and the second city in population in the Dominion. This city is noted for its picturesque scenery and severe climate. From here the tourist may, if he desires, embark for the Old World.

In 1853, the first time I touched American soil, I traveled up the St. Lawrence, and was much impressed with the falls, canals, and picturesque scenery along its shores. From that day forth the writer has been almost a constant traveler; for only three years afterward he joined the filibustering expedition of General William Walker, directed against Nicaragua. We took the steamship Texas at New Orleans. After an adventurous and somewhat stormy career, Walker was finally captured, September 3, 1860, condemned by a court martial, and shot. Some of his volunteers died, and others were shot by the natives. Those who escaped with their lives were scattered in various directions, some returning to New Orleans, and others to California. I was among the latter. In the winter of 1860 I returned East. This was before the Central Pacific Railroad was constructed. I embarked on the steamship Illinois at San Francisco, crossed the Isthmus of Panama, stopping at Acapulco and Cuba. We had a calm and pleasant voyage on the Pacific side, but an unusually stormy and unpleasant one on the Atlantic. The voyage lasted twenty-three days. Thus it will be readily seen that the writer has been something of a traveler during the last thirty years, and that he has within that time experienced both pleasure and privation. Many times has he been questioned in regard to what he considered the most desirable route to travel, and perchance this brief description of the various points of interest to be seen on the different highways may be of service to some other tourist.

There are many different routes and many different modes of travel over this continent, and to decide for others as to what route would suit them best would be a hard matter. In a word, they are all good; there is much of interest to be seen on all of them. The season of the year would always be an important factor to be taken into consideration in making a choice. The southern overland route would be preferable in winter, and the northern in summer. It isn't exactly pleasant to be snow-bound with the thermometer below zero in the winter, neither would one enjoy the extreme heat of Arizona and New Mexico in the summer.

CHAPTER II.

THE ATLANTIC AND THE BRITISH ISLES.

I DEPARTED from New York City at noon on the 11th of August, 1885, on the steamship Wisconsin, belonging to the famous Guion line, and bound for Queenstown. As we slowly steamed out of the harbor, all hands stood on deck to take a last look at the receding shore. We could see the long wharf lined with people waving their last adieu to the friends who were going far away to sojourn for a season among another people, and in a foreign land. There were 200 passengers on board, embracing many different nationalities, a variety of professions, and nearly all grades of society, from a nobleman to a California gold dig- ger. Each had an object in view; many were . going to visit their friends, to return to the home of their youth after a lapse of many years; and, once again on *terra firma*, this motley crowd would become scattered from the Baltic Sea to the Medi- terranean. Others were going with a view of making a home somewhere in Europe, to settle down and enjoy the portion accumulated in Amer- ica; but, strange to say, I was the only one in all that goodly number who entertained the idea of making an entire circuit of the globe.

The first day out we were favored with a calm sea, and we found "a life on the ocean wave" very enjoyable; but the second and third days our good ship was tossed to and fro on the boisterous billows, and, as a natural consequence, many of the passengers succumbed to that most disagreeable feature of ocean travel, sea-sickness. At such time I was generally to be found on the hurricane deck; the fresh salt air seemed to help dissipate the disagreeable feeling. The fourth and fifth days were a repetition of the first. We sighted several sailing craft, and enjoyed the unusual calmness of the sea. Nearing Newfoundland, we were enveloped in fog, and the music of the fog whistle could be heard every few minutes. A man stationed at the bow was on a constant lookout, and every once in a while we could hear him sing out, "All well, forward." In every direction now could be seen fishing boats, with their occupants busy gathering in the spoils of the deep. We also passed two dismantled hulks, which caused me to ponder on the possible fate of their occupants, and to wonder if we were to be consigned to the tender mercies of old Neptune. On Sunday we had religious services on the quarter deck. It is the custom on English steamers to hold some sort of service every Sabbath. If there happens to be a clergy-

man on board, he generally conducts the services ;
if not, the captain generally reads a chapter from
the Bible.   On the seventh day out we had a cool
breeze, and sighted quite a number of steamers
and sailing craft.   The passengers were now getting somewhat accustomed to the motion of the
boat, and were able to be out on deck.   They were
also becoming well acquainted, and many different kinds of amusement were devised for passing
away the time.   We had several very enjoyable
concerts.   For much of our pleasant times we were
indebted to a few interesting and jolly Philadelphia
ladies.   On the eighth day we were introduced to a
gale which watered the hurricane deck, and sent us
all back to bed.   We had no inclination to venture
out of our state-rooms, but were contented with
peeping through the port-holes at the storm.   On
the ninth day we had a head wind, which impeded
our progress, and a defect was discovered in the
boiler.   It is rather monotonous, I assure you, to
be obliged to stop in mid-ocean for repairs.   However, accidents are liable to occur ; and, if one is
fired with an ambition to travel extensively in
foreign lands, he must fortify himself with patience,
courage, endurance, and last, but not least, *coin.*

On the morning of the tenth day we caught our
first glimpse of the coast of Ireland, a very welcome
sight to those who did not enjoy ocean travel, and
there were many.   We cast anchor on the same

day in the harbor at Queenstown, 3,000 miles from New York. Queenstown has a poor harbor, and heavily laden vessels are obliged to anchor quite a distance from the shore. Passengers and freight are transported to the mainland in tenders. The waters in this vicinity were dotted with fishing boats, and I was told that fishing was the principal resource of the people who live along this coast. After a brief survey of Queenstown, I was soon *en route* for Dublin. The entire country between these two places is densely populated and well improved. The landscape, dotted with cozy homes, and gilded by the rays from an August sun, was simply beautiful. To a Californian accustomed to broad fields of waving grain, with only an occasional farm house, this door-yard farming seemed very small business indeed. Here 8,000,000 people are crowded together, and derive their livelihood from less than half the acreage on the Pacific slope, which has a population of less than a million. But thorough cultivation and fertilization force the soil to yield to its utmost capacity. This, combined with a diversity of crops, raising a few fine sheep and cattle, and the utmost economy and industry, enables these people to eke out an existence. In such a densely populated country the poor have a hard time to exist, and England's best statesmen have devoted much time and attention to trying to adjust the respective rights and privileges of landlord and tenant. I hardly consider myself a prophet; still, I am willing to venture the prediction that this generation will not live to see the Irish question settled. Dublin, the metropolis of Ireland, is a city of about 300,000 inhabitants. The plan of the city is singularly simple. The River Liffey flows almost through the centre from west to east, and bridges connect long lines of streets running north and

DUBLIN FROM THE LIFFEY.

south. The communication between the two sides of the city is ample, there being nine bridges in a distance of about a mile and a half, and ferries for the two miles of shipping between the last bridge and the mouth of the river. Sackville street is the finest avenue in Dublin : the houses, however, are not uniform, and the street is not long enough for its width ; while the Nelson pillar, itself a beautiful object, blocks the view and interrupts traffic. On the other side of the Liffey, across the Carlisle bridge, is Westmoreland street, with the Bank of Ireland and Trinity College at the south-ern end. At right angles to Westmoreland street is Dame street, unquestionably the best street in the city. The houses are lofty and massive, and more than one of them colossal. At one end is Dublin Castle, and at the other, the great front of the Bank of Ireland and of Trinity College. The chief drawback to Dublin as a city is the sudden transition from magnificence to meanness, and in no part of it is there freedom from this unpleasing contrast. In addition to this, the soil is so oozy that, after even a slight shower, it is melted into far-spreading lakes of mud.

The suburbs of Dublin constitute at present the chief of the many attractions which the stranger is wont to admire. Dublin is the seat of the Irish courts of law and equity, from which appeal lies only to the House of Lords. The means of edu-cation are ample. The incessant contests between the various religious denominations have had the effect of imparting energy to all engaged in teach-ing. Dublin has several noble edifices, the first and greatest of which is the Bank of Ireland, formerly the House of Parliament, which occupies five acres. Trinity College is in itself a source of pride to the city. Dublin Castle, being built of brick, the greater portion of it is dingy; but the tower and chapel are handsome. The Custom House is considered one of the chief ornaments of the city. Among the manufactures are woolen goods, silk and linen. The chief articles of export are whisky and the famous Dublin porter.

After several days of rambling on the Isle of the Shamrock, I started for London, by way of Liverpool. A portion of the distance we traveled by rail, and the remainder of the journey by steamer. On the 27th of August we anchored inside the magnificent breakwater at Liverpool, and I was soon engaged in inspecting one of the largest shipping ports in the world. The commerce of Liverpool extends to every part of the world; but probably the intercourse with America stands pre-eminent, there being five lines of steamers running to New York alone, besides lines to many other American ports. The leading feature of the city is the wharves and harbor, and here can be seen the flag of nearly every nation on the globe. The two principal railway lines between Liverpool and London, a distance of 220 miles, are the Midland and the Northwestern. I chose the latter. We traveled at the rate of sixty miles an hour, which was the fastest riding during my whole tour; and, for my part, I do not care to repeat the experience, as I consider it too fast for safety. I found the English railway system a novel, and, to my mind, uncomfortable way, of traveling. I do

THE PRINCE OF WALES AND FAMILY.

(63)

not enjoy being locked up in a compartment with half a dozen strangers.

The road between Liverpool and London runs over a fertile and somewhat level country, lined with cities and smaller towns, the whole country being densely settled, and under a high state of cultivation ; and I was again face to face with a country greatly in contrast with California in the size and cultivation of the farms. Here we see what can be done by industry and thorough cultivation; here a million exist with comfort on an area which in our country is occupied by a few thousand. Should the traveler prefer mountain scenery to that of a level agricultural district, he should travel by the Midland Railroad. We at last reach London, the metropolis of England, and the chief city of the British Empire. It is situated on both banks of the River Thames, and has an area of 123 square miles, and a population of about 4,000,000. A detailed description of the city would fill a volume, and the books written upon the subject are so numerous that they would fill a library many times over of themselves. I will content myself with mentioning a few of the principal points of interest.

I made Charing Cross Hotel my headquarters, on account of its central location. The streets within the city limits are in many cases confused and intricate ; and the total absence of plan in the construction of the nucleus of London has doubt-

less tended to aggravate the confusion outside
the old boundaries. Much of the effect of the fine
architecture of the city's streets is totally lost from
promiscuous crowding, and the main connecting
streets between the city and the West End display, at certain parts, much meanness and incon-
gruity. Regent street, the most fashionable
throughfare of London, possesses ample width,
and the splendor of its shops atones to some extent
for the plain monotony of its regular architecture.
In Oxford street, which ranks next to it in importance, there are many buildings of a more ornamental character. Piccadilly, the eastern half of
which is occupied chiefly by shops, and the western
by dwelling houses and clubs, is a medley of every
species of architecture. Close to the most fashionable regions, there are many mean back streets,
tenanted by workmen; but the principal territory
of the working classes is comprehended in the
dense and dreary districts east and southeast of
the city. I was much impressed with the activity
of business. The confusion of vehicles, such as
carts, hacks, hansoms, wagons, tramway cars, etc.,
all combined to keep up an incessant din from
dawn until dark, and from dark until dawn again.

The Metropolitan and Metropolitan District
Railway lines, which run partly under ground, and
form almost a complete belt around the inner circle
of London, with several branches intersecting it,

5

London, with St. Paul's in the Distance.

and others communicating with various suburban lines, have proved invaluable in relieving the throng of vehicles on the streets, and in affording rapid communication between important points. I was much interested in this underground railway. Every short distance the cars stop at a platform with a flight of stairs, upon which passengers can ascend to the street or descend to the cars. I consider this railway one of the greatest and most useful enterprises in London.

I can not call to mind any occurrence on the whole journey that gave me so much pleasure as did my visit to the Exhibition of Inventions. This immense building, or rather series of buildings, is filled with tools and models of machinery of every kind, from a hand saw to a steam engine. I had the pleasure of riding in a car run by electricity, and it worked like a charm. It would not be surprising if ere long many of the street cars in California should use electricity for the motive power. Nearly every nation on the globe was here represented by some invention. Among the exhibits from America I noticed a large collection of the celebrated Waltham watches. These were awarded the first prize. For the fee of one shilling, we had access to all parts of the building. The place was literally packed with people. All nationalities were represented, and the confused murmur of voices reminded me of the tower of Babel.

Another place I visited with pleasure and profit was the Grain Exchange, in Mark Lane. This might properly be called the balance wheel of the world's wheat market. Its movements are watched with interest by farmers in all parts of the world. I there saw samples of grain from nearly all the grain-growing countries. As a farmer I derived much valuable information in regard to the quality

THE TOWER OF LONDON.

and production of different kinds of grain. Here could be seen buyers and sellers from every part of Europe. It was with pleasure and satisfaction that I observed that our California wheat stood the test, and was unsurpassed in quality by that grown by our neighbors across the Atlantic. I also visited the Crystal Palace, the Tower Water Works and the various parks. Buckingham Palace, the residence of Queen Victoria, occupies the site of Buckingham House, purchased by George III. in 1761.

The Tower of London is always a great attraction to the traveler, and the place is thronged with people from morning until night, each paying their penny as they pass through the gate. This tower was, according to tradition, originally built by Julius Cæsar; but the nucleus of the present building was begun in 1078, by William the Conqueror, who erected the part now known as the White Tower. This tower was completed in 1098. Additions were made at various periods, and it now occupies an area of thirteen acres, surrounded by a moat constructed in 1190. The new Palace of Westminster, built at a cost of about £3,000,000 on the site of the old palace, which was destroyed by fire in 1835, is a vast and ornate building in the Tudor-Gothic style, covering altogether an area of about eight acres. At the northeast corner is the clock tower, 320 feet in height. Above the dome over the central hall a spire rises to the height of 300 feet; and the Victoria Tower, 340 feet high, surmounts the royal entrance at the southwest corner. The central hall, which is entered by St. Stephen's Porch and St. Stephen's Hall, separates the House of Peers, which, along with the royal rooms, occupies the western portion of the building, from the House of Commons, to which the eastern portion is assigned.

The National Gallery of Paintings, in Trafalgar
Square, contains some of the finest specimens of
the English school of painting, besides many fine
examples of the old masters.   St. Paul's Cathedral
is remarkable for its massive simplicity and beautiful proportions.   The interior is imposing from its
vastness.   Some of the monuments of the old
building are preserved in the crypt, where also are
the tombs of many of England's most distinguished
men.   This cathedral is built in the form of a
Latin cross, the length being 500 feet, and the
breadth at the transepts 250 feet ; the dome rises
to a height of 365 feet, or of 404 feet to the top of
the cross by which it is surmounted. the height of
the interior dome being 225 feet.   It can only be
equaled in grandeur by the Cathedral of Milan, or
surpassed by St. Peter's, in Rome.   The unique
commercial position of London, and its intercourse
with every quarter of the globe, have assisted to
make it financially, in a more complete sense than
it is commercially, the metropolis of the world.
The docks present a busy scene, and there can
always be seen a host of vessels, some at their
moorings, others coming and going to and from all
parts of the earth.   I also visited the Bank of
England, the largest institution of the kind in the
world.   Among the other points of interest I found
time to visit were the famous Scotland Yards, the
Exchange of Industry, the imposing statues of

Lords Nelson and Wellington, Cleopatra's Needle, the operas, theatres and museums, and Madame Tussaud's wax-works.

In so large a city as London, there is much suffering and distress among the poorer classes. I was told that a majority of the families in the tenement houses subsisted largely on bread and ale. If

WESTMINSTER ABBEY.

I should base my opinion on the number of miserable objects I saw staggering around in a state of intoxication, I would naturally be led to the conclusion that ale or intoxicating liquor of some kind formed the principal diet of these poor creatures. Much of the crime committed can probably be attributed to the same source. It would require

months to see all the sights of London, or to get
any definite idea of this immense city ; and, as my
time was limited to a few days, I could only take in
a few of the principal points of interest. Hotel
bills, car fare, and general expenses were more in
London than in any other place I visited in Europe.
The people, with few exceptions, I found to be
generous and obliging, and I was not so tormented
with runners, cabmen and waiters trying to get a
fee as in Italy and other places on the Continent.
London alone would have repaid me for visiting
England.

The next place visited was Glasgow. This city,
after London, is the most populous in Great
Britain. It is situated on the banks of the River
Clyde. Glasgow has been almost exclusively a
commercial city for the last half-century, and has a
great variety of manufacturing interests. While
no one of the great industries occupies a position
of predominant importance, so as to stamp itself
as the peculiar characteristic of the town, there are
numerous leading departments of industry which
have long been established, and are prosecuted on
a large scale, while a variety of special manufactures have found their principal centre in Glasgow
and the Clyde Valley. Ship-building is the greatest of all the industries of Glasgow, and the position attained by the ship-builders of the Clyde is
a matter of imperial consequence and national

pride. In some years about half the total tonnage built in the United Kingdom has been launched from the banks of the Clyde. The work turned out is very diversified, but, as a rule, of the highest order. It includes armor-plated and other vessels for the Royal Navy; mail and passenger ocean

THE OLD UNIVERSITY OF GLASGOW.

steamers, for the great transatlantic and other lines; river steamboats, famous throughout the world for swiftness and elegance of appointments; merchant sailing vessels; dredging plant and hopper barges. With the exception of a very small proportion of wooden vessels, the whole of the shipping built on the Clyde is of iron and steel. The thoroughbred

cattle I saw during my visit to Glasgow were superior to any that I have seen elsewhere. I had the
pleasure of visiting several breeding establishments, and seeing some of the famous Clydesdale
horses. I noticed a vast difference between these
Scotch steeds and the horses of Northern Europe.

My next destination is France. I journeyed by
the way of London to Dover, which is about three
hours' ride from the metropolis, the road traversing
a well-cultivated and somewhat broken country.
Before crossing the Channel, I hope the reader will
pardon me if I digress a little, and comment again
on the English railway system, and the highly cultivated lands I saw. Perhaps the latter struck me
more forcibly than it otherwise would have done had
it not been a sight in such marked contrast to what
I have been accustomed to see at home. I believe
I never saw an acre of land in England that was
not well and thoroughly cultivated. I suppose this
high state of cultivation is necessitated by the high
rent, which necessarily compels the tiller of the soil
to force the land to yield to its utmost capacity.
The snug and cozy homes, surrounded by a small
patch of well-tilled land, all had an appearance of
comfort and thrift. The railway tariff in England
is rather lower than in the United States, first-class
fare being about two cents a mile. However inconvenient and uncomfortable the English railway
system may appear to an American, it is generally

. adopted on the Continent, in India, Australia and
Japan. For my part, I did not admire the construction of the cars ; they are coupled closely together, and the passenger must climb in a side
door, as there is no platform at either end of the
car. Each car is divided into small compartments,
capable of holding six or eight passengers. As soon
as the train starts, the door is locked until you
arrive at the next station. I sometimes heard people complain, that in case a robbery or some cr me
was committed while the train was in motion, one
would be at the mercy of the depredator, as there
is no communication between the different compartments. However, the passengers are not kept
in "durance vile" for any great length of time, as,
in this densely populated country, the distance between stations is very short. The conductor walks
from car to car on a narrow plank, which is only a
foot or two above the ground. No one is allowed
to board the train while in motion, and this rule is
strictly enforced.

Another custom which appeared odd to me was
that of women acting in the capacity of bar-tend-
ers, at railway stations, inns, or taverns. Oftentimes when stopping at a station I would see a
half-dozen of these damsels busily engaged in deal-
ing out liquors, coffee and sandwiches to the hungry
and thirsty crowd. However strange this may
appear to a traveler from the other side of the At-

lantic, these bar-maids are considered respectable, and you never see any of them under the influence of liquor. This seems to be one of the old and well-established customs of the country, probably made necessary by the fact that the women largely outnumber the men,—more so, I believe, than in any other country in Europe. Another point in their favor is that the amount of remuneration they expect to receive is small, and they are generally more reliable and attend more strictly to business than the men.

CHAPTER III.

FRANCE, SWITZERLAND AND AUSTRIA.

At Dover I embarked for Calais, in France, and, on arriving there, for the first time realized that I was a stranger in a strange land. Traveling in Great Britain, where the English language was continually spoken, I felt more at home than in a country where on either hand I heard people talking in an unfamiliar tongue; and, as I had never been taught to *parlez Français*, not a single word uttered was intelligible to me. Calais is a fortress of the first class, and was formerly a place of great strength; but it would now probably not be able to defend itself long against modern artillery. Steamers carrying the mails cross twice a day to Dover, and return. It is the principal landing place for English travelers on the Continent. In traveling from country to country, the first business I found it necessary to engage in was to have my money exchanged for the coin of the country I was traveling in, as it is almost impossible to turn around without spending money. I now had to convert my pounds, shillings and pence into francs and centimes; and here I will say that I found the most useful friend and companion on a journey like mine to be a long letter of credit. In Europe, Africa, India and Australia, I found English coin preferable to any other. In a tour around the world one travels more in English territory and on English steamers than on any other; and, as English coin is largely circulated, and its value well known in the Oriental world, one is less liable to be swindled by money exchangers and brokers, in using it, than he would be if he was continually having his money exchanged. Japan and the Sandwich Islands are the only countries in which I found American money to be the most desirable.

I had no sooner landed on French soil than I found myself surrounded by swarms of guides, or runners, who all offered their services in a most polite manner. It was " *Monsieur* this," and " *Monsieur* that;" "May I show you the cab," "the hotels," "the sights," "attend to your baggage;" and they even wished to hang up my hat. As they expect to be remunerated for the slightest service, it is sometimes preferable, being more profitable, to wait upon one's self. At times their officiousness became so annoying that I was tempted to wish the last servant out of sight. On my first attempt to leave Calais for Paris, I failed, by some mischance, to get aboard the train in time; and, as I saw it leaving the depot, I realized that

the train and my baggage were gone, and that I
was left behind. As the train was not yet fully
under motion, I thought I would try the American
plan of running, and jumping aboard; but I was
promptly stopped by a French official, who informed
me that I must wait until the next train. He was
very polite, however, and, after a long string of
words, pointed to his watch and made me understand that another train would soon be along. In
a very short time I was on another train, speeding
swiftly along in the direction of Paris.

After five hours' ride over a beautiful agricultural country, I found myself in the gayest city in
the world. I first turned my attention to my luggage, which was safely deposited in the Custom
House. After using a mixture of several languages
and a variety of signs, and paying a fee of one
franc, it was handed over. I always found it more
convenient and safer to keep in close proximity to
my luggage. My next step was to hire an interpreter; and there proved to be an abundance of
them, rendering it unnecessary to go for them, as
they always came to you. After a certain amount
of bargaining and bickering, I agreed to pay mine
six francs a day; and he, in return, agreed to show
me all of the sights and curiosities, both ancient
and modern, in the city of Paris. He recommended himself very highly, and said he was an
expert in the English language, and one of the

Paris.

best guides in Paris. As a matter of fact, he spoke about ten per cent. English, and the balance French.

He first piloted me to an hotel of his own choosing, which bore the name of Hotel de Strasbourg. The host was French, and so were the guests. My breakfast was served at eight o'clock in my room, lunch at one, and dinner at from seven to eight. We had every imaginable dainty from a horse to a hare; the tables were resplendent with silver and glassware, the waiters were polite and attentive; and the spacious dining hall, lighted by electricity, in the evening presented a brilliant scene. The waiters always expect to be "tipped," especially by American travelers. The cafés in the boulevards, I found to be one of the most interesting features of Paris. Here are tables strung out along the sidewalks the length of several blocks, where the Parisian men and women sit and sip their wine, apparently oblivious to the crowd around them. If one should sit down at one of these tables and call for coffee instead of wine, they would be served with black coffee in a wine-glass, and then be provided with another glass filled with brandy to mix with the coffee.

Among some of the first-class restaurants are the Café Americaine, on the Boulevard des Capucines; Anglo-Americaine, Rue de la Chaussée d'Antin; and the Grand Hotel, near the Louvre. Hotel rates

vary from one franc and fifty centimes to five francs,
according to the bill of fare and hour of meals. It
is generally well to make a bargain beforehand
with landlords, guides and cabmen, as there seems
to be a tendency among all of them to fleece
strangers, especially Americans. The principal
mode of traveling between different portions of the
city is by cabs, omnibuses and tramways. The
tops of the coaches have comfortable seats, and
about as many passengers ride outside as inside.
The tramway fare is thirty centimes, or six cents
for an inside fare, and about half that amount for
an outside fare.

The grandest of all the grand sights which I saw
in Paris was the Palace of the Louvre. This is
occupied by the richest museum in the city. On
the ground floor are museums of ancient sculpture.
There can be seen such treasures as the Venus of
Milo and the Pallas of Velletre, the most beautiful
of all statues of Minerva. Special rooms are devoted to early Christian monuments and Jewish
antiquities. On the first floor there is a magnificent collection of pictures, furniture, drawings, pottery, terra-cotta ware ; as well as objects in bronze,
glass and ivory. The second floor accommodates
the naval museum, part of the French school of
painting, and rooms for the study of Egyptian
papyrus-rolls. The Luxembourg Palace has a free
museum containing one of the finest art collections

(88)

in France, and the grounds, comprising eighty-five acres, are laid out in beautiful gardens.

Paris has about sixty theatres, of which the Grand Opera House, or National Academy of Music and Dancing, is the largest and most beautiful. This magnificent structure covers two and three-fourths acres, and is the finest in the world. The next place I had my guide point out to me was the Place de la Concorde. This occupies rather an elevated situation, and Paris can be seen in almost every direction. The chief point of interest in the square is eight imposing statues representing the chief towns of France. From the centre, where stands the Cleopatra Needle, many of the most imposing edifices of Paris can be seen. One has a fine view of the Chamber of Deputies, the Madeleine and the River Seine. The Palace of Trocadéro, which was built for the exhibition of 1878, also occupies an elevation on the right bank of the Seine. The central rotunda contains the largest music hall in Paris, and a colossal organ. It will hold 15,000 auditors. An exceedingly fine view of the city and the suburbs can be had from the dome.

The Champs-Elysées is an attractive promenade, lined with elm and lime trees. The Elysées Palace, in the Champs-Elysées, is a vast edifice, built in modern style, and is the residence of the President of the French Republic. The Palais Royal is

(85)

also a favorite place of resort, both for the Parisian
and the tourist. The court and square are lined
with shops, which present a most brilliant display
in jewelry and every variety of trinkets. At night
these arcades are a blaze of light, and presented
one of the most magnificent sights of my whole
journey.

My guide now, for a change of scene, piloted me
across the River Seine. This beautiful river flows
for seven miles through Paris, and, as it enters and
as it leaves the city, it is crossed by a viaduct, used
by the circular railway and by ordinary traffic.
That of Point de Jour has two stories of arches.
Two bridges, the Pont des Arts and the Passerelle
de Passy, are for foot passengers only, all the others
being used for carriages as well. The most famous of all these bridges is the Pont Neuf, the
two portions of which rest on the extremity of the
island called La Cité, where the river is at its widest (961 feet). On the embankment below Pont
Neuf stands the statue of Henry IV. Between
La Cité and the left bank the width of the lesser
channel is reduced to 161 feet. La Cité also com-
municates with the right bank by the bridges of
Notre Dame and Au Change ; with the left bank,
by that of Archevêché, the so-called Pont au
Double, the Petit Pont and the Pont St. Michel.
The banks of the Seine are lined with palaces and
mansions, the water is dotted with boats of every

description, and its numerous bridges are constantly thronged with people.

I visited the tomb of the first Napoleon. This grand memorial is placed in the Church of the Invalides ; a stately dome is erected over the sarcophagus which contains his remains, and over the entrance is this inscription (taken from his will) : "It is my wish that my ashes may repose on the banks of the Seine, in the midst of the French people, whom I have loved so well." In various parts of the city there are magnificent statues representing Napoleon on horseback.

While in Paris I attended the funeral services of Admiral Courbet, who died in China, and whose remains were brought to Paris for burial. The funeral was almost as imposing as that of General Grant, which I had attended in New York City. In fact, this Admiral was almost as famous in France as General Grant was in America. One of his latest deeds of prowess in the French Navy was to sink eleven ships in the China Sea in about as many minutes. In return for this friendly act the Emperor of China offered a reward of $100 for the head of every Frenchman sent him. The majority of my readers will call to mind the brief Franco-China conflict that occurred a few years ago. Since then travel in the interior of China has been considered unsafe for Europeans, especially Frenchmen.

The largest and finest religious building in Paris is the Cathedral of Notre Dame. The attractions and places of interest worthy of attention are so numerous that it would require more time than I had then to see, or have now to describe, them. I certainly saw people dressed more elegantly and in more fashionable attire than I ever saw before or since. One of the happiest thoughts of my visit to this great city was that there seemed to be more wealth and less poverty than in any other city visited by me. Considering the fact that I was a stranger to both the customs and the language of the French people, my stay in Paris was a very enjoyable one, and I hope, some day in the near future, to revisit this charming city. I agree with other travelers, that the Parisians deserve the reputation they have long enjoyed of being the politest, gayest and most fashionable people in the world.

On leaving Paris, I boarded the cars for Berne, in Switzerland. On this route we passed many towns and cities. We journeyed over a rolling country; the soil was fertile, and vegetation everywhere luxuriant. The land was planted principally to grape-vines and vegetables, and had very much the appearance of a garden. No matter in what direction you travel in France, you find a lovely country, a pleasant climate and a hospitable and polite people. On every side can be seen evidence of the thrift and industry of the French people,—

well cultivated fields and cozy and comfortable homes.

Arriving at the end of the French Division, we found ourselves at the city of Wilhausen, which is near the border line between France and Switzerland. Continuing our journey over a beautiful country, we arrived at the city of Basel, the second largest city in Switzerland, situated on the banks of the Rhine. Its inhabitants are largely engaged in the manufacture of silk

Switzerland is chiefly a land of mountains, and is one of the most remarkable countries on the globe for its magnificent and picturesque scenery. The higher Alps rise to a distance of from 8,000 to 15,000 feet above the level of the sea, and are covered with perpetual snow. The glaciers of Switzerland are the reservoirs which feed some of the largest rivers of Western Europe. No country possesses greater interest for geologists. To the tourist it presents a great abundance of natural curiosities. There are many points of view whence the semicircular array of Alpine peaks presented at once to the eye, extends for more than a hundred and twenty miles, and comprises between two and three hundred distinct summits capped with snow, and bristling with bare rocks. Of the heights commanding such Alpine panoramas, the Righi is probably the finest, as it certainly is one of the most accessible.

Switzerland has numerous waterfalls. The fall of the Rhine deserves the first rank on account of the volume of water; but it is rather a cascade than a cataract, as it lacks height. There are many other celebrated falls. The principal and most interesting of the Swiss Alpine passes are the Simplon, the St. Gothard, the Splugen and the Bernardin, both as regards their scenery and the magnificent and skillfully constructed carriage roads which have been made over them. Switzerland contains a considerable number of lakes, among the most important of which are Lakes Geneva, Lucerne and Zurich. In many places we see the land cultivated clear to the hill-tops. The mountain side is dotted with cottages, and one is almost inclined to wonder that the houses built upon these steep slopes do not roll off into the gulch below.

On August 27 we arrived at Berne, the third city in size, and the capital of Switzerland. It is surrounded by vineyards, and has a mild, balmy climate and a rich soil. Berne is an old city, and its architecture is certainly odd as well as old. The houses are chiefly constructed of stone or granite, as this is a region of quarries, and this material is both cheap and plentiful. Many of the houses have broad porches which project over the sidewalk below. This gives the streets, which are narrow, a somewhat gloomy appearance. One of the chief

attractions of the city is the number of playing
fountains. These are ornamented with bears'
heads and various other figures. Berne is also
quite a manufacturing centre, and a large number
of watches and toys are manufactured here. I
visited several establishments, and found the greater
proportion of the operatives to be women. There
are also several large mills driven with water-
power derived from the River Aar. This swiftly
flowing stream runs through the lower portion of
the city.

The people chiefly spoke the German language.
This language I found easier to understand without
an interpreter than any other. The people were
apparently kind hearted and good humored ; the
hotel bills and servants' fees, the most moderate of
any place on the Continent. Five francs, or one
dollar, per day, is all the first-class hotels charge.
Here, again, I saw women acting as bar-keepers,
porters and waiters in the public houses. On
many occasions they have come into my room at
dawn of day, got my shoes, and given them a fine
polishing. It was something of a novelty to me
to have my shoes blacked by a rosy-cheeked
maiden. I also visited Aar, another interesting
city. It is surrounded by grand and picturesque
scenery. This ended my first visit to Switzerland,
the playground of Europe. I returned, however,
three months later, after I had made the circuit of

the Continent. The incidents of that visit to this interesting republic I will briefly mention in another chapter.

LETTER FROM SWITZERLAND.

Special Correspondence Modesto Herald.

BERNE, SWITZERLAND, Sept. 1, 1885.

This time I will only have room to give you a glimpse of the outline of my trip since I left Modesto. I have been in constant motion from rail to steamer, and from steamer to rail, until I have traveled over nine thousand miles, and I have only made a good beginning of my tour around the globe

I steamed out of the Golden Gate on the 27th of July for Portland, Oregon, 800 miles on that coast. The Pacific was not pacific, as was noticed by so many passengers feeding the fishes,—myself included. Portland, twelve miles above the mouth of the Willamette River, is a stirring city of 40,000 inhabitants. Ships are seen along the wharves loading wheat for Europe.

From Portland I left by the express train for St. Paul, on the Northern Pacific Railroad, and soon found myself hurried over the Cascade Mountains into Eastern Oregon. Cascades along the Columbia River have the grandest scenery in the West. At Wallula Junction I crossed the boundary line into Washington Territory, where I traveled for 100 miles ; but, after leaving the Snake River, the land seemed unimproved and barren of vegetation until I got to the Idaho line. Spokane Falls is the largest and one of the most important places in Washington Territory. I crossed the corner of Idaho for eighty miles, and found it thickly timbered, and adapted more for grazing than grain growing. We next moved into Montana, the finest stock country on the Northern Pacific Railroad. At Heron we entered the slopes of the Rocky Mountains, and the scenery was imposing when viewing those towering peaks and glittering streams. Helena, the capital, is a flourishing city of 10,000 inhabitants, located near the headwaters of the Missouri River, and surrounded by mountains pointing to the skies. East of Helena I was much impressed with the extensive grazing valleys, green meadows and gravelly hills. At Livingston we left the main line for Yellowstone Park. Here I met tourists from many parts of the globe, investigating the grandest pyramidic sights in the world. Even here in Switzerland I haven't seen anything to compare with it. I now resume my journey on the main line. Glendive, an important trading post, is the last station in sight after traveling 800 miles,—the extreme length of Montana. The iron horse has now sent me across the boundary line into Dakota. Medora is the first station in sight from here for fifty miles. The soil is of all varieties and colors, called the bad lands, and presents an interesting appearance to sight-seers.

The next important station we passed was Dickson, located in a fine grazing region. It also had the appearance of a good game region, from the variety of stuffed deer and wolves in sight and for sale at the depot. On the east bank of the Missouri stands Bismarck, the capital of Dakota. From here on to the Minnesota line, Dakota made a favorable change to a level, productive farming country, but barren of timber along the line. The main attraction in Dakota was the large Dalrymple farm, with 75,000 acres under cultivation. This reminded me of our extensive farming in California, —the garden-spot of the earth, on account of her even climate and natural resources. Moorhead, on the east bank of the Mississippi, was the first glimpse of Minnesota, after traveling 350 miles through Dakota. This great green State showed signs of wealth and prosperity by the many improved farms, especially in the Red River Valley ; and, were it not for its high latitude, Minnesota would equal any State in the Union.

I soon found myself in Minneapolis, the Queen City of the Northwest, with a population of 125,000, and the largest milling point in the world. St. Paul, the same size as Minneapolis, is also a great city, with its large whole-sale houses, and has the largest hotels north of Chicago.

From here I resumed my journey to Wisconsin, where I made a brief stay among old friends. Thence to New York City, via Washington City and Philadelphia, where I inspected the United States Mint, and the seat of our government. I arrived in New York August 8, in time to take a part in General Grant's funeral procession,—the most imposing affair of the kind ever known in America. After looking over New York, with its million and a half inhabitants, and thickly planted with houses for twelve miles, from Harlem River to Castle Garden, I left the harbor on the 11th of August, on board the steamship Wisconsin, for Queenstown, with about 200 fellow-passengers of different nationalities,—all going to Europe to enjoy the benefits of the portions they had accumulated in America. After eleven days, in which we had journeyed 3,090 miles over the stormy Atlantic, I found myself safely landed in the Old World. Since that I have visited Ireland, England and France. Have spent the most of my time in London and Paris ; but I am now among the lofty mountains of Switzerland. From here I am going to Vienna, and so on until I have been over the whole Continent of Europe.

Notwithstanding the difficulties I have met with in contending with strange tongues, and being a stranger in strange lands, I have enjoyed my trip to the fullest extent, and all the objects of interest in this realm I will speak of more particularly in my next. OSMUN JOHNSON,

I next visited Bavaria. Arriving at Boden See, a beautiful lake situated between Switzerland and Bavaria, I embarked on one of the small steamers that traverse the lake. This boat was crowded with tourists of various nationalities, all intent on pleasure and sight-seeing. On this boat I participated in one of the biggest dinners I had spread before me while in Europe; it consisted of thirteen courses, and would have satisfied the most fastidious epicure. After steaming across the Boden See, I landed in Lindau, a beautiful pleasure resort, surrounded, on one side, by picturesque mountain scenery, and, on the other, by the waters of the lovely lake. The streets are crooked and narrow, and the inhabitants slow-going and easy. The low stone buildings have an ancient appearance.

After a brief stay in Bavaria I made preparations to visit Austria. After passing the town of Bludens, we began to gradually ascend a lofty range of the Alps, where the scenery, for sublimity and grandeur, exceeded anything I have seen. Nothing in the Sierra Nevadas or Rocky Mountains can begin to compare with it. Among the higher peaks from which we obtained a fine view were Katzencliff, Davena and Raggler. These snow-capped peaks tower for thousands of feet above the level of the sea. As the train wound its way up the steep and narrow grade, a glance out of the car window almost made one shiver; on every side were deep gulches, steep cliffs and crags. The engineering on this road is a magnificent piece of work. Tunnels are numerous, and many of them difficult to construct. The longest one, called Alberg, requires twenty minutes to pass through.

Every little while we would pass small patches of land cultivated by the industrious peasants, who know nothing else but work. Here the women work in the field, and do all kinds of manual labor. By close economy and untiring industry these poor people manage to exist. One suit of homespun clothes for Sunday wear, is supposed to last a man a lifetime. They are always worn on holidays and on all ceremonious occasions, when they are deco-rated with ancient jewelry which has been handed down from generation to generation.

We soon arrived at Innsbrück, where we changed cars for Kufstein and Salzburg, where the road skirted the shore of a little lake, partly enclosed by rugged hills. From here the road traverses the level valleys of Austria, which seemed to be devoted to agriculture. I often saw women plowing in the field with a team composed of a horse, steer and cow. The grain is cut and threshed principally with hand tools. Very little machinery is used or seen in these districts, and the farms in these tucked-up kingdoms of Europe have the appear-ance of paddocks to one acquainted with the vast grain fields of California, where machinery is used exclusively in the cultivation of the soil and the harvesting of the crops.   Here in the whole realm main strength and stupidity seemed to be the motive power.

I arrived in Vienna on September 5.   It is a distance of 600 English miles from Paris to this city. I must confess that it was a rather uncomfortable journey.   The cars were constructed on the English plan, and I never quite enjoyed being locked up in these small compartments, with three or four strangers in such close proximity.   I have already praised the American system, which I consider the most comfortable in the world.   On the other hand, the European conductor is a much more civil individual than his American contemporary; he will answer questions freely and politely, and will talk to a stranger like any other mortal. On the other side of the Atlantic, the average conductor prides himself on his gruffness and individuality.

Vienna, one of the most interesting and enterprising cities in Europe, is situated in a fertile plain on the southernmost branch of the Danube. The great bulk of the population consists of German Roman Catholics ; but all nationalities and denominations are represented.   Vienna is divided into the old city, which is nearly encircled, and about three miles in circumference, and the new city, consisting of thirty-four suburbs.   The old city was, up to 1858, surrounded by a deep fosse, and high walls with projecting bastions, which, in later times, served as terrace walks ; but these fortifications have, in a great measure, long since been filled up or leveled, thus enlarging the glacis, a broad and pleasant esplanade, by which they were encircled, and separated from the suburbs. Of the numerous gates which formerly led from the old city to the suburbs, the Burgthor (castle or palace gate) is justly celebrated.

In the arrangement of its streets, Vienna has been compared to a spider's web, the principal thoroughfares radiating from a central point near the Cathedral of St. Stephen, to the bastions across the glacis, and through the suburbs to the outer lines, and being intersected by numerous minor streets and alleys. Contrary to the general rule in modern cities, the old part of the town is the more fashionable of the two. It has narrow streets, mostly lined with lofty houses, but also some splendid squares, and contains the oldest churches and the palaces of the emperor and the highest nobility.

The Hofplatz (court square) has a colossal statue of the Virgin, and two fountains ; the Josephplatz, an equestrian statue of the Emperor Joseph I. The square called Freiung contains a beautiful fountain with five bronze figures representing Austria and her four principal rivers. The Graben,

7

near the centre of the city, has, among other ornaments, a beautiful column in honor of the Trinity.
The Graben and the Kohlmarkt, a street leading
from it to the imperial palace, contains the finest
shops. The Imperial Library, a handsome building on the Josephplatz, contains upward of 350,000
volumes, and about 300,000 engravings, the largest
and finest collection of the kind in the world. It
also contains numerous and valuable curiosities.

The most conspicuous and most interesting
church in Vienna is the Cathedral of St. Stephen,
considered by many to be the finest specimen of
Gothic architecture on the globe. It was begun
five centuries ago ; but the two turrets flanking the
west portal, called the Giant gate, are the remains
of a church built two hundred years earlier. The
length of the cathedral is 345 feet, its breadth 230
feet. Its steeple is a masterpiece of architecture,
and is 444 feet high. The largest bell, cast from
hundreds of cannon taken from the besieging
Turks in 1683, weighs 380 hundred weight. The
view from the steeple extends over the Danube,
and many old battle-fields, also a number of palaces, gardens and bathing establishments.

Vienna has extensive manufactories. I visited
several of them, including the extensive fan factory carried on by Mr. Grunbaum, brother of our
Modesto merchant, B. Grunbaum. Here they employed 300 operatives, men and women, who were

busily engaged in manufacturing fancy fans, which are exported to all parts of the world. I am much indebted to Mr. Grunbaum for his kindness in piloting me through the bustling city, and pointing out many of the principal points of interest, among others the Grand Opera House, erected in place of the one burned down seven years ago. The majority of my readers will remember when the news of this terrible catastrophe was telegraphed to all parts of the world, and of the sad fate of the thousands of people who were buried in its ashes.

We next visited the museum. This contains seven apartments, three of which are filled with ancient armor. The other departments embrace old paintings, curiosities of nature and art, carvings, trinkets, remarkable dresses, and many objects of historical interest. Had I not so lately visited the Louvre, in Paris, I should have been all the more struck with admiration in viewing this wonderful collection of curiosities, relics and magnificent works of art.

The dancing, ball and concert rooms of Vienna, as well as other places of amusement, are very numerous and well attended, the inhabitants being distinguished by a cheerful and jovial disposition above those of all other capitals of Europe. The coffee houses are spacious, and generally thronged. The great promenades are the Glacis, the Volksgarten (people's garden), the Augarten, Brigettenau, and especially the Prater, a natural park on a series of low islands formed by the arms of the Danube. The Prater, especially on fête days, with its coffee houses, panorama, circus, swings, jugglers, rustic kitchens, long rows of tables and benches, trains of carriages, and its laughing, drinking and dancing multitudes in all the various national costumes of the Austrian Empire, is the most characteristic part of the capital. There are also fashionable cafés that are frequented by the aristocracy and nobility, who never mix with the common people. Among other features of interest that I had pointed out to me were the Palace of Justice and the House of Parliament.

During my brief stay in Vienna I made the Wienberger Hotel my headquarters, where I was charged five guldens, or two dollars, per day.

The narrow streets are thronged with people all day long. I frequently saw a woman and a dog side by side pulling a loaded wagon together. The dog would be in regular harness, and the woman would wear a shoulder strap. This was a common sight, even in the most fashionable streets, and never seemed to attract attention except from a stranger like myself. In no other city did I see a wider contrast between the rich and the poor. The former occupy costly palaces surrounded by all that luxury and wealth can give, while the latter are clothed in rags, and perform all kinds of menial labor. The open market presents a scene of much interest. Here hundreds of women are daily engaged in buying and selling all kinds of produce. These women are certainly industrious, but, unlike the Parisians, can make no pretensions to feminine beauty.

In company with some other tourists, I had a pleasant ride on the Danube, and we had a fine opportunity for viewing the city, which borders the stream for several miles.

CHAPTER IV.

GERMANY AND DENMARK.

I NOW bade farewell to the Austrian capital, and set out for Berlin, a distance of ninety German, or about 350 English, miles. The route I traversed took me through Bohemia and Saxony. Bohemia is a kingdom of the Austrian Empire, and has a population of between five and six millions. We traveled through a level and fertile valley, where the rank vegetation and the thrifty growth of its diversified crops bore evidence to the richness of the soil. As usual, the women were everywhere industriously laboring in the fields, where they could be seen with some implement in hand, some using the scythe, the sickle or the pruning knife, while others were engaged in hauling hay or plowing. It was no longer a matter of surprise to see women and men working together doing the work that in America is supposed to belong to the men exclusively. I understand, however, that in these countries this custom is a matter of necessity.

The mineral springs of Bohemia are justly famous. The industries of the kingdom are highly developed in various directions. Most important of all is the manufacture of woolen goods, principally carried on at Reichenburg and in the neighborhood of that city. The cotton manufacture is also extensively prosecuted in the same district, and at Rumburg and other places linen stuffs are largely produced. Bohemian glass has been celebrated for centuries, and is still exported to all parts of Europe. The climate is healthful, but varies considerably in different districts.

As many of the kingdoms of Europe are smaller than an ordinary county in California, it takes very little time to travel from one to the other; consequently I was soon in Saxony. This is the third constituent of Germany in point of population, and the fifth in point of area. Saxony is one of the most fertile parts of Germany. In regard to the productive occupation of its soil, it stands among the most advanced nations in the world. It also claims to be one of the most highly educated countries in Europe. Its schools and universities were founded among the earliest in Germany, and education is compulsory.

Dresden, the capital, is situated in a beautiful and richly cultivated valley on both sides of the Elbe. It is approached on almost every side by avenues of trees, and the distance is bounded by gentle eminences covered with plantations and vineyards. On account of its delightful situation

BERLIN.

and the many objects of interest it contains, it is often called the "German Florence." Dresden owes a large part of its fame to its extensive artistic, literary and scientific collections. Among the chief branches of industry are manufactures in gold and silver, straw plait, scientific and musical instruments, artificial flowers and painter's canvas. There are several large breweries, a considerable corn trade is carried on, and there is an extensive traffic in books and objects of art.

At Dresden I met a great many tourists from America, also quite a number of Americans who reside here. It was a pleasure and a relief to be able to converse in my own familiar tongue. For weeks I had been laboring with a foreign language, and had been obliged to depend on an interpreter. As one was not always at hand, and as they generally understood just about enough English to enable them to fleece a traveler, I labored under many disadvantages.

My next stopping place was Berlin, the capital of Prussia, and since 1871 the metropolis of the German Empire. It is situated on both sides of the River Spree, and is built on what was originally in part a sandy, and in part a marshy, district. By its canals it has direct communication with the Oder River. This river, with its canals and branches, is crossed by about fifty bridges, very few of which have any claim to architectural beauty. Among these latter may be mentioned the Schlossbrücke, which was built in the years 1822, 1823 and 1824. It has eight colossal figures of white marble, representing the different stages of a warrior's career. These statues are for the most part of high artistic merit; they stand on granite pedestals. The Kurfürstenbrücke is another bridge which merits notice on account of the equestrian bronze statue of the Great Elector, by which it is adorned.

Berlin covers an area of about twenty-five English square miles, and now takes its place as the third greatest city of Europe, surpassed only by London and Paris. In secular buildings, Berlin is very rich. It differs, however, from all other capitals, in this respect: that, with the exception of the castle, a large building enclosing two courts and containing more than 600 rooms, and which dates its origin back to the sixteenth century, all of its public buildings are comparatively modern, dating, in their present form, from the eighteenth and nineteenth centuries. The public buildings and monuments which render it famous, date, almost without exception, from 1814, the close of the great conflict with Napoleon I. Its churches are the structures which lay claim to the highest antiquity, four of them dating from the thirteenth and fourteenth centuries. But in respect to churches, both in their number and beauty, Berlin

THE SIEGESSAULE.

(107)

is, relatively speaking, probably the poorest of the
capitals of Christendom.

Up to a very recent date, Berlin was a walled
city.   Those of its nineteen gates which still
remain have only an historical or architectural
interest.   The principal of these is the Branden-
burg gate, which is 201 feet broad and nearly sixty-
five feet in height.   It is supported by twelve
Doric columns, each forty-four feet high, and surmounted by a Car of Victory, which, taken by
Napoleon I. to Paris in 1807, was brought back by
the Prussians in 1814.   The streets, about 520 in
number, are, with the exception of the districts in
the most ancient part of the city, long, straight and
wide, and lined with high houses; for the old typical Berlin house, with its ground and first floor, is
fast disappearing.

Among the most imposing structures are the
Admiralty, the upper house of the Prussian
Legislature, the Imperial Parliament, the royal
palaces, the Jewish synagogue, the Opera and the
Royal Museums.   The public buildings are superior
to those in most cities of Europe.   Berlin possesses
eight museums, in addition to the Royal Museum
and the National Gallery.   The Royal Museums
are the old and the new museums.   The former is
the most imposing building in Berlin.   The new
museum is connected with the old by a covered
corridor.   In its interior arrangements and decora-

tions, it is undoubtedly the most splendid structure in the city. The National Gallery is an elegant building, situated between the new museum and the Spree, and is intended to receive the collection of modern paintings, now exhibited provisionally in the apartment of the Academy.

The public monuments are the equestrian statues of the Great Elector on the Large Brücke; the celebrated statue of Frederick the Great, probably the grandest monument in Europe, opposite the emperor's palace, Unter den Linden; and the statue of Frederick William III. in the Lust Garten. On the Kreuzberg, the highest spot in the neighborhood of Berlin, a Gothic monument in bronze was erected by Frederick William III. to commemorate the victories of 1813 and 1815, and in the Königsplatz the present Emperor has erected a Column of Victory in honor of the triumphs of 1864, 1866 and 1870. This monument rises to the height of 197 feet, the gilded figure of Victory on top being forty feet high.

Next to Leipsic, Berlin is the largest publishing centre in Germany. It is not only a centre of intelligence, but is also an important centre of manufactures and trade. Its trade and manufactures seem to be at present in a transitory state; old branches are dying, and new ones springing into existence.

I was much pleased with my sojourn in Ger-

EMPEROR WILHELM.

(110)

many. I found the people, as a rule, polite and hospitable. They appeared to be much interested in American travelers. As a rule, there seemed to be less extortion practiced in Germany than in any other country I visited. The tramway fare was a trifling sum; and the fee to porters, guides and hackmen, and the railway fare throughout the whole German empire, the most reasonable on the Continent. Among the leading hotels are the Auburn and Chalsber Houses, where the traveler can have his meals served either on the European or American plan. One can fare well for eight marks, or about $1.75, per day.

I left Berlin, September 11, for Hamburg. My route lay over a level country, the soil of which seemed to be of a swampy and marshy character. The principal resources of this section seemed to be hay-making, turf-digging and turf-drying. The turf is largely used for fuel, on account of the scarcity of timber in this part of Germany. Of course, the women had a hand in both industries, and many of them could be seen busily engaged in piling turf or mowing hay.

At Würtemberg, half way between Berlin and Hamburg, I had the pleasure of seeing the venerable Emperor William, the first crowned head I had, up to this time, had the pleasure of seeing while in Europe, but far from being the last. Thousands of people were awaiting the arrival of

the Emperor. The militia was out in full force
ready to salute him. The gorgeous decoration of
the station, the drilling, the thunder of artillery, the
holiday attire of the people, all helped to make this
one of the most brilliant and striking incidents of
my journey through Prussia.

A few hours later I found myself in the city of
Hamburg, one of the most remarkable cities of
Germany, and, in fact, of Europe, ranking, as it
does, as the first of all the seats of commerce on
the Continent. It is situated on the right bank of
the northern branch of the River Elbe, about
ninety-three miles from the mouth of that river,
just where it is joined by the Alster and the Bille.

The oldest portion of the city is that which lies
to the east of the Alster ; to the west lies the new
town. The old town lies low, and is traversed by a
great number of narrow canals, or "fleets," which
add considerably to the picturesqueness of the
meaner quarters, and serve as convenient channels
for the transportation of goods. They generally
form what may be called the back streets, and they
are bordered by warehouses, cellars and the lower
classes of dwelling houses. As they are subject to
the ebb and flow of the Elbe, at certain times they
run quite dry, and afford a field of operation for a
certain class who wander the oozy channel to pick
up any articles of value. At other times they are
filled from fifteen to twenty feet above their ordi-

nary level. As soon as the telegram at Cuxhaven
announces high tide, three shots are fired from the
stintfung, at the harbor, to warn the inhabitants
of the "fleets;" and, if the progress of the tide up
the river gives indication of danger, three other
shots are fired to add emphasis to the warning.
Then the dwellers on the lower levels make a rapid
escape with their property. At the time of the
equinoxes the inundation may be repeated for several days in succession ; but, when all is over, the
people return like rats to their oozy and dripping
abodes. In fine contrast to the dull and dismal
fleets, is the bright and handsome appearance of the
Inner Alsten, which is enclosed on three sides by
handsome rows of buildings.

In the extent of its commerce, Hamburg ranks
among European ports immediately after London,
Liverpool and Glasgow. The river and harbor
are continually crowded with vessels of all descriptions, from the smallest river craft to the largest
ocean steamer.

Of the many churches in Hamburg, St. Peters,
St. Michaels, St. Nicholas and the Dutch Reformed
Church are among the largest, and probably the
most worthy of note. The Church of St. Nicholas is remarkable, more especially for its tower,
which rises to a height of 473 feet. Both interior
and exterior are elaborately adorned with sculptures. St. Michaels has a tower which almost

8

rivals that of St. Nicholas, as it rises to a height of
428 feet. It surpasses all the other churches of
Hamburg, being 229 feet long and 179 feet broad,
and produces a fine effect by the colossal proportions of its four principal pillars. Among other
buildings of interest are the Hamburg Bank, the
Grand Opera House and the Museum. The principal hotels are the Hamburger Hoff and Hotel
Europe. Here accommodations can be had in
thorough European style, and one can live
luxuriously for the moderate amount of eight
marks per day.

An extended stroll over the city left the impression upon my mind that it did not deserve much of
a reputation for either cleanliness or godliness. I
was told that vice and wickedness prevail in Hamburg to a greater extent than in any other city of
the same size in Europe. A noticeable feature of
Hamburg is the cheap prices which seem to prevail
in every branch of business. A suit of clothes
that would cost fifty dollars in San Francisco,
could be bought for twenty here.

After visiting Bremen, an important seaport
within a short distance of Hamburg, I started for
Copenhagen, traveling by the way of Kiel, a city
with a population of about 50,000. It is picturesquely situated at the southern end of Kielov
Föhrde, about sixty-six miles northeast of Hamburg by rail. Kiel is the most important naval

harbor of Germany, and the station of the German Baltic fleet, and the port and its approaches are very strongly fortified. The safety and' excellence of Kiel harbor, whose only drawback is that it is frozen in winter, have made the town one of the principal ports of the Baltic. Here I embarked for Korsör, in Denmark, a distance of eighteen German, or seventy-two English, miles.

Since landing in the Old World, I had been constantly in motion, endeavoring to see all that was worth seeing, and had traveled by all the different modes of transit the various countries afforded. As we, steamed out of the harbor of Kiel I watched the fast-receding German shore with something akin to regret ; for I had spent several very pleasant weeks among the German people. The knowledge I had acquired of their language I found afterward to be of great benefit to me when traveling in the German settlements in Asia.

After a few hours' sailing over the boisterous Baltic, we anchored at Korsör, and I was soon treading on Danish soil. The first thing was to go through the regular custom-house formality of having my baggage searched by its officers, to see if it might by any possibility contain dynamite, or some article on which a duty might be levied. Before starting out in quest of new scenes I was obliged to hunt up a money broker, and provide myself with the coin of the country For each

English pound, I obtained eighteen cronor, or
crowns, which was equivalent to five dollars in
United States gold coin. This would go twice as
far here as the same amount in the United States.

The coasts of Denmark are generally low and
sandy, and the whole western shore of Jutland is a
succession of sand ridges and shallow lagoons, very
dangerous to shipping. On the eastern side the
coast is not so inhospitable. On the contrary,
there are several excellent harbors, especially on
the islands. There is little variety in the surface
of Denmark, as it is uniformly low; and the highest point in the whole country, Himmelbjerget, in
Jutland, is only 550 feet above the level of the sea.
It is not as low, however, as Holland is. The
country is pleasantly diversified, and rises a little at
the coast, even though it remains flat inland.

The landscape of the islands and the southeastern part of Jutland is rich in beech woods,
corn fields and meadows, and even the minute
islets are green and fertile. In the western and
northern districts of Jutland this gives place to a
wide expanse of moorland, covered with heather,
and ending at the sea in low, whitish cliffs. There
is a melancholy charm even about these monotonous tracts, and it can not be said that. Denmark is
wanting in natural beauty. It is obvious that in
such a country there can exist no rivers; the
longest of the Danish streams is little more than
a brook. Nor are there any large lakes.

The people are honest, economical and industrious; every one works. The majority of them
are rosy-checked, healthy and seemingly happy in
their slow-going way. They seem devoid of any
ambition to acquire wealth. Their motto seems to
be to do good, to feel good, and to enjoy life as it
comes from day to day. Denmark, small as she is,
is the most independent little country in Northern
Europe. It is pre-eminently a corn land, all kinds
of grain are grown, and the potato is largely cultivated. The produce of grass is not very large, the
fertility of the soil tempting the farmers to use it
all for grain. The exports are largely in excess of
the imports.

From Korsör to Copenhagen is a distance of
eighteen Danish miles, or fifty-six English miles.
The road lies over a densely populated agricultural district. Men, women and children work
in the fields together. The most important
towns we passed on this route were Slagesingele,
Soro and Roskedal. I arrived at the Danish
capital on the 15th of September. Copenhagen
is situated at the southern extremity of the
sound, which is at that part about twenty miles
wide. The main portion of the city is built on
low-lying ground on the east coast of the island of
Zealand, between the sea and a series of fresh-
water lakes. It is becoming more and more the
commercial centre of Denmark, and its local indus-

tries and its foreign trade are both making rapid advances. The harbor is large and commodious, and, by the aid of canals, large vessels can enter almost to the centre of the city. The principal streets were thronged with people of every grade and rank.

At the time I was in Copenhagen the Czar of Russia was visiting his father-in-law, the King of Denmark, the public buildings were all decorated, and the people generally seemed to have donned their holiday attire. I had a glimpse of the carriage and body guard of one of the greatest rulers in the world. A few days later, while in Christiania, I saw the Prince of Wales and the Crown Prince of Norway. For all they were only ordinary mortals, I was glad I had had an opportunity of seeing them. Strange how one human being sometimes enjoys even seeing the footprints of another. The King of Denmark is blest with a royal son, the King of Greece, and with two royal sons-in-law, the Czar of Russia and the Prince of Wales. I hope on my next tour to see this royalty converted into a republic. It would infuse new life into the people to be able to breathe the air of freedom.

Among the most interesting public buildings are the Royal Palace of Christiansborg. This palace contains the council chamber and the apartments in which both houses of Parliament hold their sittings. The Palace of Rosenberg is an irregular building in Gothic style, with a high, pointed roof, and flanked by four towers of unequal dimensions. The Palace of Charlottenborg is a huge, desolate-looking structure, built in 1672. Here the annual exhibition of painting and sculpture is held. The Thorwaldsen Museum is two stories in height, and 230 feet long, and 125 feet broad. In the centre is an open court containing the artist's tomb. The exterior walls are decorated with groups of figures illustrative of events connected with the formation of the museum. The front hall, corridors and apartments are painted in the Pompeian style, with brilliant colors and with great artistic skill.

The principal theatre is the Royal, on Kongens Nytory, a beautiful edifice of modern erection. This I visited, and saw some of the ablest actors and the most brilliant assemblage of people since leaving Paris. The play was grand, and the people dressed in the most costly attire. The Royal Family might properly be considered the feature of the evening. I also visited the Tivoli Gardens, which are situated immediately beyond the western gate, and form the favorite place of resort in the summer evenings. The market square was crowded with people, and produce of every kind was exhibited. Butter and cheese occupied a prominent place, and they are among the principal exports.

CHAPTER V.

SWEDEN, THE BALTIC AND RUSSIA.

SEPTEMBER 19 I embarked on a small coast steamer for Malmö, a seaport town in Southern Sweden. It is situated on the eastern shore of the sound, opposite Copenhagen, from which it is sixteen miles distant. I paid my fare of two cronor, and, after a couple of hours' pleasant sailing, found myself at my destination. Here again I was in a new country, and my baggage had to be inspected by custom-house officers. This was done so frequently while traveling in Scandinavia that I began to look upon it in the light of a nuisance, and I resolved, that, if I ever visited the country again, I would confine my luggage to a valise, and thus save myself much annoyance. However, I was subject to less imposition and extortion in Northern Europe than in the countries south of the Alps and in the Orient, where there are whole armies of loafers and hangers-on whose sole object in life is to fleece the traveler.

Malmö is inferior only to Stockholm and Gothenburg in importance, and was formerly the most important town on the sound. It is built on a level plain, and is backed by an agricultural country. One has a fine view of the water, which is dotted with vessels. From Malmö to Stockholm is about 350 English, or fifty Swedish, miles. The distance to Gothenburg is about the same.

As we advance eastward the land is rolling and sometimes rocky, and large strips of country are timbered with stunted birch, fir and pine trees. Although to me the soil appeared unfit for cultivation, it was densely settled and fairly improved. The red houses and red barns add much to the picturesqueness of the rocky hills. The farms and fields are enclosed by stone fences. The grain is cut with a sickle, and generally harvested by women. Often in the busy harvest season, the leading farmers select a dozen women, who, with sickle in hand, cut the grain and tie it in bundles. A given number of bundles is considered a day's work. Many of these peasant women occupy little homes on the outskirts of the farmer's domain, for which they pay a yearly rent. The wages they receive for a day's work in the harvest field is fifty örer, which is equivalent to thirteen cents. The laboring classes are meagrely compensated for their work. The usual wages for a man who is employed by the year is from thirty to forty dollars, and a woman generally receives about half that amount.

Gothenburg, the second city and the chief commercial town of Sweden, is situated in a low valley surrounded by bare hills, on the south bank of the Götha River. It is well and regularly built, mostly of stone or brick, with wide and well paved streets, and in its general appearance much resembles an English town.

From Gothenburg to Stockholm by way of the canal is an interesting journey. This canal connects with Lake Wetter, a large sheet of water. The canal and lake are girted with hills, principally covered with tamarack and pine. Stockholm is situated at the junction of Lake Maelar with an arm of the Baltic called Skaengard. The city is built chiefly upon a number of islands. It is handsomely designed, and built with several squares and public walks, ornamented with trees and statues. The city has been likened to Venice. There are several points of view which recall the Southern City of the Sea ; but the resemblance is imperfect. The approaches by water are uncommonly beautiful, both on the lake side and from the Baltic, commanding views probably unsurpassed of their kind.

The most striking object from every point, is the great rectangular palace, an immense structure, standing upon an eminence on the central island. Its vast and massive walls rise far above the neighboring buildings. There are few cities in Europe whose general aspect is more attractive than that

of Stockholm. Vast ranges of buildings are relieved and over-shadowed in the Stad by the
majestic palace and church towers rising from their
midst. Nowhere has nature disposed of her undu-
lations of soil and curves of water boundary with

THE ROYAL PALACE, STOCKHOLM.

more endless variety. In the compass of a single
evening one may pass through sombre forest and
smooth pasture slopes, climb tall granite cliffs overhanging glassy lake and bay, and glide through
the busy seaport filled with sails and moving
industry, the granite quays lined and adorned

with architectural beauty, with statues and monuments of art.

The various subdivisions of the city, intersected by the waters of the lake, are chiefly islands connected by bridges, some of which are of superb granite masonry. Picturesque ferry boats, propelled by women in their showy provincial costumes, add greatly to the scene in summer. In winter the waters are compact plains of snow-clad ice, covered with all the moving activity of thoroughfares. One of the most interesting objects is the Riddarholm Church, which contains the tombs and trophies of many historic personages. The harbor is one of the finest in the world, and the largest-sized ships may penetrate into the very heart of the city.

There are several fine theatres and other places of amusement. A strong military garrison of life guards is always quartered in the barracks. A naval squadron, chiefly of gunboats, is stationed at an island opposite the palace. The city, covered by a strong fortress, is perhaps impregnable by water. Stockholm is the chief seat of Swedish manufactures, which are here extensive. Translated into English, Stockholm would be Log Island. Tradition has it that it derived its name from a stock, or log, which was sent adrift on the stream. The city was to be built wherever the log landed.

On leaving Stockholm, I crossed the Baltic, and paid a hasty visit to Russia. We had a stormy sea voyage of 375 miles. St. Petersburg, the capital of the Russian Empire, is situated in a thinly peopled region at the head of the Gulf of Finland, and at the mouth of the River Neva. The bulk of the city is on the left bank of the river, and includes the best and the busiest streets, the richest shops, the great bazars and markets, the palaces, cathedrals and theatres, as well as railway stations, except that of the Finland Railway. Among the principal objects of interest are the memorial to St. Peter and the Cathedral of St. Isaac. This city has a population of nearly 1,000,000 people. I had planned to go from St. Petersburg to Moscow, and thence to Constantinople ; but the near approach of winter induced me to give up this plan. So, after a brief but interesting stay in the brilliant Russian capital, I recrossed the Baltic to Stockholm.

CHAPTER VI.

NORWAY.

ON arriving at Stockholm, I took the cars for Christiania. On this journey I visited the Trolhatta Fall, one of the grandest sights in Sweden. At Frederickstad I had my first glimpse of Norway. I was now fast entering one of the most picturesque countries of the earth. The first sight of interest we passed in this romantic region was the celebrated Sarf-foss, on the River Glommen. This remarkable fall, or foss, is surrounded by some of the most picturesque mountain scenery in Norway. In fact, the principal features of Norwegian scenery are fjeldes, fosses and fiords, or, as we would term them, mountains, falls and rivers. On account of the mountainous character of the country, the rivers are navigable only for short distances, and even then, only exceptionally by large vessels. It is only in those comparatively frequent cases where the rivers expand into lakes, that they can, strictly speaking, be navigated by ships. On the other hand, the waterfalls in Norway are exceedingly numerous, and many of them remarkable for their height, body of water, and great beauty.

The mountains are covered with some of the finest pine timber in the world. Logs are floated down on the rivers to the saw-mills, which are everywhere in operation. The lumber is exported to all parts of Europe. This trade and the famous iron mines and extensive fisheries form the most important industries of Norway. Very little grain is raised here, and fully one-fourth of the cereals consumed must be imported.

Norway has no extensive railway system, the railways having a total length of only 973 miles. At Frederickstad, an important lumber port, I took the train for Christiania, traveling by way of the famous Kijolberg bridge, where a battle was fought in the stormy days of 1814, between Norway and Sweden. We traveled through an elevated and thickly timbered region, where we had a fine view of the long, open bay, called the Christiania fiord. This was one of the most interesting railway rides I had enjoyed in Europe.

Christiania is beautifully situated at the head of the fiord of the same name, an arm of the Skager Rack. The streets are broad, and the houses, except in the suburbs, are built chiefly of brick and stone. It is the seat of the Crown Prince and of the Storthing, or Parliament, of the Hoieste-ret, or final court of appeal, and of the bishop of the Stift. It has a population of about 125,000.

I stopped at the Victoria Hotel, where I paid

eight cronor, or about $2.25, per day.   The accom-
modations were fine, and guests are served in
Scandinavian or American style.   Among the public buildings may be mentioned the royal palace ; the
cathedral, a brick edifice in the shape of a Greek
cross ; the museums and the National Gallery, all
fairly good buildings for a small city.   The Parliament or Storthing building is substantial, but not
grand.   The palace of the Crown Prince is a
spacious wooden structure, but is not at all imposing.   After visiting the Louvre in Paris, and Buckingham Palace in London, these seemed very
small affairs.   The Fish Bazar is quite an enterprise.   Here live fish are kept all the year round,
and people get their fish here instead of buying
them at the ordinary fish markets.   The fortress
of Agershuus defends the fiord and the greater
part of the town.   It contains the regalia and
national records, and its ramparts afford an agreeable promenade   It is remarkable more for its
strength and antiquity than for its architectural
finish.

   In the northern portion of the city I visited
Agers Elv, a swiftly flowing stream, the water
power of which is utilized by the various factories.
The operatives in these factories are principally
girls.   My visit to St. John's height was the most
important event to me that occurred during my
visit to the city.   From this lofty eminence I had

a fine view, not only of the entire city, but of the shipping in the harbor. It happened while I was viewing the city from this height that there was a large crowd of people waiting for the arrival of the Prince of Wales, who was visiting Christiania. At two o'clock the carriages containing the royal personages appeared in sight, followed by a large concourse of people, all arrayed in holiday attire.

The tourist generally takes Christiania for a starting point when he decides to venture into Northern Norway to see some of the wildest scenery under the sun. Forty miles north of Christiania is a large body of water called Mjösen, where small steamers are busily plying in every direction all summer long. The general character of the whole country is extremely rugged, particularly in the North. The valleys are short and abrupt. Precipices, cascades and torrents are met with in every direction, and grand and picturesque scenery abounds.

Among the most striking natural curiosities is the mountain of Kilhorn, a remarkable pyramidal peak, terminating with a long, sharp, spire-like summit, and having a large perforation about three-fourths of the way up its side. Some of the mountain passes are extremely picturesque. The Voringfoss and Rukanfoss are cataracts, each nine hundred feet in perpendicular descent, and several of the rivers have falls of less height. The rivers and lakes are abundantly stocked with many varieties of excellent fish, among which are trout and salmon. Game of all kinds is very plentiful. Norway is a favorite resort for the European nobility, who, satiated with pleasure and sight-seeing, come here in the summer to hunt and fish.

The numerous, and in many cases very extensive fiords give to the different parts of the coast of Norway a remarkably varied character. For long distances the mainland does not come in contact with the sea. Among the most noteworthy is Hardanger Fiord, which pierces the country for eighty miles in a northeasterly direction. The climate is less severe than might be expected from the high latitude and the elevation of surface, being considerably tempered by the sea and warm southwest winds. Perpetual snow is found only in elevated localities. It is a wonderful sight to see the sun rise in its majestic beauty among the glaciers. The broad mountains running up into sharp peaks, covered with clear coats of crystallized ice, glitter in the sunshine, and present a grandly magnificent sight.

I visited Drammen, a bustling city of about twenty thousand inhabitants, situated at the head of Drammen Fiord, thirty miles west of Christiania. It has quite a number of industrial establishments, and an active trade in wood, pitch and iron, is carried on. My next stopping place was

Skien, situated at the extreme western end of the railroad, and 130 English miles from Christiania. The railroad follows the line of the sea-shore, passing through numerous tunnels, climbing hills, and crossing pretty little valleys dotted with small farms. We were continually sighting streams and waterfalls.

On this route we passed Holmestrand, Sane-Fiord and Kongsberg, situated on alvs, or rivers, and in close proximity to the coast. Here are situated the rich and famous silver mines of Norway. These mines, as well as the railroads, are owned and controlled by the government. From Skien small steamers travel by way of a canal to an inland lake called the Inland North Sea. This takes the tourist as far north as Ule-foss, in Tellemarken. Many tourists avail themselves of the opportunity to visit this attractive body of water, and view the grand and striking scenery among the lofty mountains of Central Norway.

It is exceedingly interesting to visit the country during the summer season, and inspect the satras. These are situated four or five English miles from the main farms. Here they keep the cattle temporarily during the harvest season, and have their dairies, where they make butter and cheese. While the herders are watching their flocks in the grassy meadows and on the wooded hills, they are constantly tooting their horns, partly for amusement and partly in accordance with an old custom, as it was formerly supposed that the noise of the horn was useful in keeping bears, wolves and other wild animals away from their herds.

In the temporary cabins you will hear the maids singing as they churn or spin. You will find women in the meadows raking hay or on the hill-sides, sickle in hand, cutting foliage to be cured and stored for food for the stock during the long, cold winter. The boys are engaged in fishing, and the smaller children in picking berries. The men are busy mowing, or felling timber, which is hauled, tandem fashion, by the chubby ponies to the neighboring fiords. Evening life in these cabins presents a lively scene. The time is spent in playing on the flute and violin and in dancing; when wearied of that, in spinning yarns and telling ghost stories. Some are engaged in making boasts as to who is the strongest man, who owns the fastest horse, the sharpest knife, or has the best-looking girl. This is a fair description of satra life in Norway; and is what I have seen with my own eyes, and heard with my own ears.

On returning to Skien, which is the terminus of the railroad, I embarked on a small coast steamer for Kragerö, only about four hours' ride on the Fiord. We kept close to the shore, and had a fine view of the peculiar formation of the coast. The harbor of Kragerö I found to be surrounded by

fjelds and islands. This city impresses one as
being odd, ugly and old ; the streets are crooked
and narrow, and it looks as if it might have been
pretty well shaken up at some time by an earthquake. It has a background of rugged and rocky
hills. The city has, however, several wealthy
merchants and owners of ships, and does a thrifty
business in exporting lumber to foreign countries.

On leaving Kragerö, I journeyed into the interior.
The only mode of travel now was by stage. There
is a compulsory law or rule in Norway requiring a
stage to be furnished any traveler who will pay for
the use of it, the price generally charged being one
crono and fifty örer, or forty cents, for every ten
miles, which is generally about the distance between stations. The tax-payers all along the line
of the mail road have to furnish these stages, each
as their turn comes around. The traveler usually
gives notice of his coming, by mail, the day beforehand. The stage outfit consists of a pony horse
hitched to a cariole or sleigh, according to the season of the year.

On this occasion I occupied a cariole, a narrow
two-wheeled vehicle used in Norway, just wide
enough to hold one person. I enjoyed the ride
more on account of its novelty than for its comfort. My baggage was placed at my feet ; the
driver stood upright behind me on a step, holding
the lines, with which he guided the spirited horse,

over my head ; and we rattled along at a lively
gait on a narrow road, which was but a few inches
wider than the vehicle. It is customary at the end
of the journey to tip the driver with fifteen örer
(about four cents). After a varied experience in
traveling and riding, I have learned to enjoy all the
various styles, from comfortably sitting in a palace
car to riding a pack donkey,

Arriving at Gjerestad, I was, after a lapse of
many years, in the place where I was born, and
where the earlier part of my childhood was spent,
surrounded by lofty mountains and inland fiords.
I went sleigh riding and skating, and engaged in
all the varied amusements that so delight the heart
of boyhood, utterly oblivious of the grand mountains towering above us, or of the picturesque
beauty of the fiord, whose waters glittered in the
summer sunlight or became a vast sheet of ice in
the chilling grasp of winter. Little did I dream,
that, in after years, I should travel thousands of
miles to visit other scenes less grand and inspiring,
or that my home was to be in the far-off, golden
West. The events of my childhood had almost
faded from my memory years before, and old play-
mates and schoolmates were now gray-haired men,
known to me only by their names.

On all sides I was treated to a hearty hand-
shaking and a shower of questions, a few of which I
will repeat. The first query nearly always was :

"Well, Mr. Johnson, how came you to get so rich?" to which I would reply that I was not aware of the fact that I was rich, but that what means I had acquired were due to energy and industry; that, if we desire gold, we must go where gold abounds; that "we must make hay while the sun shines;" rise early and plow deep to get corn to sell and corn to keep.

They would next inquire who was going with me around the world, and I told them that my only companion was a full purse. They would often ask me if I did not know that few travelers ever returned from such a long and venturesome journey. I answered that this was true, but that also it would be more remarkable and more to my credit if I could accomplish it; that I was fortified with courage, fortitude and endurance; and that I did not care to follow in the beaten tracks where there was no risk and nothing to encounter.

I was looked upon with as much curiosity and interest as if I had been the long-lost prodigal son. Although they put no ring on my finger, they nearly killed me with kindness in the way of over-feeding me. Here at Gjerestad two of the pleasantest weeks I had in Europe were spent; either tongue or body were in constant motion, and invitations were extended from all sides.

No matter at what hour you make a call, you must stop and eat a meal, or it is considered no visit; and, hungry or not hungry, you must eat. After leaving the table it is customary to take the host and his wife by the hand, and thank them for the meal. At the dawn of day a cup of coffee and a sandwich were brought to my bedside. Breakfast and dinner, the two best meals, are served at the regular hours. After the latter meal is over, it is customary to lie down for a couple of hours' sleep. At two o'clock coffee and sandwiches are served. This is the custom in nearly all parts of Norway, particularly in the rural districts. Even the servants eat five times a day, though often of the plainest food. Well, they need plenty to eat, as they are poorly paid for their work in Norway, as in Switzerland and Denmark.

I was now busily engaged in visiting and sight-seeing. I went from one farm to another, and was always given the chubbiest horse and best cariole, and thus was rapidly whirled along the narrow roads, which run over rolling hills, through deep dales, among fjelds and along fiords. As soon as one attraction was out of sight a grander one appeared in view. In this country a polite custom prevails; the people always lift their hats to a stranger traveling along the highway. The driver, who stood behind me holding the lines over my head, often prevented me from lifting mine very high as I returned the salutation.

Northern Gjerestad is situated at a considerable

altitude. The highest mountain in this vicinity is called Myre-ausen, and is a summer resort for the aristocracy, who come up into this picturesque region on account of the grand and romantic scenery. I stood on the very highest peak of this eminence, and enjoyed the most magnificent and the most extended view that I had had from any peak in Europe. From this point I could get a glimpse of Tellemarken's highest peaks, and see the vessels in the ocean west of Jomfruland hastening on their way over the North Sea.

The scenery was wild and picturesque, on every side towering mountains and cataracts ; and the long fiord of Gjerestad, which pierces the country for many miles, appeared like a glistening streak of silver. I concluded that this must be the Switzerland of the North, so far as grand and romantic scenery is concerned.

The marriage ceremony is probably the most curious of the many strange customs that prevail in this far northern country. The contracting parties must have the bans announced in church three Sabbaths in succession, preceding the day. This gives ample time for investigation or objection if there is any one desirous of preventing the match. A wedding is always a most brilliant affair in Norway. The wedding festivities take place at the house of the groom ; and, as all the friends and relatives at home and abroad are invited, there is generally a goodly number of people assembled.

The wedding is called a "brylüp," and feasting and dancing are kept up for two or three days. The first day the entire company march to the church, where the marriage ceremony is performed by the minister. On returning home every one is in high glee, and eating, drinking and dancing are indulged in to their hearts' content. The fattest calves and beeves are killed, the best beverages served, and the most skillful musicians employed. I have been fortunate enough to be one of the guests at a Norwegian wedding, and I assure you that a "brylüp" is a thing much to be enjoyed, and long to be remembered. This marriage custom prevails throughout Scandinavia, and in many other parts of Europe.

Education is compulsory, and, upon the whole, well cared for. Every parish has its schoolmaster, paid partly by small contributions from each pupil, and partly from the proceeds of a tax on householders. It is rare to find any one who can not at least read and write. The towns have superior schools. Great pains are taken by the clergy with the religious education of their parishioners. The religion of the people is Lutheranism, almost without exception. Probably the good seed sown in childhood is not without its beneficial effect in after years, as there are fewer criminals in the prisons in Norway, in proportion to the population, than in America and many countries in Europe.

The chief resource of Gjerestad is the lumber trade. All winter the logs are hauled from the extensive pine regions to the fiords, and, as soon as the ice breaks in the spring, the timber is tumbled into the fiords, and rafted and floated down to the seaport, and exported by the merchants.

Owing to the mountainous character of the country, there is comparatively very little level land; consequently, grain farms are small, machinery can not be used to advantage, and the crops are planted and harvested mainly by hand. The hay is mowed with a hand scythe by the men, and raked up by the women.

The crops are planted by both sexes. In the harvest season the women cut the grain with sickles, and the men tie it in bundles. It is left a few days to dry, and then hauled into the spacious barns. This is done with two rigs. A species of rack is placed either on a sleigh or a two-wheeled rig, and on this the bundles are loaded. The man drives into the centre of the barn, unhitches the horse from the wagon, and then goes back to the field for the other one. While he is away a servant girl unloads. This is kept up until the last bundle is removed from the field, and stored in the barn. In the winter the grain is threshed on the barn floor with flails by the maid servants. In the evening, when they are resting from their labors, they are busily engaged in spinning. These small farmers take great pride in building lofty houses, which they paint mostly red.

While the people in Norway, as a rule, are not wealthy, neither does extreme poverty exist. The people are happy, industrious and honest; they are simple in their tastes and habits, but kind and hospitable. They are among the best sailors in the world, large numbers of the population being engaged from early life in coast fisheries, which are an excellent school for seamen, the navigation among the islands, shoals and narrow channels, being intricate and dangerous.

Though Norway is situated in a comparatively remote region, and is the most sparsely populated country in Europe, she is on the steady road to prosperity.

I was so busily engaged in visiting and sight-seeing that the days rolled swiftly by, and, almost before I was aware of it, the time had come for me to leave one of the most interesting places on my whole journey. The last good-bye was said, and I started once more on my journey around the globe, with forty thousand miles of it yet to travel before that journey could be accomplished.

From Gjerestad I traveled westward to Christiansand, a distance of eighty-five miles. Part of this journey I traveled by land, and the remainder by water. At Risör, the first seaport, I embarked on a coast steamer for Christiansand. On the way we made landing at the following towns : Twedestrand, Arendal and Lillesand. The scenery all along the coast is picturesque in the extreme.

Christiansand is a fortified town on the North Sea, in Southern Norway, ranking next to Christiania and Bergen as an important seaport of the country. It is situated at the mouth of a deep and well sheltered harbor, and is surrounded on three sides by cliffs of uniform height. The houses, mostly of painted wood, are regularly built, and the streets are wide. There is a fine cathedral and a cathedral school. The ship-building and the fortifications are among the principal attractions.

CHAPTER VII.

ACROSS THE NORTH SEA, GERMANY AND THE ALPS.

On the 7th of October I embarked on the Bergen steamer Palace for Hamburg. On this voyage we had to travel over the North Sea for a distance of four hundred English miles. It was a very rough passage, as a heavy gale was blowing; and, if one desired a promenade on the lower deck, he would have to take it knee deep in .water. Under such circumstances I preferred to remain in my small state-room, for the cabin was small and uncomfortable for passengers. We had on board a heavy cargo of fish. The North Sea was the stormiest body of water I had sailed on up to this time, and it has the reputation of being the roughest water in the northern world.

I had now been on shore for several weeks, and had again to get accustomed to the sea. Seeing me in one of my worst spells of sea-sickness, the captain said : "Well! Mr. Johnson, I can not see where you can find any pleasure in your tour around the world if you can not stand the sea any better than this." I told him I probably would not find much amusement were the North Sea to follow me all the way around, but that in the beginning I had expected to experience many unpleasant things. The sights I saw and the pleasures I experienced in all the countries and amongst the various nations I visited were sufficient in all instances to repay me for the comparatively few uncomfortable days I had to endure while traveling on the ocean. This rough passage, however, was not without some attraction ; for I was much interested in watching the multitude of vessels which were traversing the waters of this sea, each with spreading sails hurrying along to its destination.

On the 9th of October we steamed up the Elbe River to the busy city of Hamburg, one of the free cities of Germany, and I once more found myself on German soil. I gave a brief description of this city, however, as I made my northward trip.

At Hamburg I took the cars for Frankfort-on-the-Main. We traveled over a level and moist valley for a hundred miles, when we arrived at Hanover, a city of about 150,000 inhabitants, situated in a sandy, fertile plain. The River Leine flows through the city, having the old town on its right bank, and the new town between its left bank and the River Ihme. The old town is irregularly built, with narrow streets and old-fashioned houses ; while the new town has wide streets, handsome buildings and beautiful squares. Of the latter the most remarkable is the square at the railway terminus, which has an equestrian statue of King Ernest Augustus.

The distance from Hanover to Frankfort is 200 miles. The road runs through a fertile valley, which is almost as densely populated as the suburbs of a city. This vast expanse of country is as uniformly level as Stanislaus County, in California, and struck me as being the finest agricultural country in Europe. The roadways are lined with shade trees, and on every side can be seen the comfortable homes of the industrious farmers. The first city of importance on this route is Göttingen, which is quite a railway centre. Here we changed cars for Frankfort, as I had decided to travel by the way of Bebra and Fulda. At the southern end of this road the country is inclined to be hilly, the soil is of a reddish character, and is planted to fruit trees and vines.

Frankfort-on-the-Main is one of the principal cities of the German Empire. It is situated in the Prussian province of Hesse Nassau, and was, until 1866, one of the four free cities of Germany. It occupies a position of no small natural beauty in the midst of the broad and fertile valley of the Main, its northern horizon being formed by the soft outlines of the Taunus range. The surrounding country is richly clad with orchard and forest, and, in the spring season especially, presents a prospect of indescribable luxuriance. I found

10

Frankfort an interesting and attractive city, with a population of about 150,000. It has the reputation of being the richest city in the world in proportion to its population. The bulk of the capital of Germany is concentrated here.

In the modern portion, Frankfort will compare favorably, both in the general appearance of the streets and the architectural character of individual buildings, with all except a very few of the greater cities of the Continent. Among the most attractive features of the city are the princely mansions of the Rothschilds and other opulent citizens. The dingy and unpretentious house which saw the rise of the Rothschild family still stands in the famous Judenstrasse, or Jews' street. The principal ecclesiastical building is the Cathedral of St. Bartholomew. The date of its foundation is not precisely known; but a church was erected on the site at least as early as 874.

Of the secular buildings, perhaps the most characteristic is the Rathhaus, or Romer, dating from the fifteenth century. It was here, in the Wahlzimmer, or election-room, that the electors or their plenipotentiaries decided the choice of the Emperor; and here, in the Kaiser Halle, or Emperor's Hall, that the coronation festivities were held. The palace of the Prince of Thurn and Taxis is a large building of considerable historical interest. The Eschenheim Tower is a picturesque relic of the ancient fortifications, dating from the middle of the fourteenth century.

Few cities of the same size as Frankfort are so richly furnished with literary, scientific and artistic institutions, or possess so many handsome buildings appropriated to their use. The museums, the zoölogical gardens and the beautiful pleasure grounds are all worthy of a visit. There are four railway stations, which, with the exception of the one at Stuttgart, are the finest depots in Germany. The climate in this portion of the empire is similar to that of France or Italy.

I left Frankfort for Italy on October 12, going by way of Heidelberg, Carlsruhe, Stuttgart and Baden-Baden. These are all important cities, situated in a productive valley in the south of Germany. On the south bank of the Neckar, about twelve miles from the junction of that river with the Rhine, and at the opening of the winding Neckar Valley, the situation of Heidelberg is one of romantic beauty. Behind it and before it rise lofty hills covered with vineyards and forests, and between their fertile slopes the Neckar rushes swiftly along. To the left the country opens out into the broad Rhine plain, cultivated like a garden, and bounded by distant and hardly perceptible mountains.

The chief building in Heidelberg, and, indeed, the principal attraction for the stranger, is the famous castle which overhangs the western part of the town. It is situated on the castle hill, more properly called Jettenbuhel, 330 feet above the Neckar. Though now a ruin, yet its extent, its magnificence, its beautiful situation, and its interesting history render it by far the most noteworthy, as it certainly is the grandest and largest, of the old castles of Germany. The University of Heidelberg is the oldest in the German Kingdom.

Carlsruhe, the capital of the Grand Duchy of Baden, I found to be an enterprising city of 55,000 inhabitants. It lies on an elevated plain about five miles from the Rhine, and is surrounded by beautiful parks and gardens. It has several public gardens and some fine squares. In the centre of the market place is a pyramid in honor of Charles William, the founder of the city. Carlsruhe carries on a considerable trade, and has quite a number of manufactories.

Baden-Baden, a celebrated watering place, stands on the side of a hill, near`the Ovs, or Oel, in a beautiful valley of the Black Forest, eighteen miles southwest of Carlsruhe. The superiority of its situation, its extensive pleasure grounds, gardens and promenades, and the brilliancy of its life during the fashionable season, have for a long series of years continued to attract visitors from all parts of the world. The hot springs, which were among the earliest attractions of the place, are twenty-nine in number. They flow from the castle rock at the rate of ninety gallons per minute, and the water is conveyed through the town in pipes to supply the different baths. The gaming tables, for so many years a striking feature of Baden-Baden, are now abolished.

Stuttgart, the capital of the Kingdom of Würtemberg, is situated on the River Nesan, a tributary of the Neckar. It stands in a very beautiful valley, surrounded by vine-clad hills, with well-wooded mountains in the distance. The town is encircled by a wall and ditch, is entered by eight gates, and consists of two parts, the ancient and modern, with two suburbs. In the chief square is a fine old Gothic church, with a high tower and many ancient sculptures and monuments of the princes of Würtemberg. In the vicinity are numerous parks and gardens, where the public are admitted, including Rosenstein, the summer palace of the King.

Stuttgart is a very ancient town ; but the date of its foundation is not known. It has one of the finest and most spacious railway depots in the world. On arriving at the station, we had to descend a long flight of stairs, go underneath the track, and come up on the other side of the station. Many of the depots in Europe are constructed on this plan. However odd this may seem to be, it guards against accidents that might otherwise occur,

The country is very thickly settled, and one is hardly ever out of sight of villages or towns. I had now traveled the whole length of the German Empire twice in two months, and had seen much of the life and resources of these industrious people. I did not see much of the mountain scenery, but was greatly surprised in finding such a vast area of level land. Much of it was irrigated, and all well cultivated. Notwithstanding that the country is densely settled and seemingly over-populated, the people appeared to be happy and prosperous. I concluded that economy and industry did it all.

I crossed the River Rhine, and once more found myself in Switzerland. Before leaving the Rhine, however, I must not neglect to mention the delightful ride I had on this most beautiful river. I found its banks lined with gigantic trees, their branches projecting over the water's edge. The sources of the Rhine are found in the Swiss Canton of Grisons. It is about 800 miles in length, and drains an area of 75,000 square miles. It connects the highest Alps with the mud banks of Holland, is the chief river of Germany, and has been one of the most important waterways of Europe from the earliest times, to which the long array of ancient and flourishing towns along its banks bear witness.

Politically the Rhine has always played a great

part, and it would require no great strain to write
a history of this majestic river which would also be
a history of the western half of Continental Europe. In military history constant allusion is made
to the Rhine. Every general who has fought in
its neighborhood has at one time or another had
to improvise a means of crossing it, from Julius
Cæsar, who crossed it twice, down to our own
time.

It has always exercised a peculiar sort of fasci-
nation over the German mind, in a measure and
in a way not easily paralleled by the case of any
other river. "Father Rhine," as it is sometimes
called, is the centre of the German's patriotism.
In his literature it has played a prominent part,
and its weird and romantic legends have been alternately the awe and the delight of his childhood.
It was the classic river of the middle ages, and
probably the Tiber alone is of equal historical
interest.

In crossing the Alps the second time, I traveled
by way of the St. Gothard Tunnel, the longest tunnel in the world, having a total length of ten miles,
and requiring forty minutes to pass through it.
While I have said much in praise of Germany's
stately cities, extensive and fertile valleys, and
majestic rivers, the palm must be accorded to
Switzerland for grand and picturesque mountain
scenery, and beautiful lakes. At the foot of the

Alps on this route, is a pastoral region, the chief resource of which is stock-raising. Here I saw the largest breed of cattle in Europe. They were feeding on mountain sides so steep that one wondered how they managed to maintain their equilibrium.

Lake Lucerne was my first stopping place. This lake has extraordinary interest for the lover of natural scenery, and for all who feel a sympathy with the story of Swiss independence. The irregularity of its form is the chief cause of the unequaled variety of its scenery; but the structure of the mountains that enclose it much enhances the effect. Its eastern portion lies amid limestone rocks, which are marked by sharp peaks and ridges and precipitous crags; the middle part is enclosed by such mountains as the Righi and the Burgenstein, which show steep faces, with gently sloping summits; while the western extremity is surrounded by swelling hills, richly planted, and dotted with bright-looking hamlets or solitary farm houses.

The forests which once covered the greater part of this region have been extensively thinned out; but enough yet remains to add another element to the charms of the scenery. Vineyards are scarcely seen on the shores of the lake; but orchards surround most of the houses, and the walnut grows to great perfection.

On the shores of this lake were nurtured the

men who commenced the heroic efforts that secured freedom for their country. Here, at the beginning of the fourteenth century, in an age when nearly all Europe was in the hands of feudal oppressors, a handful of mountaineers drove out the local tyrants and leveled their strongholds, and, a few years later, on the fields of Morgarten and Sempach, confronted and put to flight the chivalry of Austria.

I had the pleasure of riding with some tourists from America on one of the small steamers which traverse the waters of this lake. There are many other Alpine lakes of great beauty which I visited while journeying across the Alps. The whirlwinds of the Alps are worthy of notice, not only on account of their terrific violence, often overwhelming the hapless traveler with blinding snow, but on account of their frequently setting in motion the dreaded avalanche. So precipitous are the slopes of many of the Alpine peaks that the giving way of a slight barrier, a tree or a boulder perhaps, is sufficient to detach from its original position a vast mass of snow and ice. This, gathering force from its fall, brings sudden and inevitable destruction on whatever may be on its track, burying at times whole villages, crushing extensive forests, and filling up the beds of rivers.

CHAPTER VIII.

ITALY, GIBRALTAR AND MALTA.

On descending the Alps into Italy, the first city of importance is Milan, lying in the middle of the fertile plain of the Lombard. It has a population of nearly 300,000. Seen from the top of the cathedral, the surrounding country presents the appearance of a great garden, divided into square plats by rows of mulberry or poplar trees. Milan is built in a circle, the cathedral being the central point, and is surrounded by a wall seven miles in circumference. Immediately outside the wall, a fine broad thoroughfare makes the circuit of the city. The streets inside are, for the most part, narrow and crooked.

Among the noted buildings the cathedral is the most important. It is built of brick cased in marble from the quarries which Visconti gave in perpetuity to the Cathedral Chapter. It is 447 feet in length and 183 feet wide ; the cupola is 226 feet high, and the tower 360 feet. The roof is built of blocks of white marble ; is supported by fifty-two columns, with canopied niches for statues ; and is ornamented with turrets, pinnacles, and 2,000 statues. The name of the original architect is not known ; but it is certain that many German master masons were called to Milan to assist the Italian builders.

There are four other churches of interest in Milan. St. Ambrose's, the oldest, was founded by St.

MILAN CATHEDRAL.

Ambrose, in the fourth century, on the ruins of the Temple of Bacchus. The royal and archiepiscopal palaces are both worthy of note I also visited the Arsenal, the Crematory and the theatres. With the exception of the St. Carlo, at Naples,

Milan has the largest theatre in Europe. Milan is rich in works of art, and it has been the home of many excellent sculptors and architects. The picture gallery of the Breva is one of the finest in Italy.

As I was again in a new country, my baggage must be examined at the custom house. At the time of my visit to Italy the cholera was raging, and all baggage was put into an intensely hot cell for about ten minutes. This was required as a precaution against the epidemic. While undergoing this process of purification, my leather valise had a hole burned in it.

Once more I had to contend with new customs, new coin, and, worst of all, an unfamiliar language. I had to employ an interpreter to point out the objects of interest and explain the many strange sights. The ordinary fee for such services is five francs a day, and as much more as they can get out of the unwary stranger. The traveler on the south side of the Alps is subject to constant annoyance from beggars, and all sorts of imposition from runners and guides.

From Milan to Venice was a ten-hours ride on the cars. The northern half of this route was over a moist and level valley, thickly planted to vines and fruit trees. All kinds of vegetation grow in profusion, and the roadway for miles was lined with ornamental shade trees. I was almost tempted to think I had found the Paradise of Europe. The Italian women are not behind their sisters on the other side of the Alps so far as out-door labor is concerned. Everywhere in the fields or gardens they could be seen busily engaged in hoeing, raking or pruning. For this hard and constant toil they are poorly remunerated.

One of the most interesting cities we pass be-tween Milan and Venice is Verona. This is a very ancient city, and the date of its foundation is un-known ; but Julius Cæsar established a colony here, and under the Romans it became a flourish-ing city. It has a population of about 65,000. Verona is situated on both sides of the river Adige, which is crossed by four stone bridges. The town is surrounded by extensive fortifications, and has five gates. Many of the streets are nar-row and dusty ; but some are wide and well kept. It stands in a beautiful country at the foot of the hills which form a portion of the Tyrolese Alps.

Venice is on the Gulf of Venice, which is prop-erly a portion of the Adriatic Sea. About four miles from the coast is a long and narrow belt with a number of openings through which the waters of the Adriatic Sea make their way, forming a lagoon from twenty-five to thirty miles long and about five miles broad and containing seventy-two small islands. Into this lagoon, piles have been driven, and upon them Venice has been built, so that from

THE CITY IN THE SEA.

(178)

any point the city seems to be floating in the water. It is an extremely interesting place to the sight-seer. Communication between the various parts of the city is by water. There are only two streets worthy of the name,—Mauria, which is situated in the centre of the city, and is from twelve to twenty feet wide; and the Piazza of St. Mark, with the Piazzetta leading from it to the canal. The Piazza is surrounded on all sides by handsome buildings, and is a favorite resort for loungers and tourists.

The Grand Canal is from 100 to 180 feet wide, and is lined on both sides by magnificent buildings, many of which come down to the water's edge, so that people step from them into the gondolas. There are 146 smaller canals, which are crossed by 360 bridges; but over the Grand Canal, there is only one, called the Rialto. This is a magnificent marble structure, built in 1590, at a cost of more than half a million dollars.

The gondolas, which in Venice take the place of carriages and fast horses in other cities, are a species of barge. They are flat bottomed, usually about thirty feet long, are as narrow as a canoe, and are always painted black. The bows terminate in sharp points, ornamented with brass, which curve upward like a goose's neck to the height of several feet. Near the centre of the gondola is a small cabin with glazed windows hung with black curtains. The gondoliers, or boatmen, are gener-

ally barefooted and half clad. They are so expert
in the management of their craft that a collision or
accident is almost unknown, notwithstanding the
fact that in some quarters the water is fairly
swarming with boats. The city is full of gondoliers, runners, guides, beggars and peddlers, all
lying in wait for an opportunity to squeeze the
loose change from the traveling public.

Venice was at one time one of the proudest and
wealthiest cities in Southern Europe, and carried
on an extensive commerce ; but for several centuries her commerce has been declining, the majority of her people have relapsed into indolence
and vice, and her magnificent palaces are slowly
falling into decay.

The public buildings are numerous and splendid.
The most important of the churches is the Cathedral of St. Mark. The foundations of this church
were laid in 977 ; but it was not entirely completed
until 1111. It is built in the form of a Greek
cross, with the addition of porches. While it was
building, every vessel returning from the East to
Venice was obliged to bring pillars and marble for
its construction. The principal front is 170 feet
wide, and has 500 columns of various shapes and
colors. Over the central vestibule stand the celebrated bronze horses which were brought from the
hippodrome at Constantinople when that city was
taken by the Crusaders: They are said to have

been cast twenty-seven years before the birth of Christ. In 1797 they were carried to Paris by Napoleon, but were restored in 1815. The interior of the church is exceedingly beautiful, the floor is of tessellated mosaic work, and the walls and columns of different kinds of marble.

In nothing is the past greatness of the Venetian Republic better illustrated than in the Arsenal, a large building on an island in the eastern part of the city. It is surrounded by extensive ramparts. Near the principal entrance stand four lions in bronze, which were brought from Greece in 1685. At one time 16,000 workmen were employed at the Arsenal. At the close of the eighteenth century many of the curiosities of the model-room were destroyed by the revolutionists, among them the Bucentoro, the vessel in which the doge annually espoused the sea. This ceremony was intended to illustrate the dominion of the republic over the Adriatic Sea.

One of the most imposing public buildings is the ducal palace. This palace contains many magnificent rooms, and is enriched with splendid paintings, some of which are among the earliest specimens of oil painting on canvas. Opposite the palace, and connected with it by the Bridge of Sighs, are the public prisons, capable of containing 500 persons. At the right of the Cathedral of St. Mark is a lofty bell tower, ninety-eight metres high,

11

built in 1494. It contains a curious clock, above which are two large bronze figures which strike the hours upon a bell. I also visited the museum, the Academy of Fine Arts, and the glass manufactories. Up to the close of the last century, Venice was the teacher of Europe in the manufacture of glass, and her wares were the most perfect and elegant in use. All kinds of glassware can be seen here, from the daintiest bijoutry to the largest French plate mirror.

I was importuned on every side to purchase expensive presents for my friends of the feminine persuasion in America ; but, as much of my journey was yet to be accomplished, and with the inevitable custom house always looming up before me, I resolutely declined to handicap myself with more luggage. The guides, of course, were always anxious to assist the salesmen in disposing of their wares, and for this assistance they generally receive commissions. The hotel which leads all others in Venice is the Hotel de Italy, a stately structure of two hundred rooms. Accommodations can be had for fifteen francs per day. The dining tables were beautifully decorated with glassware. The population of the city seems to be a mixture of almost every element and every nationality, and numbers about 144,000.

On the 26th of October I left Venice for Florence, which is ten hours' ride from the former city.

Midway between the two cities is Bologna. This city is about two miles long, and a mile and a half broad ; it is surrounded by a high brick wall, and has twelve gates. The streets are generally narrow and crooked, but clean and well paved ; the houses mostly three stories high, and all public and private buildings built of brick. It has a population of 160,000. This city contains no less than 130 churches, the largest of which is San Petronio, an unfinished but splendid structure, which dates from 1390. Bologna has long been famous for its sausages and its soap, its manufactures comprising many other varieties of articles as well. It is the birthplace of many famous men, and is very ancient. It is said to have been founded by an Etruscan king.

From Bologna to Florence the road runs over a mountainous country, and we passed through twenty-four tunnels, some of them very difficult of construction. Florence is situated on both sides of the River Arno, which here flows through a wide valley. On the north the city is bounded by spurs of the Apennines, on the south by low hills belonging to the same range. The climate is salubrious. The situation and surroundings are extremely beautiful, the soil in the vicinity is remarkably fertile, and corn, vines and olives cover hill and valley ; while the mountains, which rise 3,000 feet above the city, are covered with cypress, chestnut and pine. The country is noted for its abundance of flowers.

The Florentines are gentle and courteous in their manners, and were seemingly the most refined people on the southern side of the Alps. The city is well supplied with parks and squares. The Casino, a large extent of ground planted in long avenues of trees, is the fashionable resort of the nobility of Florence. The Boboli Garden, which belongs to the royal palace, is open twice a week to the public, and, with its statues, fountains, terraces and trim alleys, is the delight of the Florentines. The streets are paved with stone, which for centuries has been obtained from quarries south of the city.

There are many stately and beautiful mansions here, and among the most princely structures is one belonging to Mackay, the Nevada Silver King. Florence contains over 170 churches, among the most remarkable being the Badia, or ancient abbey; the cathedral, Sta. Maria Novella, San Marco and the Annunziata. These churches are very ancient, and of enormous size.

The Art Gallery contains some of the finest paintings in the world, including several of Raphael's and Titian's masterpieces. A room called the Tribune contains the greatest treasures of the gallery, and here are placed the most celebrated statues of antiquity. The Egyptian Museum is small, but contains many objects of interest. The Museum of Etruscan Art, which is situated under the same roof, contains a collection of ancient mosaics and bronze, the most important of which is a life-size bronze statue. It also contains a marble Greek sarcophagus.

The Campanile, or bell tower, of the Cathedral, was commenced in 1334. This tower is 275 feet high and 45 feet square. It is entirely veneered with black, red and white marble, and has five stories. On the basement story are two ranges of tablets in relief; one representing the creation of Adam and Eve, the other the seven virtues, the planets and the seven sacraments. Take it all in all, Florence is one of the most beautiful and interesting cities in Italy, and generally one of the first visited by travelers.

From Florence to Rome is a seven-hours railway ride over a mountainous and barren region, destitute of timber, and unfit for cultivation. On this route we passed many ancient and picturesque ruins. The first thing I did on arriving at the Eternal City was to select my guide; and here let me remark that, although in Rome, I did not always do as the Romans did.

The first object of interest which I visited was the Cathedral of St. Peter, the mother of all churches, at least so far as size and grandeur are concerned. The interior of this church is 602 English feet long, and 445 feet wide at the transept. The circumference of the circle of pillars which support the dome is 232 feet, and the cupola is 193 feet in diameter. From the pavement to the top of the cross the dome is 430 feet in height. It is encircled and strengthened by six bands of iron; it is surmounted by a balustrade six feet high, and adorned with statues representing Christ and the Apostles. The interior is magnificent; it is ornamented in bronze and mosaic. Near the altar are several gilded portraits of the ancient popes, which have long Latin inscriptions on them. On the floor of the church are figures marked giving the dimensions of the large churches in the world, these proving conclusively that St. Peter's is the largest of them all. The building of this church, from its foundation, in 1450, until its dedication, in 1625, occupied a period of 175 years. Visitors congregate here from every part of the world.

Next to St. Peter's, one of the most imposing and interesting structures is the Vatican, or papal palace. This palace, which is one of the most magnificent in the world, is rather a collection of separate buildings than one regular edifice. It occupies a space of 1,151 by 767 feet, and has over 200 staircases, 20 courts, and 4,422 rooms. Many of the rooms are decorated with frescoes by famous artists. It contains a gallery of statues, a museum filled with the relics of the ancient inhabitants of Italy, and a picture gallery which has more treas-

St. Peter's at Rome.

ures than any other gallery in the world, although the whole catalogue only numbers fifty paintings.

The Capitol, on the famous Capitoline Hill, is chiefly remarkable for the collection of art it contains within its walls. The two Capitoline museums are very rich in classical sculpture, bronzes, coins and pottery. Prominent among the many statues is a colossal figure of Mar-forises, the river god. There are many squares in the city consisting of small paved areas, generally adorned with fountains and monuments. The fountains are numerous, and form one of the most attractive features of the city. They are plentifully supplied with water by three aqueducts which yet remain in operation of the many that poured their streams into the ancient city.

The Piazza Colonna is one of the finest open spaces in the city; it is ornamented with a gilt bronze statue of St. Paul, which is 135 feet high. At the Piazza di Pietra can be seen the ruins of the Temple of Neptune. The Church of the Twelve Apostles is also called the Church of Constantine, after the name of its founder. Under the portico can be seen the fine monument of Vopato, and the figure of an eagle brought from the Trojan Forum. The Roman Forum, Campus Vaccino, was formerly used as a market place, and contains many ancient and interesting ruins.

On the Palatine Hill are the remains of the

palace of that name. The gardens are open to the public on Sundays and Thursdays. They are generally thronged with visitors. The ancient city of Rome was originally founded on this hill, and, as the city grew, it spread over several of the adjoining eminences, and finally became known as " the City of the Seven Hills." The Lateran, a museum of classical sculpture and early Christian remains, was, until the fourteenth century, the residence of the pope. In this museum were fine statues of Hercules and Neptune. The Pyramid of Cestius is a grand sepulchral monument, built of concrete, and faced with white marble. It is 118 feet high, and contains a small chamber decorated with stucco. On the marble facing is an inscription in large letters stating that this is the tomb of C. Cestius.

The Circo Agonalis is one of the largest open spaces in Rome, and was probably formerly used as a circus. It is ornamented with fountains, and has other interesting features to attract visitors. Palace Spadra contains a collection of antiquities, pictures and statuary, among the latter a statue of Aristotle in a sitting posture. The Collosseum is one of the most interesting of the Roman ruins. It has been stripped of its exterior ornamentation, the interior is entirely dismantled, and much of the outer wall has been carried off for the sake of the material ; but it still remains a most imposing and sublime ruin.

The city is divided into ancient and modern Rome. Ancient Rome is a city of traditions, and full of historical interest. At one time it covered a circuit of thirteen miles, and embraced a population of nearly 2,000,000. Corso street was the principal street in old Rome. Extensive ruins, magnificent palaces and public buildings testify to her former greatness. Ancient Rome was built on a series of low-lying hills, while the modern city is built chiefly on still higher land. The streets are clean, well paved and well lighted. The principal business streets are full of life and activity; but for hundreds of years to come the old city will prove the attraction to travelers and tourists.

In no other city did I see a wider constrast between wealth and poverty; one portion of the population living in opulence and splendor, the other in rags and filth. The streets are filled with beggars, and venders of small wares, all struggling with the problem of existence, presenting a novel scene of confusion to the stranger.

It would require volumes, and years of research, to do justice to this old city; and, as my time was limited to the space of a few days, I am unable to give a detailed account of much that would prove of interest.

The following was written to the author's home paper, the Modesto *Herald:*

LETTER FROM ROME.

Special Correspondence of the Herald.

ROME, ITALY, Oct. 15, 1885.

EDITORS HERALD :—I must send you a few more lines about my rambles in the Eastern hemisphere. Since I wrote you from Switzerland I have been interestingly sight seeing on the Continent of Europe, and have traveled thousands of miles on land and water as fast as express trains and steamers could carry me. I have crossed the Baltic and the North Seas. In Norway I remained the longest and traveled the most. I find that country consists chiefly of fjelds, fosses and fjords. From Christiania to Doverfjeld the picturesque scenery is extremely grand, and presents to the eye a pano-rama. I also traveled extensively in Sweden and Denmark. These countries are densely populated; but I found no great attractions for tourists to feed their eyes upon. I have been over the length of the whole German Empire, by two different routes, and have been in all the leading cities, including Berlin, Bremen, Stuttgart, Hamburg, Frankfort-on-the-Main, Carlsruhe, Hanover, and many others, in my journey. Frankfort, a city of 155,000 inhabitants, is beautifully located in the heart of a level valley. It has wide, well-paved sidewalks, stately mansions, richly furnished stores, and the inhabitants equal those of any city of its size in Europe for dress, style and elegance.

Germany, south of Frankfort, is well improved, and the soil of the most productive kind, as was shown by the valley being dressed in the finest pro-ductions for many miles on the River Rhine. In all Germany, there is a fine, level farming country, but destitute of mountain scenery. Next comes Basel, the finest city in Switzerland, which country I have also been over in two different directions. As I have just recommended Germany for its beautiful level valleys, I will reverse my praise to Switzerland for its attractive mountain scenery. While Germany has few scenes, Switzerland has enough to make up for the whole of Europe, including her Alps and glaciers. She has many interesting attractions to sight-seers. A strange feature is that this elevated country is not of a rocky character, except on the Alps. Small farms may be seen almost to the hill-tops, dressed in green, produce of all kinds, and fruits and vines.

Oxen and women are often seen working together in the fields. Some-times see a mixed team of horses and oxen, but seldom more than three in number.

This is the second time I have crossed the Alps. The first was to Aus-tria, and this time to Italy. In coming to Italy I passed through the St. Gothard Tunnel, the longest tunnel in the world. As the railroads are built much on elevated ground, it gives the tourist a fine view of the many scenes, from the pyramidic peaks to the glittering streams at the foot of the great Alps, and rugged chain of mountains. As a consequence the railroad tunnels are many, and difficult of construction. Some of them are made in the shape of loops, and in corkscrew style.

After leaving the Alps, the first city I sighted in Italy of importance was Milan. It has a population of 300,000, and is a great terminal point for railroads. Here I found many points of interest, but did not see the place of cremation. From Milan I resumed my journey to Venice. The country on this route is mainly attractive for its moist, rich soil, and thickly planted in fine rows of trees and grape-vines. I begin to think I have struck the Paradise of Europe. The city of Venice I find located in the Adriatic Bay, several miles from the mainland, built on small islands, and it is said to be one of the oldest cities in the world. It has 144,000 inhabitants. The main street in Venice is the Grand Canal, where little steamers take passengers and goods and land them at their doors. Hundreds of other small row boats, or gondolas, are used in smaller streets and alleys to convey people and their luggage to any part of the city. No horses or vehicles are seen or needed here. The chief attraction here is the fine glass works and the St. Marquis Square. It is said to be the finest square in the world. Next is the Bell Tower, ninety-eight metres high ; the Royal Palace, the Doge's Palace, the Grand Museum, the Hotel de Italy and the Grand Opera. These are some of the leading objects in Venice. The city is full of porters and runners lying in wait to squeeze the loose change from the traveler.

From Venice to Florence was ten hours' run on the cars. A large portion of this was over a broken and mountainous country. We went through twenty-four tunnels before we arrived in Florence. This city has 160,000 inhabitants. I was much impressed with the beautiful location and appearance of Florence; and, after I had my Italian guide along to point out and show me all the fine arts and leading points of interest over the city, I concluded I had at last found a good second to Vienna, in Austria.

From Florence to Rome was seven hours' run over the roughest country I have found in Italy. At last in Rome, and I must do as the Romans do. Among the grandest attractions in Rome are St. Peters, and the Pope's Palace, or the Vatican. The many departments and galleries of fine arts, painted and ornamented in gilt and bronze, are the grandest sights I ever saw. Nothing in London or Paris can compare with this imposing edifice, nor do I expect to see in my whole trip around the globe the grandeur I see here in Rome. St. Peter's Church is the largest in the world, ornamented also in gilt and bronze. St. Paul's is the next largest church. Rome has five hundred church buildings, and it is full of statues, sculptures, fountains and museums. I have paid my guide five francs per day to take me all over the city, and show me the ruins and points of interest, until I am satisfied that this is Rome, Rome. So soon as I see the Pope, the monks, the marquises and counts, I will resume my journey to Naples; and, when I have done that city justice, I will take a steamer for Constantinople, thence to Egypt, and extend my travels around the world. When I get to the land of the Pharaohs, you may hear from me again.   OSMUN JOHNSON.

Naples is situated on the northern shore of the Bay of Naples, and fanned by the spicy breezes of the Mediterranean. It is 169 miles distant from Rome by rail, and is the largest and most populous city in Italy, having about 600,000 inhabitants. It disputes with Constantinople the claim of enjoying the most beautiful site in Europe. The Italians say: " See Naples and die." While I am not quite ready to shuffle off this mortal coil, I am willing to admit, that probably no other place in the world combines so much natural beauty with so many objects of interest to the lover of antiquity.

Naples is built at the base and on the slope of a range of hills which are divided by a ridge into two natural crescents. The western crescent is a narrow strip of land between Vomero Hill and the sea. It is the fashionable quarter, and is most affected by foreign residents and visitors. The eastern crescent is by far the largest as well as the oldest part of Naples, and includes the ports, the arsenal and the principal churches. A magnificent view, both of land and water, can be had from the hills, which form a background to the city; though the city it-

(174)

self is seen to the best advantage from the water, and the approach from the sea is famous for its loveliness.

Naples has most interesting surroundings. In the near distance is Mount Vesuvius, which presents a scene of matchless grandeur. It has been in action at intervals for 1,900 years. Its first eruption is said to have occurred in 79 A. D., at which time Pompeii was destroyed. Another place of interest is the famous Blue Grotto, on the Island of Capri. The scenery throughout this island is of unusual beauty, and it is said to have been a favorite resort of Cicero, Nero, and other historical characters. It is chiefly celebrated, however, as the retreat of Tiberius, the last ten years of his reign having been spent here.

Principal among the buildings of especial interest is the National Museum, better known as the Muser Borbonico. This contains a large collection of household utensils, statues, vases, gold, silver and bronze coins, made 79 years after the birth of Christ; in fact, everything that would bear removal from Herculaneum and Pompeii. It also contains a number of celebrated statues, among which are those of Alexander the Great, Tiberius and Hercules. This museum is a treasure house of early Italian and Roman antiquities. Note-book in hand, I followed my guide from room to room, he pointing out and explaining the various objects of interest.

The Egyptian room contains a collection of Egyptian furniture, cooking utensils and agricultural implements, the latter of the rudest construction. In viewing this ancient collection, one could not but remark on the wide difference which exists between *then* and *now*. In this room are also many fine pictures, including the Farnese Bull. This picture is an exemplification of a Greek legend, which runs as follows: Dirce, the wife of Lycus, King of Thebes, sorely persecuted Antiope, who finally escaped to Mount Cithæron, where her twin sons, who were unconscious of their parentage, were being brought up by herdsmen. Dirce, who had come to the hill for a Dionysiac ceremony, proposed that the sons, Amphion and Zethus, should tie Antiope to the horns of a wild bull, to be dragged to death. They were about to do so, when a herdsman announced their relationship, and they then tied Dirce to the bull instead.

The third and fourth rooms are chiefly filled with large equestrian statues. Principal among them are those of Julius Cæsar, Tiberius and Vespasius, also a fine statue of Nero after a victorious battle, and the marble statue of Balbi. A large room in the upper story is filled with small bronzes. This collection contains a large variety of articles suggestive of the domestic life of Pompeii and Herculaneum. The mosaic pavements in this section are of peculiar interest.

The collection of sepulchral vases comprises upward of three thousand specimens. The gallery of painting comprises a collection of masterpieces by the world's most renowned artists. In the hall of Flora is the Flora Farnese, one of the master-pieces of ancient sculpture. The collection of ancient glass contains nearly every article into which glass can be worked. The library is very large, and contains many thousand books in both the ancient and modern languages, as well as many ancient and valuable manuscripts. I have neither time nor space for a detailed description of the many wonderful and valuable objects of interest in this museum, but have given a brief description of those which most attracted my attention.

Near the museum is an imposing memorial of the revolutions of 1799, 1820, 1848 and 1860, con-sisting of four colossal lions in bronze, and sur-rounded by a high iron fence. A few steps from here brought me to a public park, which adjoins the sea. It is much frequented by tourists and sight-seers. One of the main features of this park is a lofty statue in the shape of a dome, which is ornamented with small sculptures from the base to the top. In many directions statues, fountains and other interesting curiosities can be seen. Here also is the largest church in the city.　.

The streets are generally well paved with square blocks of lava ; sidewalks, where they exist, are

nearly always narrow; the houses are more remarkable for their size and solidity than for their
elegance, and no other city in the world possesses
such a mass of houses of the same description and
so densely crowded with all sorts of people.

The business portion of the city presents a
most animated and interesting appearance to the
sight-seer. Owing to the balmy climate, and the
fondness of the people for out-door life, a great
deal of the trade is carried on on the sidewalks,
both in selling and manufacturing goods. One of
the queer features of this custom is that you frequently see hundreds of little boys, sitting or
standing on the walks, and industriously engaged
in learning a trade. An expert mechanic can be
had for three francs a day. A laborer receives
twenty pennies, or forty cents. The streets are
crowded with venders of worthless wares, who sing
out at the top of their voices the articles they have
for sale. The beggars and guides help to swell
the number, surrounding a stranger like a swarm of
bees, and are a source of great annoyance. One
is forced to the conclusion that Naples, in addition
to being one of the most interesting cities in Italy,
is also one of the most annoying ones.

A great deal of poverty exists among the lower
classes; but the people in general seem to be
happy and contented. They consume little, and
that little is cheap. For three cents a day a man

can get his fill of macaroni, and for three cents more he can have very good fish or vegetables fried in oil. These can be procured at any of the innumerable stands of itinerant cooks about the streets.

The upper classes are refined in appearance, generally well educated ; as a rule, tastefully dressed ; and the men are better looking than the women. The scholars and men of science in Naples are celebrated throughout Italy for their devotion to their respective branches of study.

At the Bristol Hotel, which is situated on an overhanging bluff, we had a splendid view of the busy life on the bay and in the brilliant city. We could also see the reflection of the Blue Grotto, on the Isle of Capri, twenty miles distant ; and Mount Vesuvius, which has been in action for nearly two thousand years. In the distance could be seen the Mediterranean, the harbor teeming with vessels carrying the flags of all nations. Naples is justly regarded as one of the most interesting cities of the world, on account of its classical associations, its numerous palaces and public buildings, the picturesque animation of its principal streets, and the beauty of its situation. I was fortunate in securing the services of a good guide who had all the points of interest at his fingerends. He was sure not to lose me, as I paid him the enormous salary of five francs per day.

At Naples I had an opportunity of joining an excursion party to Gibraltar, and visiting the extensive fortifications that the world has heard so much about. They are certainly formidable. Gibraltar is situated on the European side of the narrow strait which forms the entrance to the Mediterranean. The rock, as this promontory is generally called, rises abruptly from the low, sandy isthmus

THE TOWN AND ROCK OF GIBRALTAR.

which connects it with the mainland, to a height of 1,200 feet. The eastern side needs no defense beyond its own precipitous cliffs, and the northern and southern sides are so steep as to be almost wholly inaccessible. The western side slopes down toward the water, and here are situated the town and the principal fortifications.

Inside the fortifications are two ranges of galleries cut out of solid rock, and portholes are cut at intervals of twelve yards, and are so contrived that gunners are safe from any possible assailant. This fortress is almost impregnable; any fleet of modern artillery attempting to take it would find it a hard nut to crack.

The town of Gibraltar is chiefly inhabited-by Spaniards. At the time of my visit they were suffering with cholera. The whole population, whether civil or military, is subject to certain stringent rules. For even a day's sojourn a stranger must obtain a pass from the town mayor; and, if he wishes to remain longer, a consul or householder must become security for his good behavior. Licenses of residence are granted only for short periods; but they may be renewed if necessary. Gibraltar is a mean-looking town, with narrow streets and lanes. The houses are a mixture of English and Spanish style. The people may at any moment be called upon to give up their houses and grounds to the military authorities; so they are naturally deterred from spending much money on their dwellings or buildings.

On this excursion we also visited Malta, one of Great Britain's Mediterranean possessions. This island is seventeen miles long, and nine miles broad at its widest part. We landed at Valetta, the capital, which is situated on a splendid natural harbor. No sooner had the steamer dropped anchor than we were surrounded by a swarm of small row-boats, whose dusky boatmen were scrambling and yelling, each endeavoring to get passengers to convey to the shore, a distance of about 100 yards. For this service they will demand a shilling, but, after some hard bargaining and much bickering, they will take threepence, or six cents, instead of fifty. On landing, we were again surrounded by natives of various professions, from a cabman to a beggar. However, after selecting a guide, we proceeded to view the town.

The first thing that I observed was that the narrow streets were thronged with beggars. This annoyance extended to all the Oriental towns. Among the places of interest we visited were the Governor's palace, a comfortable structure, containing many portraits and paintings of former knights of the island; and the Cathedral of St. John, famous for its rich inlaid marbles, its Brussels tapestries and its painted roof, and containing some fine paintings and sculpture. We next visited another church, where we were shown the dried remains of a number of priests, some of whom had died as recently as 1870. It was customary, when a priest died, to put his body in a slow oven, and there let it remain for one year, when it was taken out and exhibited in the collection. They are now prohibited from continuing this custom.

We inspected the fortifications, which seem

almost impregnable, and visited the Garden of San Antonio, where we saw a large quantity of tropical fruits, which were growing in profusion. Another point of interest is the catacombs, which are hewn out of the solid rock, and extend 200 yards under the ground. The guide pointed out a chamber said to have been occupied by the Apostle Paul. Here also is an underground passage extending for a distance of seven and a half miles.

No river, brook or lake exists on this island, and it is destitute of forests. Malta is excessively hot in summer, and the sirocco prevails, especially in autumn. The climate, however, is not considered less salubrious than that of other parts of Southern Europe, and in the winter it is delightful. The atmosphere is so clear that at all times of the year the summit of Mt. Ætna, 130 miles distant, may be seen during the rising and the setting of the sun.

On leaving Malta, we returned to Naples, where I took the cars for Brindisi, a thirteen-hours railway ride from Naples. Of course, I was locked up in a compartment, in English style, which to my mind is an uncomfortable one, but which seems to prevail on both sides of the Alps. This route runs principally over an agricultural country occupied by the industrious peasant, who seems to prefer work to rest, although poorly compensated for his labor. In every direction, in field and garden, both sexes could be seen toiling in the hot sun.

The most important cities on this line are Foggia and Bari. Foggia is situated near the centre of the great plain of Apulia, 122 miles by rail from Naples ; is well built, and the main streets are wide and clean. It has become a great railway junction, just as it was formerly the meeting place of the principal roads of the country. It is a staple market for corn and wool, and the corn magazines are very extensive, consisting of vaults lined with masonry, built under the principal streets and squares.

Bari is situated on the Adriatic Sea, and is quite an important commercial town. The inhabitants are skillful seamen, and carry on a large traffic, in their own ships, with different parts of the Adriatic. The older part of the town is gloomy and irregular ; the new portion has wide streets and handsome buildings.

Brindisi is situated at the head of a bay of the Adriatic. The streets are narrow and crooked, and the town presents a somewhat dilapidated appearance. Since the restoration of its maritime importance, which is principally due to the fact that it forms the great transit station in the overland route to Asia by the way of the Mount Cenis Railway and the Suez Canal, some improvement has taken place. It has some ancient ruins of considerable interest, principal among which is a remarkable column supposed by some to have marked the termination of the Appian Way.

CHAPTER IX.

THE MEDITERRANEAN, EGYPT, RED SEA AND ARABIAN SEA.

ON the 30th of October I embarked on the spacious steamer Gwalior, for Egypt, via Greece. The Mediterranean was as calm as a mill-pond, and the voyage was much more enjoyable than the one over the stormy Atlantic, North Sea or Baltic. On this ship were tourists from every quarter of the globe, and all ranks were represented, from an English nobleman to a California farmer. It seemed singular to me, that, out of such a large number of tourists, I was the only one who represented the "Golden State;" and, more singular still, the only one from America; and, strangest of all, the only one who expected to make an entire circuit of the globe.

This short voyage over the Mediterranean was a very pleasant one, as I had many agreeable companions, and had several most interesting conversations with some of these aristocratic passengers on board the ship. I was the only one who could answer the hundreds of questions they found to ask in regard to the resources and wonders of California. It is strange how well a man will remember all the good points of his home country when he comes to travel abroad, and it did not take me long to convey the information that California was gifted with all the blessings that Nature could bestow.

I was not far behind my European companions in asking questions, for their country and their customs were as new and strange to me as were mine to them, and I derived much information from my new-found friends. Every vocation has its own range of thought and talent, and one can hardly fail to be interested and improved by an interchange of ideas. In pursuing the ordinary routine of daily life, we ofttimes let our thoughts and ideas follow one particular channel, and we need to get out among our fellow-men and widen our experience. We shall then find that much that had seemed of importance to us will grow small and insignificant.

The vessel on which I was now traveling, and the Kiserhind, on which I made the last and longest portion of my journey, belonged to the Peninsular and Oriental Steamship Company, which goes by the name of the P. and O. Line. This line runs about sixty large vessels, and is said to be one of the safest and most reliable lines whose vessels traverse the Eastern waters. Accidents are almost unknown on this line, even on the

Bay of Biscay and the Red Sea, where shipwrecks are of common occurrence.

The traveler will have no trouble in keeping his body together, as he is surrounded by luxury and plenty. It is the rule on these steamers to have five meals a day. Coffee and sandwiches are served at 6 A. M., breakfast at 8 A. M., and lunch at 1 P. M. This lunch consists of a long list of dainty dishes which will compare favorably with the viands served on the Mississippi steamers, which once had the reputation of having the best tables of any boats in the world. Dinner is served at seven o'clock, and this is, of course, the principal meal. We were often served with a dozen different kinds of meat, including fowl and fish. The evenings were spent in promenading on the deck, or in various amusements and pastimes, and at 9 P. M. sandwiches are again served.

If the traveler desires any beverage to keep him in a good humor, he will find the bar supplied with liquors and wines of all kinds, including stout and Dublin porter at sixpence a bottle. This bar was certainly well patronized, if one could judge from the large stock of empty bottles which rapidly accumulated from day to day. The cabins, saloons and state-rooms on this steamer were spacious and comfortable, which is more than can be said of many of the steamers which sail on Eastern seas. Two of the worst habits in which sea-going people generally indulge, are intemperance and profanity. The former seems more prevalent on English, and the latter on American, steamers. Swearing, by either officers or crew, is strictly against the rule on the English passenger lines; but there seems to be no objection to their drinking to their hearts' content. On the American vessels the rule seems to be reversed; as I saw very little tippling, but the crew, from the captain to the cook, indulged in profanity on all occasions.

The first country we approached after leaving Italy was Greece. This country is small in space, but wonderful in physical advantages, and the beauty and variety of its scenery are unequaled. The coast line is broken by numerous bays and harbors, which give it unusual maritime facilities. The climate is salubrious, the soil fertile, and olives, figs, and other tropical plants grow luxuriantly. The methods of tilling the soil are still primitive, and modern implements are not employed to any extent.

This little kingdom has been subject to more than its share of turmoil and strife; but at present it is blessed with prosperity and peace. Want of time prevented me from visiting Athens, the great political centre of the country. The cities at which we stopped were Navarino, Zante, Candia and Ghazze. After leaving the latter place, Greece soon faded from our view and we had had our last glimpse of Europe.

As we neared the land of the Pharoahs the water was dotted with sailing craft of every description. Vessels of all kinds were seen on every side, from the stately man-of-war to the boat of the Algiers pirate. I noticed that nearly all nations had their men-of-war stationed in the ports of the Mediterranean to look after their subjects and the interests of their respective countries. We soon sighted the low coast of Egypt, and I was to have my first glimpse of the Orient.

The first port at which we stopped was Alexandria. This city was founded by Alexander the Great, 332 B. C. The ancient city contained magnificent buildings, and was for centuries the centre of commerce and of learning. Few of the remains of the ancient city are now visible. Among the most striking is the column called " Pompey's Pillar." It stands on a mound of earth about forty feet high, has a height of ninety-eight feet, and consists of a single piece of red granite. The greatest drawback to Alexandria is the shallow and uncertain harbor, where it is often a difficult task for vessels to get in and out. The population numbers 250,000, and is of a very mixed character, consisting of people of nearly every nationality.

I visited the museum, which is filled with Egyptian antiquities and many curious relics of an ancient civilization. My Arabian guide kept me moving from object to object. I also visited the various

mosques, and many ancient and curious ruins,—
sights which, at first interesting, after a time become monotonous.

From Alexandria to Cairo is a distance of 150
miles by rail.   Cairo is the capital of Egypt, and
is situated on the east bank of the Nile, about
twelve miles from the apex of its delta.   The
Nile is the chief natural feature of Egypt, and the
yearly inundations are the great feature of the
country.   With the exception of a few fertile
oases, nearly all the cultivated land of Egypt lies
in the valley and the Delta of the Nile.   Twelve
miles above Cairo the river separates into two
streams, which continue to diverge until they reach
the Mediterranean, where they are nearly eighty
miles apart.   The triangular space enclosed by the
two branches of the river is called the Delta.

The soil is unsurpassed in fertility, and its richness is annually renewed by the inundations of the
river, which deposits on the land a coating which
enriches the soil.   In many parts plowing is dis-
pensed with, the seed is thrown upon the mud, and
sheep or pigs turned loose in the fields to trample
in the grain.   On this annual inundation depends
the success of the crops, as, by either falling or
rising too high, it causes much damage and distress.

Cairo is partly on a plain and partly on the
lower slopes of a rocky range of hills.   The cita-

THE CITY OF CAIRO.

(191)

del stands on an eminence 250 feet above the level
of the city, and the view from its ramparts is one
of great beauty and magnificence. On the eastern
side the Desert of Sahara extends almost to the
gates of the city.

In every street I chanced to stroll, I was surrounded by beggars, and they tormented me the
most of any of this class that I ever had 'the misfortune to meet. No matter which way you turn,
they keep following you, shouting *backsheesh, backsheesh;* and, were it not for the fact that they are
innumerable, one would be glad to give them the
money they demand, in order to get rid of the
sight of their dusky faces. They are clothed in
rags, and covered with dirt and filth.

Cairo is an interesting city to tourists. It is
walled off into quarters, deriving their names from
the character and condition of their occupants.
The houses of the poorer classes consist of miserable mud hovels, which are generally filthy and
dilapidated. The houses of the wealthy citizens
are generally very elaborate and elegant. A winding passage leads through an open doorway into
the court, in the centre of which is a fountain
shaded with palm trees. The principal apartment
is generally paved with marble.

Among the important public buildings is the
University of Islam. The students are said to
number 11,000, and the majority of them are pre-

paring for the priesthood. They are taught theology, the exposition of the Koran, the traditions of Mahomet, and are well grounded in civil, moral and criminal laws With the exception of professors of literature, few Egyptians are taught to read and write. The women are very rarely taught to read. The palace of the Khedive is a stately and imposing building. The city has 500 mosques, of which the most magnificent is the Mosque of Sultan Hassan, dating from 1357, and famous for the grandeur of its porch and cornice. The Mosque of Tulon was founded in 879, and exhibits some very ancient specimens of architecture. The citadel was built in 1166, but has since been frequently altered. It now contains a palace and a mosque erected by Mehemet Ali on the site of Joseph's Hall, in the centre of which is Joseph's Well, which is sunk in solid rock to the level of the Nile. Bazaars, temples, shrines and old ruins are numerous.

Here can be seen people of every nationality, sect and creed, and the population presents a very picturesque and interesting appearance. The majority of the streets are narrow and irregular, although in the newer portion of the city an effort has been made to straighten and widen them.

I next visited the pyramids, which rank among the grandest wonders of the world. They are about eight miles from Cairo. The Great Pyramid,

13

or Cheops, as it is called, from the name of its builder, dates from 2,300 years before the birth of Christ, and was built at an enormous expense. It is 450 feet high, and covers about twelve acres of ground. My guide informed me that it required 300,000 men and twenty years to build this vast structure, and that 100,000 men were employed ten years in constructing the causeway by which the blocks of stone were transported from the quarries to the banks of the Nile, from whence they were taken in boats to the other side. Here these pyramids have stood through all the succeeding centuries, defying the elements, and remaining as perpetual monuments of the greatness of a by-gone civilization.

As I desired to make the ascent to the top of the Cheops, I secured the services of three Arabs for the sum of two and one-half francs apiece to aid me in the undertaking. Two of them were occupied in pulling me up by the hands, and the third boosted me from behind. The ascent from the foundation to the top consumed eleven minutes, including the intervals of rest. From this height we had in one direction a fine view of the beautiful valley of the Nile, dotted with groups of trees, and covered with green fields; on the other side lay the Desert of Sahara,—as far as the eye could reach, a limitless waste of sand.

As I stood gazing out over the country, my

thoughts traveled back over the long line of years to the time when Joseph was the ruler of Egypt, and this was the land of the Pharaohs; and in imagination I could see the waving fields of corn which grew in the seven years of plenty. But these people have long since crumbled into dust, with only here and there a monument left to mark the scenes of their former greatness.

Near the Cheops are two smaller pyramids, varying in height from 250 to 350 feet, but large enough, however, to do justice to any country outside of Egypt. Here, also, is the Sphinx, with its head turned toward the Nile, carved out of solid granite rock, and supposed to represent King Cephren, the builder of the second pyramid. The soil has accumulated around the base until only the head and shoulders are visible above the sand. To my mind, the Sphinx is fully as interesting as the pyramids.

In traveling in Egypt, one finds that camels and donkeys are largely used as a means of transportation by both the stranger and the native, and the tourist who is desirous of visiting the sights and objects of interest in the surrounding country has no difficulty in obtaining an outfit and putting his desires into execution.

From Cairo we took a trip up the River Nile as far as the First Cataract. This I very much enjoyed, as it enabled me to get an insight into the

life and customs of the Arabs who live along the
banks of this famous and beautiful stream.   I
shall not soon forget these dusky denizens of
Egypt, if for nothing else than their begging pro-
pensities.   They were certainly the most intolerable nuisance that I had come in contact with during my journey.   I also visited the island of
Rhoda, a short distance from Cairo.   It was on
the southern shore of this island that Pharoah's
daughter discovered the infant Moses.   I had
intended, on leaving Cairo, to visit Jerusalem and
its historical surroundings ; but at that time the
cholera was raging there, and I thought it best on
that account to give up a journey which otherwise
promised so much of interest and profit.   So, with
much regret, I left Egypt without visiting the
sacred city, but still hope to be able to do so
sometime in the future when I have again earned
a recreation.

From Cairo to Suez is a four-hours railway ride
over a level and uninteresting country.   Camels
laden with packs, and driven along by their Arab
masters, were the chief sights on this route.   The
city of Suez is situated on the Red Sea, at the
southern end of the Suez Canal, and is 140 miles
from Alexandria.   It stands in a desert.   The
population, which numbers about 12,000, is a mixture of European and Oriental races.

The Suez Canal is eighty-eight miles long, and

extends from Port Said, on the Mediterranean, to Suez, on the Red Sea. It passes through two lakes, Lake Timsah and the Bitter Lakes. These, however, were dry before the cutting of the canal. The channel through the lakes was excavated partly by hand labor, and partly by dredging ; the remainder of the canal was cut out through the desert. This canal is one of the greatest of modern enterprises, was constructed at a vast expense, and shortens the distance for ships traveling from Western Europe to Asia 3,751 miles, which is a saving of thirty-six days on a voyage.

There is a constant stream of vessels passing through this canal, and a heavy tax is levied on each vessel for the privilege of going through it. The stockholders gather in an enormous revenue from this investment. The city of Suez owes its prosperity to this canal, as a large number of steamships anchor here, and it is a connecting point for travelers visiting Africa, Europe, Australia and India. From the lighthouse a panoramic view can be had of the long and rugged ranges of mountains on both the Arabian and African sides of the Red Sea.

At Suez I embarked on the floating palace Kiserhind, a vessel belonging to the P. and O. Steamship Company. The anchor was raised, and we were soon speeding away over the Red Sea. The first point of historical interest we passed was the place where Moses, leading the children of Israel, is popularly supposed to have crossed, when pursued by Pharoah. If Pharoah and the Egyptians were drowned in the Red Sea, they certainly had a salty grave, as this sea is said to be the saltiest water in the world, with the exception of the Dead Sea and the Great Salt Lake. On the Arabian side is a well called Moses' well. This well is much frequented by tourists, and the waters are said to be very bitter. The next point of interest was Mount Sinai, where Moses received the ten commandments. Aside from its historical interest, this mountain and its surrounding peaks are impressive in their sublimity. From a distance it has the appearance of a long, red streak in the Arabian mountains, and is apparently barren of vegetation. The hot rays of the sun, shining upon it, gave it a smoky, hazy appearance.

The first two days sailing over the Red Sea the fervid African sun poured down upon us, and the heat was almost unendurable. The thermometer registered ninety-five in the shade at 7 A. M. In my state-room, at midnight, the heat was almost enough to suffocate me, and the perspiration poured from every pore. A sea voyage of this kind is more to be endured than to be enjoyed, especially in the warm season of the year. I was told that persons in delicate health had died from the effects of the heat while crossing this sea. The lady passengers, seated in their easy-chairs, spent most of their time on the hurricane deck, where they were protected from the blazing sun by a canvas awning. We spent most of our time trying to catch a breeze, which was about as scarce as green grass on the Desert of Sahara.

However, on this occasion, the heat was of but short duration ; for, suddenly, the smooth, calm sea was swept by a raging storm, which sent most of the passengers to their berths, and sea-sickness prevailed with the majority. But for once I did not succumb, and reported regularly at the table when meal time came around, not always an easy thing to do in a heavy gale. This storm occurred near the Gulf of Aden, where, a few months before, two steamers were swamped, and, with the exception of one man, all on board were lost. However, accidents are expected to occur here at any time, as this is a treacherous sea, full of rocks and islands, where vessels have been stranded, and shipwrecks are of frequent occurrence, especially during the monsoon season. In the last few years they have begun to erect lighthouses on the various islands, and these beacons of light, shining out over the dark sea, will prevent much disaster in the future.

There is not much in the way of scenery along the shores of the Red Sea. There is generally a narrow, sandy plain along the coast, backed by ranges of barren mountains, abrupt in outline and of moderate height. We passed a group of twelve islands called the Twelve Apostles, which are named accordingly. As the smallest island is almost covered up in the sea, and the waters in its vicinity are consequently more treacherous and dangerous to vessels, it is therefore called Judas Iscariot. There are several physical features about this body of water from which its name may have been derived, one being the abundance of red coral, and another the red fish which abound in its waters. The Red Sea is about 1,200 miles long, and 200 miles broad at its widest part.

The last object which attracted our attention as we steamed into the port of Aden was the Island of Perim, which divides the sea into two channels, called respectively the Great and Little Channels. The former is ten miles broad, and the latter narrow and shallow. This island is a bare black rock, three miles and a half long, and probably a little over two miles wide. It is almost destitute of vegetation, and is without water.

Aden belongs to Great Britain, and is one of the coaling stations of the P. and O. Steamship Company. It has a population of about 35,000, and considerable trade is carried on here in the products of Arabia, such as coffee, gum, feathers, pearls and ivory. Coal, for the use of the steamers is its most valuable import. One of the principal occupations of the inhabitants seems to be begging. In this art I found them not far behind their Egyptian brethren. They also have trinkets and jewelry to sell, for which they expect to receive many times their actual value.

On leaving Aden, we had a long sea voyage before us, as our next destination was Colombo, in Ceylon. We passed through the Gulf of Aden into the Arabian Sea, then out upon the Indian Ocean, and found traveling much pleasanter on this body of water than on the sultry Red Sea. We had on board several passengers of high rank, among the most noteworthy being Lord Byron, a relative of the famous poet; and Lord Carrington, the newly appointed Governor of New South Wales, in Australia. There were also other lords and noblemen of more or less importance, who were going as representatives of the English Government to India and China, and the majority of these gentlemen were accompanied by their wives. They all helped to swell the number of what I believe to be one of the jolliest lot of passengers that ever sailed in the Oriental seas. We devised various amusements and entertainments to fill up the time, and break the monotony of the slowly passing days.

We traveled at the rate of about 275 miles a day, passing Cape Guardafui, on the African coast, and the Island of Socotra. The country in the

vicinity of the cape is said to be inhabited by cannibals.   In this torrid climate the evening is the
pleasantest part of the day; for, as soon as the
tropical sun begins to ascend the horizon, the cabin
and state-rooms become uncomfortably warm, and
the majority of the passengers ascend to the hurricane deck, where they are somewhat protected from
the sun's rays by the canvas awning, and try in
various ways to while away the long hours.   Some
are engaged in reading or writing; others, in spinning yarns about the past, or telling conundrums.
Some are speculating on the latitude or longitude
we are in, on the depth of the sea or the height of
the barometer; wondering how many miles we
traveled yesterday, and whether we are going to
have a storm to-morrow, etc.   And so the days go
by until the novelty wears away and the jokes
grow stale.   We begin to tire of new friends, and
long for the old, familiar faces.   We weary of the
seemingly boundless waste of water, and sigh for a
glimpse of land.   We grow impatient for new
sights and scenes.

On this voyage we had several preachers aboard,
and, as a natural consequence, had religious services
on Sundays.   Every Sunday at six bells, or eleven
o'clock, the fire alarm was sounded, and the crew
hurried out in full force, and, for a brief space of
time, the decks were a scene of great confusion.
This, of course, was in every case a false alarm,

but was part of the ordinary routine, as it is necessary to keep the crew well drilled, so that, in the
case of a genuine fire, they will be able to obey
orders promptly and efficiently. Of all the calam-
ities liable to occur at sea, fire is the most to be
dreaded, and every precaution is necessary to be
used to guard against it. Finally, after a voyage
of 3,500 miles from Suez, we entered the harbor of
Colombo.

Here we drew a sigh of relief, and hailed with
joy the termination of a long and somewhat perilous voyage. We had crossed the barren deserts
of Egypt, endured the heat on the Red Sea, and
stood the racket of the monsoon on the Indian
Ocean ; so that now the prospect of landing on
terra firma, and enjoying the shade of the dense
masses of tropical foliage, seemed pleasant indeed.

CHAPTER X.

CEYLON AND INDIA.

As soon as the steamer cast anchor, we were surrounded by natives, each in his rickety little boat, who swarmed the harbor like sea dogs, and looked about as rickety as their boats, which are long and narrow as a canoe. They kept up an incessant yelling and scrambling, each trying to secure his share of the passengers to convey to the shore. In a short space of time, after entrusting yourself to one of these wretched little boats, you are landed on shore. For this service the boat-man will charge you a half a rupee, or twenty cents. If you do not come up to his expectations in the matter of an extra fee, you are threatened with a ducking. Should the boat capsize, it would have no more effect on the natives, who are principally Singhalese, than throwing a cork into the water. They are apparently not born to be drowned.

On landing, you are importuned by guides and half-naked beggars, both an unmitigated nuisance in their way. On the streets you are followed by venders of curios and cheap jewelry. The latter they try to palm off as genuine jewels, and charge enormous prices in proportion to their actual value ; and, should the unwary traveler allow himself to be beguiled into purchasing the wares of the dusky merchants, he will depart from the Island of Ceylon a sadder and a wiser man.'

Colombo is the commercial metropolis, and at present the capital, of Ceylon, and has a mixed population of over 100,000. The people consist of descendants of the Portuguese and Dutch, who have both at different times controlled the island, Singhalese, Chinese, Arabs, Persians, Parsees and half-castes of all colors. There are a large number of English residents, many of them belonging to noble families. They are mainly dependent on mercantile or political occupations, although some of them are planters. This city lies north of the Equator, in latitude seven. Tropical fruits and all kinds of vegetation grow luxuriantly. On approaching the city, one would scarcely believe that it could contain such a large population, as many of the native dwellings are merely small huts which are hidden from view by the overhanging palm and cocoanut trees.

One of the greatest enterprises of Colombo is the magnificent breakwater lately constructed by the British Government, the first stone of which was laid by the Prince of Wales in 1875. Vessels can now lie at anchor in safety in this harbor, even when the monsoon is at its worst. Among the places interesting for a stranger to visit are the fortifications, the barracks, the parade ground, the cinnamon gardens, the museum and the clock tower. I also visited the prison, and had a conversation with Arabi Pasha, the noted Turkish General who was captured in Egypt by the English, and sent to Ceylon, where he is detained as a prisoner. He is a large man, and has a very determined appearance.

In the various countries I had visited, I had ridden in the vehicles peculiar to each country, and I was now about to enjoy the privilege of riding in what, so far, was to be the most novel of them all. This consisted of a clumsy sort of a cart drawn by a buffalo, and, of course, driven. by a native driver. I paid my half-rupee to the driver, boarded the cart, and started to inspect the suburbs of the city at the rate of about two miles an hour. This particular buffalo was as docile as a kitten, and about as swift as a snail. The driver looked a great deal wilder than the steed. The least I can say for this expedition is that it made up in novelty what it lacked in comfort. In Ceylon, buffalo, native oxen, or cows, generally take the place of the horse, and are usually driven single in a clumsy kind of a cart.

The Singhalese are, as a rule, well formed, and, were it not for their brown skins, good looking.

They are more intelligent than any other of the Oriental races, and most of them have more or less knowledge of the English language. Ceylon was the only country in the Orient where I could travel to good advantage without an interpreter. The native food is similar to that used by the Chinese, and cooked and served in about the same manner. Rice, fish, tea, and different kinds of bread-fruit are their staple food.

As Ceylon is situated in the tropics, very little clothing is needed, and very little used by the natives. The peculiar costume of the women attracts considerable attention from the stranger, and they resemble our Indian women in their fondness for brilliant colors. Before you get fairly acquainted with the feminine style of dress, you will hardly be able to distinguish the men from the women. However, if they do not beg, you may be pretty sure that it is a woman, as the men are nearly all inveterate beggars. The children have no costume to attract attention from any one. You can see them playing or running along the streets entirely destitute of clothing of any kind. It requires very little time, however, to become accustomed to these things, which at first seem so peculiar, and ere long one ceases to notice them at all.

From Colombo, I visited Kandy. This town is situated in the interior of Ceylon, seventy-five miles by rail from Colombo, and over 1,700 feet above

the level of the sea. The road between the two
places is remarkable for its beauty, and the wonderful engineering skill shown in its construction.
On the last thirty miles of this road, there are
eight tunnels, the track winds around the mountain tops, and, with each succeeding mile, the
scenery grows wilder and grander. We pass peak
after peak, until Bible Rock, which towers hundreds
of feet above them all, is left behind, and we find
ourselves nearly 2,000 feet above the level of the
sea, in one of the most picturesque countries in the
world. Here we had a commanding view of rice
fields, coffee and tea plantations, which are situated
on steep hillsides and in deep gulches, and everywhere could be seen the natives busily engaged in
tilling the soil. As I gazed on this beautiful tropical panorama, I concluded that I had at last found
something to equal in grandeur Cape Horn in the
Sierras, the Alps, and the grand mountain scenery
in Norway.

Kandy is beautifully surrounded by hills; it is
built around the margin of an artificial lake constructed in 1805 by the last king of Kandy, and is
situated in the heart of the coffee and tea plantations. Tropical fruits grow in profusion. Here
can be seen the cinnamon tree, the cocoanut, the
pine-apple and the bread-fruit. This fruit the natives boil, using it largely in the place of bread.
The palm, with its spreading branches, affords a

fine shade; and the lantena, a species of berry fruit, grows rank all over the island.

Among the most striking objects of interest at Kandy are the temples, of which there are sixteen, twelve Buddhist and four Brahman. Of the Buddhist temples probably the one most worthy of mention is Dalada Malagawa, as it claims to be in possession of a tooth of Buddha. I was shown the casket which contains the tooth, which has been guarded for centuries as a memento of the famous teacher. Ceylon was converted to Buddhism 500 B. C., and may properly be called a Buddhist country, as the majority of the Singhalese, who number seventy per cent. of the population, are Buddhists.

When I visited the temples the priests very politely and willingly showed me their images and sacred curiosities; but from the time I entered the temple and commenced my investigation of the sacred relics until I left it, the priests followed me around with musical instruments, which to my mind resembled cow-bells and tin horns, and beat the tom-tom until I was almost distracted with the noise. I was frequently enjoined not to touch the images or relics, as they were all sacred; but the priests themselves, I found, were not too sacred to beg. After they had got all the pennies they could possibly squeeze out of me, I was led out through a succession of iron doors in a grandly ceremonious style, followed up in the meanwhile by the beating

14

of the tom-tom. This was a visit that I have no longing to repeat.

The only hotel in Kandy is the Queen's Hotel, which is kept partly in European and partly in the Oriental style. The servants were natives. The charge at this hotel for accommodations was six rupees, or three dollars, a day. A native servant lies down in the hall outside the bedroom, acting, I suppose, as a body guard. I had my mind and eyes as much on the guard as on the thieves, from which he was supposed to be a protection. However, he expected to be tipped with a few annas for this service, on my departure from the hotel. This detestable custom of feeing the servants, which prevails in France, Italy and Egypt, also extends to every country in Asia.

The first thing that attracted my attention upon my arrival in Kandy, was the absence of white men. The streets were black with natives, who came swarming around me trying to sell their worthless trinkets, and, when I positively refused to buy, then they would begin to beg. I was very much interested in studying the manners and customs of the natives and their life, both in town and on the plantations. The problem of life is a serious, and to me an interesting, study.

Many travelers are afraid to venture into the interior of the Oriental countries on account of the treachery of the natives, and are content with visiting the seaport towns, and keeping along the beaten line of travel. On several occasions I have had European tourists agree to visit interior places with me; but in every instance, when the time came to start, they would "fly the track," and say that it was too dangerous, that we might be murdered, etc. For my part, I would about as soon stay at home as to be obliged to follow closely in the beaten track of other travelers. I like to digress; a little danger and uncertainty gives spice to an adventure. However, when I saw the timidity with which other travelers viewed these trips into the interior, I concluded that I deserved some credit for bravery.

Since 1817 the entire sovereignty of the Island of Ceylon has been in the hands of the British, and they controlled the principal forts along the seaboard as early as 1796. I have noticed that law and order seem to prevail in all of Great Britain's possessions, and Ceylon is no exception to this rule. The natives seem to be perfectly satisfied with their strict but good government. The government of Ceylon maintains a large number of public schools, and there are also schools under the management of the Roman Catholics and other missionary bodies. I was told that the Singhalese children are, as a rule, very bright, and learn the English language quite rapidly. Some of the wealthier natives send their sons to Oxford to be

educated. I had an interview with a Singhalese
graduate who had just returned from that institution, and had been awarded an important position
by the British Government. Native students are
often given official positions when qualified to fill
them, and are thus encouraged to perfect themselves in a knowledge of the English language and
English institutions.

Ceylon is now, like the balance of British India,
on the high road to civilization. Nearly all of the
producers of the islands are English planters, who
employ native servants at very meagre wages.
A sixpence a day is the most that is paid for ten
hours' work. The natives, however, do not seem
to need much money, as they are not at all enterprising, and are satisfied with a mere existence.
Food is obtained at a trifling expense, and in this
warm climate much clothing is not needed. These
European planters have rather a fine thing of it, as
they have been enabled to purchase this land at a
very low price, and native labor is so extremely
cheap.

Ceylon is rich in resources, and well able to support her population of 3,000,000. In addition
to her tropical fruits, rice and coffee plantations,
she has some mineral wealth. In the western and
southern portions of the island, iron exists in large
quantities, and is of excellent quality. In many
places it crops out at the surface in a state of great

purity. From time immemorial the Singhalese have been accustomed to work the ore into tools; and, although the means they employ are rude and imperfect, they manufacture articles which are esteemed by them far above those imported from Europe. The rudely worked Singhalese iron is equal in temper to the finest Swedish metal. Natural deposits of common salt are found in many of the provinces. It is also produced by artificial means in large quantities.

Extensive pearl fisheries exist off the northern part of the western coast of Ceylon. The banks on which these oysters are found are situated at a distance of from sixteen to twenty miles from the shore, and extend north and south for many miles. The fisheries are conducted by the government, which sells the oysters in heaps of 1,000, as they are landed from the boats. In some parts of the island precious stones are met with in great abundance, the most valuable of which are the ruby, the amethyst, the sapphire, the cat's-eye and the carbuncle. Moonstones, cinnamon stones and garnets are found in great abundance and variety.

In the hill country every valley and open plain is made to yield its crop of grain, and the steep sides of the hills are cut into terraces, on which are seen waving patches of green rice watered from the mountain streams. Tobacco is extensively cultivated in various parts of the island.

The cultivation of coffee is one of the most important industries, as the soil and climate of Ceylon are capable of yielding an excellent quality of this product.

Probably the most valuable tree which grows on this island is the cocoanut palm. The plaited leaves of this tree serve as plates and dishes, and as a thatch for the cottage of the native. The dried leaves are used as torches, and the large leaf-stalks for garden fences. The trunk of the tree sawed up is employed for every possible purpose: its fruit, when green, supplies food and drink; when ripe, it yields oil. The fibre of the cocoanut is worked up into a kind of yarn and cordage called cori, which is admirably adapted for use in salt water. The trading vessels of this country employ no other cordage or rope but this, and the planks of the small vessels are often held together by cori yarn, without the aid of a single nail.

The following review of the voyage from Egypt to Ceylon, with some other items, is reprinted from the Modesto *Herald:*

LETTER FROM CEYLON.

Special Correspondence to the Herald.

KANDY, CEYLON, Nov. 4, 1885.

EDITOR HERALD:—A few more lines about my movements in the Oriental world.

After sight-seeing among the mysteries of Egypt, I resumed my journey to India, and embarked at Suez on the magnificent steamer Kiserhind, belonging to the Peninsular and Oriental Steamship Company. The line is said to be the safest of any line that runs in the Eastern waters. Accidents are almost unknown to this line, even in the Bay of Biscay, or on the treacherous Red Sea, where shipwrecks have been of frequent occurrence.

The town of Suez, on the south end of the canal, has a mixed population of 12,000 inhabitants. Here is a general anchorage of steamers where passengers make connections and selections for their destination. From Suez we enter the Red Sea. The first two days out the African sun was almost unendurable. It is hot, without a breeze, the thermometer standing ninety in the shade at 8 o'clock A. M., and at midnight, in my state-room, I was soaked with perspiration as though I had come out of a sweat-box. Under such circumstances a sea voyage is only to be endured, but not enjoyed very highly. However, this extreme heat was only of short duration, as we were soon surprised and comforted by a raging storm and breeze that washed the hurricane decks, and sea-sickness was the result. Many of the passengers were feeding the fishes; but on this voyage I was not one of them, as I reported regularly at the table. The storm was near the Gulf of Aden, where a steamer was swamped last June, and all the lives were lost but one man. The next day the storm subsided to a usual calmness. The Red Sea is 1,200 miles long, and from 60 to 175 miles wide, and it is said to be one of the saltiest bodies of water in the world. The leading historic objects of interest on the Red Sea coast are Mount Sinai, where Moses received the law, known as the Ten Commandments, and a well where the Arabs frequent, and which they call the Well of Moses. The water of this well is bitter.

Ceylon has a mixed population of 3,000,000, composed of the dusky races. Kandy, seventy-five miles from Colombo, has many attractions for the tourist and sight-seer. The city is situated amid rolling hills, and surrounded by coffee plantations and luxuriant gardens of tropical fruits and trees. The Buddhist Temple is the grandest of all the objects to be seen in Kandy. The peculiar constructions of the railway and the scenery along the line from Colombo to Kandy on the upper forty miles are the grandest in the world. The hill country of Ceylon is bright with the rich green of tropical plantations, and presents many interesting landscapes.

Notwithstanding the heat in this tropical climate, I have found my travels enjoyable and interesting, and I have formed many pleasant acquaintances both on land and water. But a long, long letter of credit I have found to be the most useful companion.

From here I will visit many interesting points in India, thence to Australia, and extend my journey to Japan and China. I anticipate arriving in San Francisco about the 15th of January, and will have traveled in all about 50,000 miles, and thus have completed the circle around the world.

OSMUN JOHNSON.

After extended traveling along the sea-coast and interior of Ceylon ; after viewing her scenery and resources, from Peduratallagalla, her loftiest mountain, 8,280 feet high, to the coffee plantations in the deepest gulches,—I took the steamer at Galle for Madras, a distance of 700 miles. This city is situated on the eastern coast of Hindustan, ranks third among the ports of India in respect to the number and tonnage of vessels stopping there, and the value of its exports and imports, and carries on trade with every part of the world. Madras has a population of about 500,000, which includes Europeans, Hindus, Parsees, Mohammedans and a mixture of many other races.

As this city has no harbor, passengers must be transferred quite a distance in small surf boats, which are propelled by natives. As there is a heavy surf breaking on the shore all the time, the landing is too dangerous and difficult to be interesting. Here I saw a curious way of transferring the mail to the shore. Should the vessel enter the roadstead in a sea so heavy that the small boats can not effect a landing, the natives tie a pair of logs together, on which they ride to and from the boat. The mail bags are tied on to their heads. Should they roll off the logs, it would produce about the same effect on them that it would on a duck. Upon landing on shore, you are immediately surrounded and beset by beggars and guides.

Here you see the traveling chair, or two-wheeled Jin-rik-ishia, which is used in China and Japan. The natives who propel these vehicles are not behind the best of their Asiatic brethren in extortion and attempts to fleece the unwary stranger.

The leading manufacturing industries are the manufacture of silk, lace and Indian shawls. These goods can be purchased here at astonishingly low prices, mainly due to the cheapness of labor. As baggage has to go through the custom house so frequently, and import duty is imposed on articles of this kind, it is not best to accumulate too much at even low figures. One of the principal attractions in the city is the museum and the menagerie, where can be seen the wild animals common to India. Among the places I inspected were the fortifications, the Government House, the numerous and imposing mosques, the temples and the native shops. The lighthouse, which is 125 feet high, is visible from a ship's deck fifteen miles at sea.

From Madras to Calcutta, the capital of India, is a distance of 750 miles, and a three-days journey by steamer. Calcutta is situated on the east bank of the River Hugli, about eighty miles from the sea-coast. It has a population of a million souls, composed of representatives of nearly all the Asiatic races, and a large number of Europeans. It derives its name from the village of Kalighat, on account of the great mortality which existed

there for many years.   It was identified in the
mind of the mariner with Golgotha, the place of
skulls.   It is now sometimes called the City of
Palaces, a name which it richly deserves, as the
streets, in the European quarter especially, are
lined with magnificent structures.   Among the most
costly buildings are St. Paul's Cathedral and the
Government House, each erected at a cost of about
half a million dollars.

The most interesting of all sights in Calcutta is
the shipping.   The Port of Calcutta extends ten
miles along the Hugli; the average width of the
channel is 250 yards, and it has moorings for 169
vessels.   At the railway terminus on the Hourah
side of the river is an immense floating bridge,
which was built at a cost of over a million dollars.
It is constructed on pontons, and affords a continuous roadway for vehicles and foot passengers.

In the Zoölogical Gardens can be seen nearly
every kind of animal peculiar to India.   The
Botanical Gardens contain all varieties of tropical
plants, and are an attractive place to visit.   I also
visited the fortifications, the art galleries and the
museum.   I strolled through the native portion of
the city, which is densely populated, and was much
interested in what I saw of Hindu life, also in the
Oriental shops, the temples, shrines and mosques,
of which there are a large number.

The three great religions in India are Buddhism,

Mohammedanism and Brahmanism. Throughout twenty-two centuries the Brahmans have been the counselors of the Hindu princes, and the teachers of the Hindu people, and they were the depository of the sacred books, the philosophy, the science and the laws of the ancient Hindu commonwealth. In the sixth century B. C., Buddha appeared, and gained many followers. Buddhism has co-existed with Brahmanism for more than a thousand years. As a religious founder, Buddha left behind him a creed which has gained more disciples than any other system of beliefs in the world. After a lapse of 2,400 years, it is professed by 500,000,000 people, or more than one-third of the human race. Mohammedanism was born in Arabia about 600 A. D , and soon spread over a vast portion of country. It never gained a strong foothold in Southern India, but had many followers in the Northern portion of the country. It is to be hoped that the day may come when the worship of idols of brass and stone will be discontinued.

The English, on assuming the government of India, determined as far as possible to administer justice in accordance with the existing laws of the country ; and, so long as the various religious beliefs do not conflict with justice and humanity, they are not interfered with. There are many missionaries in India engaged in the work of christianizing the natives ; but, when you ponder on the fact that there are nearly 250,000,000 of them to convert, it looks as if it would require the combined forces of the whole Christian world, and as if scores and scores would come and go before such a result would be accomplished. The press and the railways will be important factors in the work of civilization.

India is the great granary of Asia, and a formidable rival to the wheat producers of California, and, in fact, of the whole United States. It has been conjectured that the total area under cultivation to wheat in India is equal to the area cultivated to the same crop in the United States. The quality of the grain is high enough to satisfy the English millers, and "Calcutta Club No. 1" commands a price in Mark Lane not much below that of the finest Californian or Australian wheat.

Railway communication is rapidly extending all over India, and there are already some 13,000 miles of road in operation. Tourists can now travel by rail from the foot of the Himalaya Mountains to the southern extremity of Cape Comorin. India has four great rivers, the Indus, the Ganges, the Irawadi and the Brahmaputra, all flowing through broad valleys, and from time immemorial the chief means of conveying the products of the interior to the sea. The competition naturally existing between river craft and the railroads is conducive to cheap transportation. In the delta of the Ganges River, navigation attains its highest development. The population may be regarded as half amphibious. In the rainy season, every village can be reached by water, and every family keeps its own boat.

Since the construction of the Suez Canal, the distance from Bombay to Liverpool is much shorter than from San Francisco to Liverpool by the way of Cape Horn. This makes a difference in the cost of transportation, and wheat can be carried from India to England much cheaper than from San Francisco to England. This has a corresponding effect on the price. Another fact in favor of our Indian rivals is that the Hindu cheap labor can be had on the sea as well as on the land, as Indian sailors can be employed for eight rupees, or less than four dollars, per month. However, when the Panama Canal is finished, the tide will turn in our favor, our wheat will have the less distance to travel, and transportation will be proportionately cheaper. Vessels passing through the Suez Canal have to pay a heavy tax on the cargo, and, under the present law, they are required to anchor over night. This, in most cases, adds one day more to the journey, so that, when everything is summed up, and we get our canal, the tonnage from India to Liverpool will not be so much lower, after all, than from California.

In addition to this, a California farmer, with his

combined harvester, can accomplish more work in one day with four men than an Indian planter can with fifty coolies, using the present rude hand implements. There is great opposition to machinery in India; for there are millions of laborers struggling for bread, who are willing to work for almost nothing. They look upon a machine which takes the place of hand labor as an innovation which deprives them of a livelihood. The producers in the Indian agricultural districts are neither so grasping nor so enterprising as our average California farmer, and are satisfied with much less. Everything is cheap; the tropical produce and the grain, as well as the labor. Planters hire coolies to work in the harvest fields at a sixpence per day apiece, and at less than that on the coffee and tea plantations and in the rice fields. In the Calcutta bag factory, wages are but threepence per day.

India has two great drawbacks. One is that communication with the interior districts is often attended with great difficulties. As the railroads are extending their lines in all directions, this disability will soon be removed. The other is the liability to drouth. In a country so densely settled as India, and where the means of communication are so limited, the failure of a harvest must always cause much distress. India lies half to the north and half to the south of the tropic, and, excepting a small fractional part of a mountainous character, is subject to great summer heat. Some parts are regularly visited by rain in season, and other parts are liable to drouth. One season of drouth is generally followed by another, and that by a third.

Out of thirty-one famines during the present century, fifteen succeeded each other in three, and sixteen in two, consecutive years, while intervals between them varied from two to ten years. The country has, of course, always been subject to famines; and history relates how in 1031 the Emperor Shah Jehan, and in 1631 the Emperor Aurungzebe, tried to mitigate their desolating effects without much success. Within the time of the present generation several very severe famines have taken place. From the year 1848 to 1878 the abnormal deaths which occurred in years of famine did not fall short of ten millions. It cost the state, to relieve the starving population during this period, not less than 21,250,000 pounds sterling, exclusive of several millions in loss of revenue. Irrigation and railways have done much to remedy the evil.

India is a great country, and possesses a great variety of resources. British India has a total area of about 1,500,000 square miles, and a population of 240,000,000. Of the area, nearly 600,000 square miles, with a population of 50,000,000, belong to the native states not under British administration; while the remainder, 900,000 square miles, with 190,000,000 people, is under direct British rule.

As my journey around the world was a long and somewhat tortuous one, my time for visiting India was soon exhausted. Had I been satisfied to follow in the usual track of travelers, and taken the most direct route to China, I would only have had to travel 1,700 miles in going from Calcutta to Hong-Kong; but I was ambitious to visit Australia, though by going in this roundabout way it lengthened the distance something over 10,000 miles. I wavered a little when I thought of the long and monotonous sea voyage, and meditated on the fact that it was the typhoon season of the year. Still, by taking the longer route, I could visit Australia and New Zealand, skirt the shores of New Guinea, take in the Philippine Islands, and see the extensive coral reefs which exist in the Southern waters. I should sail over many seas, and see many sights that would be missed by going the other way; so I concluded that the pleasures of this trip would overbalance its discomforts; and, bidding good-bye to my friends and traveling companions, as they were going to continue on the direct route to Hong-Kong, I promised, if the typhoon did not get the best of me on the China Sea (this sea is never known to behave itself), to meet them there some time in the future. I embarked on the steamer Enos at Calcutta for Colombo, a distance of 1,400 miles over the Bay of Bengal.

CHAPTER XI.

THE VOYAGE OVER THE INDIAN OCEAN.

COLOMBO is the junction of the P. and O. Steamship Company, where the various routes diverge for Australia, China, Japan or India. On leaving here, we had a sea voyage of 5,000 miles before us ere we could reach the Australian shore. On account of the extreme heat in these tropical countries, white linen clothes are worn almost entirely, and heavy clothing is of very little use. As a clean suit is needed every day, one has to have a plentiful supply. So, before starting out on my journey, I had to see that my clothes were washed and in good order for the trip, as this would be my last opportunity before reaching Australia. This washing process is a somewhat interesting one to look at, but very hard on the clothes. Every article undergoes a vigorous pounding with a long stone, and, if the garments are not of the strongest material, they are unable to stand this ordeal, and new ones become a necessity. The expense for washing, however (outside of the wear and tear of the material), is of small consequence, one penny apiece being the regular price charged in all parts of Asia for washing and ironing shirts.

It may here again be mentioned that it is well

15

for tourists to be careful about investing in finery or curiosities as presents for their friends, as such articles are all subject to import duty. Packages containing ammunition and liquors can not be shipped as baggage, and cases of these articles must be accompanied by a declaration that they contain no explosive matter. The principal lines making monthly trips from Europe to India and China are the P. and O., the East India Steamship Company, and a French line called Messageries Maritimes. These are all reliable and popular lines, and make regular trips and connections by the way of Suez and the Red Sea; but between Colombo and Australia the P. and O. steamers are the ones which run the most regularly.

Two days out from Colombo we crossed the line of the Equator. Here we felt the heat intensely, especially when on deck. For several days we had the eastern trade wind against our course, and progress was slow, 250 miles a day being an average run. This portion of the Indian Ocean is destitute of islands or any object of interest, and there is nothing to be seen but the waste of waters, and the sky overhead ; so the passengers were thrown entirely upon their own resources for amusement. At dawn of day we generally had our baths, a daily bath being an absolute necessity in this warm climate. A custom which to me seemed somewhat singular prevails on steamers which sail in these waters. In the early morning the ship's officers and the passengers promenade the hurricane deck barefooted, and in their light morning clothes. They do this in order to get the full benefit of the cool morning air before the sun rises. They keep up a lively pace for about half an hour, and then retire below, where coffee and sandwiches are served. About 2 P. M. everybody on board, except the sailors on watch, retire to their rooms for an hour's sleep, and at four o'clock coffee and sandwiches are again served. In addition to this, we had the regular meals served at the regular hours.

On this passage we had on board a jolly lot of Indian planters, from whom I gained much valuable information in regard to terrace farming, the tropical staples; seeding and harvesting, and the cost of each; the yearly average of the crops, the principal exports, and the crops from which the largest returns may be expected. I was told that the cultivation of tea must largely take the place of coffee; as, next to wheat, the former is the most profitable staple of India. Well, what you don't hear aboard one of these passenger steamers is not worth hearing, as you mingle with pilgrims of every clan and from every land, hearing a great variety of languages, and seeing representatives of nearly every industry and profession. Every day's travel took us farther away from the Equator; and, with a change of latitude, came a perceptible modification of the temperature, making the remainder of the voyage much more endurable and comfortable.

CHAPTER XII.

AUSTRALIA.

AFTER we had been out twelve days, without any especial incident to record except the head wind and the extreme heat, we sighted Cape Leeuwin, the first landmark of Australia; and on the thirteenth day we cast anchor in King George's Sound, a distance of nearly 4,000 miles from Colombo. Here we remained twenty-four hours, which gave us all an opportunity to go on shore and try terra firma once more. We were all very much tanned and about half cooked by the heat of the tropics, and quite appreciated the change after being tossed about by the restless deep for so many days. The town of Albany, on King George's Sound, has a population of 2,000, all Europeans. This town is situated on the southwestern extremity of Australia, has no particular object of interest worthy of mention, and is surrounded by low, barren hills, which appear unfit for cultivation. The town chiefly exists upon the traffic from the sea. The best feature of King George's Sound is that it affords a commodious and secure harbor, which could accommodate a much larger fleet than is likely to be needed to guard English interests and subjects in this part of the world.

It seemed pleasant indeed to be in a civilized country, and see white people once more instead of the dusky heathen we had left behind in Egypt, Africa and India. We could now see churches and stores, instead of idols, shrines, and bazaars filled with trifles. Here were to be seen a large number of enterprising, refined and well-dressed people, instead of the lazy and half-naked Oriental races, and we could now tread on wide and well-paved streets instead of narrow and filthy Oriental lanes. Here we could hear church bells ringing out the summons to divine worship, instead of witnessing the heathen clapping his hands and bowing his knees before temples and idols; and we all enjoyed very much the life and bustle incident to the transaction of business in this prosperous little city inhabited by a civilized people.

Thus far the greater part of my traveling had been done on English steamships, on English possessions, and in English waters. This government seems to be the power behind the throne in nearly all quarters of the globe. Malta, Aden, India, Ceylon, Australia, Hong-Kong and many other places and islands are in the hands of the British. They have standing armies everywhere; their flag flies on every sea, and from men-of-war in every port; their fortifications are numerous;

and their soldiers and officers, on land and water, can be counted by the million. England is often called the "Mistress of the Seas," but maintains this supremacy at an enormous expense.

Our next destination was Port Adelaide, 1,000 miles distant from Albany. We soon entered the Great Australian Bight, and were out of sight of land for two days. After three days' sailing, we anchored at Port Adelaide, which is seven miles distant from the city of Adelaide, and were put on shore by a steam tender. The harbor at this port is safe and commodious; but there is a bar at its mouth which prevents large vessels from entering, the depth of the water varying with the tide from eight to sixteen feet. With a few exceptions, the harbors on the coast of Australia are shallow, which is a great drawback to the prosperity of many of the seaports. In case of a severe gale, vessels need a safe harbor where they will not be exposed to the fury of wind and wave.

Adelaide is a beautiful city, situated on both sides of the River Torrens, which is spanned by several bridges. The two portions of the town are called North and South Adelaide. South Adelaide is the commercial centre of the town, and lies on a very level plain on the left bank of the river. North Adelaide, the smaller portion of the town, contains the chief private houses, and occupies a gentle slope on the right bank of the river. Adelaide is the capital of the British colony of South Australia, and of the county of the same name. Its streets are broad, and regularly laid out. Among the most important public buildings are the Governor's house, the government offices, the Post-Office and the theatre. The principal places worth visiting are the Botanical Garden and the public grounds, called the Park Lands, which contain over 1,900 acres.

Australia is the largest island in the world,—so large that it is often called a continent. It is 2,500 miles in length from east to west, and 1,950 miles in breadth from north to south, contains an area of about 3,000,000 square miles, and has a seaboard of 8,000 miles. As it is situated in the Southern Hemisphere, the seasons are just the reverse of what we are accustomed to. June is a winter month, and crops are harvested in December and January. The cities in Australia are of modern construction, and similar to those in America.

There are no temples, ruins or shrines, and the aborigines of this country, like the North American Indians, live in rude huts, which are either bowers formed of the branches of the trees, or are made of piled logs loosely covered with grass or bark. In the southeastern part of the island some of the huts are larger and more substantial. The numbers of the native Australians are steadily diminishing; small remnants of the race exist in each province, and a few tribes wander over the interior. It is estimated that there are not more than 80,000 of these aborigines left on the continent.

The sea-coast, except on the northern and northwestern shore, is wonderfully devoid of inlets from the sea. Along the entire line of the eastern coast there extends a succession of mountain ranges, and on the western coast there is a series of low-lying hills. Off the southern coast of Australia the waters of the Indian Ocean commingle with those of the Pacific. I would have needed no other proof than this, had I been skeptical on the subject, to convince me that the earth was surely round. I had been traveling east for many months, and now was back in the waters of an ocean whose waves washed the shores of my home in the far-off West.

From Adelaide to Melbourne is a distance of 550 miles, which can be traveled either by rail or steamer. Melbourne is the most populous city in Australia, and is situated at the head of the large bay of Port Philip, on the northern bend, which is called Hobson's Bay. The spacious, land-locked harbor of Port Philip was discovered in 1802, by Lieutenant Murray. The city of Melbourne occupies a space three miles inland, on the Yarrah River; but the suburbs extend along the shores of the bay for ten miles.

The entire absence of guides and half-naked coolie beggars was to me a very pleasant change. Instead of being surrounded by these nuisances upon my arrival at the depots or wharves, I was met by the typical English cabman, his coat glittering with brass buttons, and his head adorned with a plug hat. He was indeed a gorgeous-looking individual as he sat on the top of his hansom, to which a steed of the Clyde breed was attached. The hansom is a peculiar conveyance. There is no chance for quarreling with any one while riding, as the coachman sits on top, and there is only room for one passenger inside, and that one must not be an overgrown one. This inside space fitted me as snugly as if I had sent my measure ahead. For the privilege of riding in one of these vehicles, you pay the sum of one shilling per mile, if you make your bargain beforehand; if not, you will probably have to pay double that amount. Extortion seems to be the rule with cabmen and guides of all races and colors, and in the cities of all countries, from San Francisco (traveling eastward) to the shores of Japan.

Melbourne is the capital of the colony of Victoria, and is the most populous city in Australia, offering, perhaps without exception, the most striking illustration of the aptitude of the Anglo-Saxon race for colonization. Until the year 1835 no white man had ever made his habitation there;

MELBOURNE, THE CAPITAL OF VICTORIA.

and now the spot where the first settler made his home in the wilderness is the centre of a great city, which is ten miles in length, six in breadth, covers an area of 45,000 acres, and has a population of 283,000 people. This city is beautifully located. It is built on nearly level ground, slightly rising to the centre from every direction, giving it an easy slope for drainage; consequently it is a healthy city as well as a beautiful one.

At present there is a strong rivalry between Melbourne and Sydney, each contending for the honor of being the chief city of Australia. Melbourne has at present 25,000 more people than Sydney, and Victoria Colony contains some of the best agricultural land in Australia; there are also extensive sheep ranges, and some of the richest gold mines of the country, in the vicinity of Melbourne. Sydney, by virtue of its position, is probably destined to be the greater commercial city of the two, as it has one of the finest and most spacious harbors in the world. The surrounding country, however, is not so rich as that around Melbourne; it is thickly timbered, too hilly to be much of an agricultural country, but is a fine pastoral region, and affords an extensive range for cattle. In the near distance is situated the town of Newcastle, which is surrounded by extensive coal fields. The quality of this coal is said to be equal to that of Great Britain for most purposes, and it is largely used by steamships navigating the Pacific and Chinese waters.

I have become so interested in these comparisons, that I fear I am digressing. I will now return to Melbourne, and give a little further description of the city and its surroundings. The climate in the vicinity is considered unusually fine. The only drawback is the occasional hot winds, which blow from the north for two or three days at a time, and raise the temperature until it is uncomfortably warm ; but by far the greater proportion of the time the sky is clear and the air mild and dry. On days when the wind blows, I have seen the temperature vary from 60 to 120 degrees. I had my best view of Melbourne and its environs from Flagstaff Hill. Its numerous suburbs surrounded the city in all directions ; in the distance, on three sides, were ranges of hills, and on the fourth the waters of Hobson Bay could be seen sparkling in the sunlight.

Notwithstanding its size, Melbourne is by no means a crowded city ; the streets are all ninety-nine feet wide, and parks, squares and gardens are so numerous that it occupies an area nearly one-half as great as that of London. The two principal streets are Burke and Collins,—the first the busiest street in Melbourne, the other containing the most fashionable shops. The buildings which line these streets are of uniform height, and substantially built; but you find no such magnificent structures as can be seen in the business portion of San Francisco, nor does there seem to be the same amount of activity and bustle. I had quite an argument on this subject with one of Melbourne's enterprising citizens who had been deluding himself with the idea that his city was far ahead of San Francisco. I quietly disabused his mind of this idea, and informed him that it would have to grow with all its might for the next twenty-five years before it would be as far advanced as our Metropolis of the Golden West.

Among the objects of interest to be seen in Melbourne are monuments of Burke and Collins, two of Australia's most famous explorers; the barracks, the Parliament Houses, the Custom House, and the Town Hall, which will seat nearly 3,000 people. In this hall is a colossal organ, on which the city organist performs two afternoons in each week, the public being admitted at a nominal charge. The parks and public gardens are extensive and handsome. The Royal Park contains about 600 acres, and is timbered with gum trees. About thirty acres in the centre of this park are beautifully laid out, and contain a zoölogical collection. The Yarrah Park, which is about 300 acres in extent, contains the leading cricket grounds. Want of space will prevent me from elaborating further on interesting features of Melbourne.

I then visited the western portion of the colony of Victoria, and saw some good agricultural country. Here the wheat is harvested with strippers of three-horse power ; but larger machines are in course of construction. By these machines the wheat is stripped of the heads. On the long stubble which remains, vast numbers of sheep are pastured, and they are often brought, for this purpose, a distance of several hundred miles from the interior. Great attention is paid to sheep farming, as this is one of the leading industries of Australia. The price of labor I found to be much the same as in California, six shillings, or $1.50, per day, being the usual wages paid in the harvest season.

The two principal inland towns were Sandhurst and Belrat. Sandhurst is built on the exhausted part of the old gold fields of Bendigo. Besides gold mining, there are quite a number of local industries, including coach building, brewing and iron casting. There are nearly 7,000 miners employed in the Sandhurst district. Belrat has 181 mines, some of them 1,000 feet deep; and one in particular, known as the Pandora, is 2,000 feet deep. If the Pacific coast wants to beat those figures, I am afraid she will have to cross the Sierras to the Comstock, in Nevada. Silverton is the principal town in the dividing range, or barrier, where there are rich silver mines. The Belrat and

Hillman districts contain the richest mines in the colonies. Millions of pounds of the precious ore have been taken from these mines, and they are still worked at a great profit by the fortunate owners.

After inspecting the gold fields, I visited some of the sheep plains, or sheep runs, where they count their flocks by the hundreds of thousands. I was told that these sheep runs contain from thirty to a hundred thousand acres, and this amount of land is generally owned and controlled by one man. Many of these runs I found to be rocky, and, with the exception of the timber, apparently barren of vegetation. It seemed to me that there were two sheep to every blade of grass. This Australian grass must be exceedingly nutritious, or such a multitude of sheep could not manage to subsist. However, at the time that I visited Australia, there had been four dry seasons in succession, and all kinds of stock were in a starving condition, particularly in New South Wales and Queensland, where the water-courses had run dry. In fact, most of the inland Australian streams dry up early in the season, as there are no rainy regions or snow-clad mountains in the interior to feed the rivers. Drouths are of common occurrence, and the rain-fall is very light, probably owing to the low, flat character of the country, and the scarcity of high mountain peaks along the coast to condense the rain clouds, which are consequently blown across the country without distilling their moisture. I heard the question of constructing reservoirs, to catch the water in the rainy season, discussed in many districts. In Texas they have cisterns for rain water, and catch all they can, keeping it to use in time of drouth

The interior of Australia I found to be thickly timbered with large gum trees, the majority of them destitute of leaves, and some of bark. In many places they were ringed, and left to die and rot down. This was to make openings for farmers, probably for another generation, when the heavens will distribute moisture with a more liberal hand than at present. However interested I may have been in some of the resources of Australia, I was not favorably impressed with it as an agricultural country, not only on account of the frequency of the dry seasons, but because of the character of the soil, which is red and rolling, and has the appearance of being heavy to cultivate. It looked to me as if farming with the expectation of raising a profitable crop would be very much like buying the cat in the bag. I found, however, that the Australian residents who had never been in any other great wheat-producing country looked on the matter in an entirely different light, and from a more favorable point of view. Probably I was not an unprejudiced observer, as I had been for so many

years a farmer in California, a country in which
crops of all kinds grow to the acme of perfection.
I also visited several stock farms. I found the
cattle to be of enormous size, but was not favorably
impressed with the appearance of the horses, which,
to my mind, were disproportionately formed,
although they were said to be descendants of the
famous Clydesdale stock.

Take it all in all, Australia is a great and progressive country, and has a glorious prospect in
the near future. Her resources are many and various, and, where she is inferior in one branch of industry, she has others which more than compensate
for the difference. Australia is the greatest wool-
growing country in the world, and has more coast
line than any other. Her commercial interests are
enormous, her coal fields are inexhaustible, and she
is rich in minerals of every description. Copper,
tin, antimony, mercury, platina, bismuth, iron,
galena, quicksilver and shale, which yields kerosene
oil, are all found in Australia, and she is second
only to the United States in the extent of her gold
and silver mines. In the last few years pearl fishing has become quite an industry in Australian
seas, and has been carried on with considerable
success. Good pearls are found in Shark's Bay,
especially in an inlet called Useless Harbor; mother
of pearl shells are fished at many points along the
western coast, and an important pearl fishery has

16

been established in Torres Strait, on the coast of Queensland.

After thoroughly acquainting myself with the resources of Victoria Colony, I returned to Melbourne, where I took the train for Sydney, the second largest city in Australia, and the capital of New South Wales. The distance between these two cities is 575 miles; the railway fare, four pounds, or about twenty dollars; the time occupied in the journey, twenty-two hours. The railway system in the southern hemisphere is on the same plan as that of Europe and India. I can never cease to express my contempt for the construction of the cars,—the same inconvenient, uncomfortable compartments, where there is scarcely room enough to swing a cat. Here eight passengers are wedged in, the door locked, and we are left without water or conveniences of any kind until we arrive at the stations, which in this country are often few and far between, as the road runs through new and remote districts. I suppose I will again have to admit that I am prejudiced in favor of the American system, which I consider the most luxurious mode of traveling in the world. In these cars, which are much larger and more comfortable, the proud, brass-buttoned conductor reigns supreme ; you can take items on the physiognomy of a hundred people if you so desire, instead of half a dozen ; you have a stove to keep you warm in winter, and ice water to cool your parched throat in summer; and the windows are so constructed, that, if you feel disposed, you can raise them and put your head out to view the heavens or any earthly object.

In Eastern countries you are always surrounded, on arriving at stations, by porters who are always more than willing to anticipate your wants, and who desire to be remunerated accordingly. If the tourist does not wish to pay for learning their sharp practices, as I have done, he will give them a few pence, and they, in return, will lift their hats, favor you with a low bow and a sickly smile, and let you depart in peace, while they stand in wait for the next victim. In Australia, as in Europe, young women superintend the bars and lunch counters, and, at the large stations, seven or eight of these blushing damsels can be seen busily engaged in attending to the wants of the hungry and thirsty travelers. The price of a glass of ale or a cup of coffee is threepence, and sandwiches are furnished in proportion to the appetite of the individual.

There is very little agricultural land on the route between Melbourne and Sydney; but there is a large extent of country where coal abounds, and the greater portion of the remainder is devoted to grazing purposes. While traveling over this road, I talked with a stockman who owned 100,000 head of sheep, which were stationed in different places on his *run*. In New South Wales the coal-bearing strata cover a very large area in several detached portions, the largest of which probably exceeds 12,000 miles. In the vicinity of Newcastle, where the principal workings are, the coal seams vary from three to thirty feet in thickness, sixteen seams above three feet being known. It is estimated that the coal strata in Queensland cover an area of 24,000 square miles. Very little has been done toward their development, the districts in which they occur being too far from the settled portions of the country.

This route is not diversified enough to be picturesque, and is entirely devoid of attractive scenery. There are no mountains and dales, the country is low, and in many places the soil is stony. There are very few high mountain peaks in Australia, the highest being Mount Kosciusko, which has an altitude of over 6,000 feet. The principal attraction along the line of this road was the dried gum trees which dotted the country, some of them of immense size. The gum trees form the principal timber of Australia. There are 400 species of eucalyptus, or gum; the blue, the red, the white, the spotted, etc. They grow to an immense size, and live to be many hundred years old. The most of them shed their bark instead of their leaves, and some have neither leaves nor bark. Other species of timber are the white box, the iron bark, rose-wood, sandalwood, tulip-wood and satin-wood. These latter are used by cabinet makers for ornamental work.

Sydney, the capital of New South Wales, is a bustling commercial city, situated on rolling hills similar to those on which Rome is built. It lies on the harbor of Port Jackson, about four miles from its entrance. This harbor is completely landlocked, and the largest vessels can come close to the wharves, thus saving much inconvenience in loading and unloading vessels, and in transferring passengers from the ship to the shore. For my part, I can cheerfully dispense with the little row boat which is used to convey passengers from the ship's side to the landing, as I do not enjoy the drenching which one is frequently treated to in this process of transportation The extensive dry docks and ship yards at Sydney furnish every facility for repairing vessels. The port is well defended by several forts and batteries. The harbor is very attractive, being fourteen miles long; and the coast very irregular, with numerous small bays and promontories, which render it very picturesque.

This bay was discovered and the town of Sydney founded in 1788; but for twenty-five years the settlers of the colony of New South Wales were only acquainted with a strip of country fifty miles wide, between the Blue Mountains and the sea-coast; for they scarcely ever ventured far inland from the inlets of Port Jackson and Botany Bay. The climate of Sydney is salubrious; more rain falls here than in the southern colonies. It has a population of about 250,000, mostly Europeans, the greater proportion of them being English immigrants. These immigrants are constantly pouring into the Australian colonies. Every steamer which arrives from England is filled with people who are seeking home and fortune in this far-off country. With the constantly increasing facilities for travel, every quarter of the globe will soon cease to be remote.

A new land act has recently been passed which is intended to enable immigrants to settle on small pieces of land, and to give them ample time to pay for their farms, but to discourage and prevent the acquisition of large pastoral estates. Out of 17,000,000 acres settled under the old law, only 3,000,000 are in the hands of bona-fide settlers. The remaining 14,000,000 are in the hands of the sheep kings. By having all the favorable spots that give access to water taken up by his servants and tools, the squatter becomes practically the owner of his *run*, which he can extend to any limit in the same way. By this fraudulent device, great estates of hundreds of square miles have been acquired.

The loftiest eminence in Sydney is Flagstaff Hill, where a magnificent view can be had of the city, its suburbs and the harbor; and one can even see the Pacific Ocean. Among the principal attractions in this city are the Government buildings, with their extensive ornamental grounds. From this point the north shore and the Balmain can be seen to good advantage. Macguire street is lined by rows of fine residences on one side, and by government property on the other, is a favorite prominade, and one of the gayest thoroughfares in the city. The Museum, the Public Library, St. Mary's Cathedral, and the City Infirmary are all extensive institutions. In the suburbs are the City Park, the Zoölogical and Botanical Gardens and Belmore Park, all interesting places to visit. One thing that struck me peculiarly is the fact that the flowers, both the cultivated varieties and the wild flowers, seem to be entirely devoid of fragrance.

The most aristocratic quarter is Potts' Point and Vermalon, where the residences may be considered a good second to those on Nob Hill, in San Francisco. The most opulent citizens of Australia reside here. The leading hotels are the Pettis Hotel and the Royal, in St. George street, where you can get fair meals and a good bed for twelve shillings a day. Pitt street and St. George street, the main thoroughfares of the city, have a carriageway sixty feet wide, and are lined with handsome shops and churches and other public and private edifices. Business of every description is transacted, and, from seven in the morning until eleven at night, they are thronged with people.

New South Wales was for many years a penal settlement, and the agitation on this subject has been the only serious cause of conflict between the colony and the mother country. It ended by the latter yielding, and transportation was somewhat reluctantly abolished. Sydney is well situated to control the commerce of the Southern Pacific Ocean, occupying a position corresponding to that of San Francisco on the Northern Pacific. It has a large inter-colonial trade, and also carries on an extensive commerce with the United States. It is destined, by virtue of its situation, to become one of the great seaports of the world.

My next move was from Sydney to Paramatta, a town thirteen miles distant, on the Paramatta River. This was an exceedingly pleasant trip, as it gave me an opportunity of viewing the pictur-esque scenery of the harbor, the islands, and the beautiful gardens on the Paramatta River. Para-matta is an old town, and of little importance. Here I took the cars for the Blue Mountains, in the neighborhood of which the grandest scenery of Australia is found. The railroad which runs over these mountains is called the Zigzag Railway, and is constructed on the plan of the letter N. The first zigzag, called the Little Zigzag, is thirty-five miles from the Big Zigzag. The cars travel backward and forward before completing the ascent of the mountain, which is called the Lapstone Hill. The scenery is grandly picturesque, and would do credit to the Alps. From this hill we could look over the broad valleys into deep gulches, and could follow with our eyes the windings of the rivers. I must not neglect to mention, that, in this zigzag, a terrible railroad accident occurred six years ago ; two trains collided, and many passengers were killed.

After arriving at the summit, we followed a broken chain of mountains for many miles. All along the line of the road the country is thickly timbered, and to the left we could see far down into the valley at the foot of the mountains. The most elevated points on this route were Mount Ketoomba, which rises to a height of 3,349 feet above the sea-level; Went Falls, situated at an altitude of 2,856 feet ; and Mount Victoria, which is 3,422 feet high. This elevated region is a popular resort for Sydney people, who come up here a few weeks in December, when the heat is most intense, to cool off. The climate is said to be so healthful, that, except in case of accidents, people never die. Continuing our journey eastward, we soon arrive at the Big Zigzag. This is constructed on a steep incline of 800 feet, in the form of two N's. On emerging from one of the tunnels through which we pass, we overlook five tracks, running nearly parallel with each other. In addition to the beauties of the scenery, there are numerous caves which the tourist can visit. Of these the Imperial Cave is the most important, and the most frequented by visitors.

After rusticating a few days in the Blue Mountains, I crossed over to Burke, and enjoyed the hospitality of the people in the interior of New South Wales. Then, having seen all I cared to of the inland sights, I recrossed the mountains to Sydney. The principal resources in the Blue Mountains are the hunting grounds and the vast coal fields, which extend over a space of 200 miles to Newcastle. I was now fully convinced that the Southern Hemisphere had at least one wonder which could compare with the Yellowstone Park, the Alleghanies, Yosemite, Switzerland, or the Kandy Mountains, in Ceylon,—places which should be visited by all who wish to make a thorough tour of the globe, no matter how much pressed for time.

CHAPTER XIII.

NEW ZEALAND.

BEFORE leaving for China, I concluded to visit New Zealand, 1,281 miles distant from Sydney, so embarked on the regular mail packet Oakland. New Zealand consists of two large islands, called respectively North Island and South Island, of another smaller one called Stewart Island, and of a number of smaller islands and islets. New Zealand was discovered by a Dutch navigator in 1642; but he did not land there. Captain Cook, in 1769, was the first European who set foot on its shores. He visited the country several times, and circumnavigated the coast in the course of his three voyages of discovery, exploring and partly surveying the general outline. He introduced several useful animals and plants, including pigs, fowls, potatoes, turnips and cabbages. From Captain Cook's final departure, in 1777, until 1814, little is known of the country, except that, owing to the cannibalism and ferocity of the natives, it was a terror to sailors.

In 1814 a church mission was established at the Bay of Islands, which was followed by others, and both Protestant and Roman Catholic Missions were formed. In the course of the following thirty years the entire native population was converted, nominally at least, to Christianity. There was, of course, in after years a considerable relapse; but cannibalism ceased, and the barbarous nature of the race became softened, and capable of civilization; so, as a whole, the results of the missionary teaching were great and permanent.

The Islands of New Zealand have, since 1840, been a colony of Great Britain. It was not colonized in the usual manner, around one common centre; but there were formerly six distinct settlements,—Auckland, Wellington, Canterbury, New Plymouth, Nelson and Otago. For some years communication between them was irregular and infrequent. Three provinces are each subdivided into counties. The residence of the Governor is at Wellington, which is the seat of government. The government and Legislature have always been disposed to favor native interests, the right of the natives to their lands have always been fully recognized, and no land has been taken from them without their consent, except in the case of some confiscated lands which were taken under the authority of a special law from rebellious tribes.

The Governor is appointed by the Crown. The Legislative Council, or upper house, consists of fifty members who are appointed for life by the

Governor. The House of Representatives consists of ninety-five members elected by the people. Four members of the House must be Maoris, elected by their own race, and they are also entitled to several members in the Council. The duration of the House is for three years; but it is subject to re-election whenever the Governor dissolves the assembly. Education is free and compulsory, with certain exceptions, for children between the ages of seven and thirteen. Religion is not allowed to be taught in any of the schools.

The country is, to a great extent, mountainous, but is interspersed with fertile valleys and extensive plains, where prosperous farms can be seen growing crops of wheat and grain of all kinds. Hops are extensively raised in the Province of Nelson, which is frequently called the Garden of New Zealand. Drouths are almost unknown in these colonies, and rain is frequent. In the North the greater amount falls during the winter; in the South it is more equally distributed throughout the year. Almost every valley and plain is well watered by streams flowing from the mountains. There are countless streams of the purest water in New Zealand, but very few rivers of any depth or size. In the Canterbury districts are large runs, or stations, where hundreds of thousands of sheep are reared. Here also can be seen vast herds of cattle and horses, which seem to be roaming at will.

Gold is found in all parts; but the principal quartz mines are in the Thames and Coromandel districts, near Auckland, in the North Island. Gold is also found in the river beds and on the sea-coast, where it can be worked with comparative ease. Good coal is obtained in many parts of New Zealand, particularly on the west coast of the South Island. There are also rich copper mines near Nelson, which are beginning to attract attention. Building stone of various kinds and of excellent quality abounds. The principal articles of export are wheat, wool, barley, oats, flax, hops, gum and gold. The industry of freezing and shipping mutton has lately been entered into with great success. Kauri gum, a valuable product of the kauri tree, found in the soil on the sites of old kauri forests, and at the foot of growing trees, is much used in Europe and America as a base for fine varnishes. Fruit of every description abounds.

The scenery is very picturesque. The mountains in the North Island occupy about one-tenth of the surface, and are thickly covered with timber. Mount Ruapehu and Mount Egmont are extinct volcanoes. Mount Tongariro is occasionally active. In the South Island nearly four-fifths of the surface is covered by mountains, the greater part of them open, covered with grass, and well adapted for pasture. The Southern Alps run close to the west coast the whole length of the island. Mount Cook, which is over 12,000 feet high, is the highest peak, and has many glaciers. The main range of these mountains is crossed at intervals by low passes. On the eastern side are extensive agricultural plains, and the western slopes are rich in mineral wealth.

On the southwestern coast are several sounds which are surrounded by snow-capped mountains rising from 5,000 to 10,000 feet in height. The scenery is grand, especially in the vicinity of Milford Sound. There are also numerous cascades and waterfalls in this section, one of which is 800 feet in height. In the Province of Auckland, on the North Island, are some famous geysers and sulphur springs, which are much visited by tourists and sight-seers. The waters are warm, transparent, and of a beautiful blue color, and are supposed to contain wonderful curative power for tubercular diseases, rheumatism and nervous affections.

New Zealand abounds in birds peculiar to that country alone, and is particularly remarkable for its wingless birds. There are four species of kiwi. These birds are a little larger than a hen ; they are without wings or tail feathers, have bills like a snipe, short legs, and are covered with long brown feathers which resemble hair. The kuku is a species of owl, and is called by the settlers " More Pork," because its cry resembles those words. Parrots are abundant. Great numbers of kaka, a large brown parrot, assemble both morning and

evening on berry-bearing trees, and utter discordant
screams, which among the natives serve as a signal
for the beginning and ending of the day's labor.
The kea, another native bird, has of late years
developed a fondness for mutton.   It flies upon the
backs of the sheep, and, with its strong bill, tears
the flesh away until it reaches the fat around the
kidneys, which is all that it eats.   Dogs and rats
were the only native quadrupeds when the islands
were first visited by Europeans.   There are no
snakes.   A few lizards are found, which are harm-
less, although they are held in superstition by the
natives, who think the spirits of their ancestors
inhabit them.

The trees are almost all evergreens; consequently change of seasons makes very little difference in the appearance of the forests.   The kauri
pine, which is found only in the North Island,
grows to a great size, and is often forty feet in circumference.   Owing to the lightness and toughness
of the stem, it is well adapted for masts.   The
totard pine equals the kauri in lightness and commercial value ; the purri rivals the English oak in
hardness.

There are 2,500 miles of railway in New Zealand.   In addition to road and railway communication, intercourse is carried on between the chief
ports, two or three times a week, by swift, commodious steamers.   Telegraph wires run through

every settled district, and extend to Australia and England. There are a line of steamers which make regular monthly trips between San Francisco and Auckland, and regular mail steamers which run between the latter place and England. The time consumed in making the trip is forty-five days. There are also steamers which run between New Zealand and the different Australian ports. The distance between Auckland and Melbourne is 1,479 miles. For many years the government issued free tickets to emigrants, and thousands of people from England and Germany availed themselves of this privilege, and made themselves homes in this far-off land. The issuing of free tickets has now been stopped, and an aid-emigration bureau has been established by the government, which assists farmers, and other classes of people in need of assistance, with a small amount of capital, and enables them to get a start.

The native inhabitants are called Maori. Their hair is generally coarse and black, though sometimes a rusty red; they have good teeth, a broad nose, and brown skin, which in some instances is very fair, and in others so dark that it is almost black. They are deficient in reason and judgment, and have little imagination, but possess good memories and quick perceptions. They are fond of simple and noisy music, and have an accurate per-

17

ception of time. They are vain, arrogant and revengeful, hospitable to strangers, affectionate to their friends, and observant of their promises; they are dirty and indolent, and formerly worshiped gods, to whom they addressed prayers and offered sacrifices. Their gods were invisible, many of them deified men, ancestral chiefs of the tribe or nation by whom they were worshiped. They believe in a future state, and that there are two distinct abodes for departed spirits, neither of which is a place of punishment, as they believe that evil deeds are punished in this world by sickness and personal misfortune. They apparently more industrious and more capable of civilization than our American Indians, and are now turning their attention to farming and other pursuits

In the bush and back country are thousands of wild hogs, the increase from a few that Captain Cook let loose when he first landed on the island. Auckland is the largest city on the islands, and was, until 1865, the seat of government. All of the principal cities are well laid out ; the streets are broad, and the buildings of modern architecture. Wellington, the capital of the province of the same name, and at present the seat of the New Zealand Government, is situated on the fine harbor of Port Nicholson. It has a number of fine public buildings. The principal hotels are the Occidental and the Imperial, at each of which the regular charge for accommodations is twelve shillings per day. The country is especially adapted to agriculture, as it is never subject to drouth, and can always find a market for the surplus crops in the sister colony of Australia, where drouths are of frequent occurrence.

New Zealand is nearly antipodal to Great Britain, and resembles it in climate, only that it is more equable. The summer is longer and somewhat warmer than that of England, and the other seasons much milder. In some districts high winds prevail ; in others, the atmosphere is peculiarly serene. The climate is said to be the finest in the world. New Zealand, with her mild climate, fertile soil, fine harbors, extensive and valuable mineral deposits, and picturesque and beautiful scenery, is destined to rank first among the colonies in the Southern Hemisphere. After a pleasant and profitable visit to this country, I returned to Sydney, where I embarked on the steamer Airlie (belonging to the Australian and Eastern Steamship Company) for China.

CHAPTER XIV.

THE AUSTRALIAN COAST.

THE distance between Sydney and Hong-Kong is 4,500 miles; so I was in for another long sea voyage, and the most dangerous one I had yet undertaken since beginning my tour. First, we had to travel for a distance of 2,000 miles with the Australian shore on one side and the Great Barrier Reefs on the other,—the most extensive coral reefs known in the world. There are frequent and often dangerous passages in this barrier which permit the entrance of vessels into the sea lying between it and the mainland. This body of water varies in breadth, from its southern entrance, where the reefs lie at a great distance from the shore and it is a broad, open sea, to its central point, at Cape Tribulation, where it hardly affords a passage for vessels. Going north, it widens again until it stretches far away from the coast, and extends across the east end of Torres Strait. Many vessels have been stranded on these reefs in the last few years.

Secondly, we had to face the typhoon in the China Sea. These winds are generally preceded by a peculiar haziness of the atmosphere, and an ominous stillness. When the storm has arrived at its greatest severity, the confusion of the scene is almost indescribable; the wind fills the air with a deafening roar, and there occur gusts, the violence of which equals or exceeds the force of the strongest wave ; everything gives way before this terrific wind, and the ship that can weather it is indeed fortunate. The Chinese call these storms *tac-fun ;* they are of frequent occurrence in the China Sea, and many ships are wrecked by them every year. To make matters still more dangerous on this particular voyage, the ship was loaded down, to within two feet of the water's edge, with coal and other heavy material. As a large share of this cargo was to be distributed at different ports along the Northern Australian coast, it gave us ample time to take in all the coast towns of New South Wales and Queenstown.

On leaving Sydney, we steamed down the harbor, and soon found ourselves in the South Pacific Ocean. After traveling seventy-three miles, we arrived at Newcastle, where we loaded the steamer down to the brim with coal to feed the furnaces on this long and boisterous voyage. Newcastle is the principal seaport town on the northern coast of New South Wales. There are two lines of steamers which run daily between this place and Sydney. It is a well built town, and has a population of nearly 25,000. The harbor is defended by a fort, and protected by a breakwater, which renders it more easy of access in stormy weather. Besides the agricultural produce of the Hunter River district, the principal export is coal. It is a common thing for vessels in this part of the world, after discharging their cargoes, to go to Newcastle and take in a cargo of coal for the return trip.

After leaving Newcastle, the next city of importance we arrived at was Brisbane, the capital of the Colony of Queensland. It is situated on both banks of the River Brisbane, about twenty-five miles from its entrance into Morton Bay, and consists of four parts,— North and South Brisbane, Kangaroo Point and Fortitude Valley. The river opposite the town is about a quarter of a mile broad, and is navigable for vessels of considerable burden. This town was founded in 1825 as a penal settlement, and named in honor of Sir Thomas Brisbane. In 1842 the penal establishment was abolished, and colonization set in. Brisbane is a prosperous seaport town, and has a mixed European population of about 47,000. It is backed by vast mineral resources, and also by extensive pastoral districts, where sheep farming is largely engaged in.

The chief gold-mining towns in Queensland are Palmerville, Ravenswood, Charter Tower and Olympia. Queensland lies between Torres Strait and New South Wales. It was separated from the mother colony in 1859. For many years there existed a natural but unfounded prejudice against the supposed warmer climate of this colony, which retarded its progress. But the discovery of its great wealth in mineral and sugar lands, and the fact of the remarkable salubrity of the climate, removed this prejudice, and greatly advanced the prosperity of the colony.

The main range of mountains consists of a broad plateau extending from north to south at a distance of from 20 to 100 miles from the coast, and varying in height from 2,000 to 5,000 feet. This region is the seat of mining, and will be of agriculture. The Coast Range is less elevated. Cape York Peninsula is a fair sample of Queensland. Good land alternates with bad. The hills are rich in mineral wealth, and the forests are very valuable. The flats near the mouths of the majority of the streams are admirably adapted to the growth of rice and sugar-cane, while the hilly slopes are suitable for coffee trees. Pastoral farming is the leading industry of the colony, and until the last few years little attention was paid to agriculture, on account of the high price of labor, and the difficulty of finding a market for agricultural products.

There is a vast section of country which is especially adapted to stock-raising. These lands are nearly all owned by the government, and leased to stock-raisers, for a small rental, for a term of years.   In settled districts, or within thirty miles of the coast, a " run " is subject to resumption by the state, on giving six months' notice, should any part of it be required by actual settlers for the purpose of cutting it up into farms.   But in the unsettled districts a lease of twenty-one years granted by the government, is pretty secure to the lessee.   The rent advances every seven years of the term from about a half a farthing to a penny an acre.   Within certain distances of the principal mountains the rains fall regularly; but the central and southern districts of Queensland are not so well favored, and the western part of the colony depends on occasional thunder-storms, although nature provides this section with a species of grass which resists drouths for a long time.   At the time of my visit to Brisbane, I was told that little rain had fallen in this vicinity for several years ; the hills had a bronzed appearance, and many of the water-courses had run dry.

The Great Barrier Reef, which follows the line of the northeastern coast for 1,200 miles, protects it from the violence of the ocean's storms, and forms a natural breakwater.   Inside of this reef the water is very smooth.   As we continued our journey northward, we were the greater part of the time in plain sight of the mainland on one side, and the reefs on the other.   On this passage I saw the wreck of an American bark which had been stranded some three months before on a hidden reef, the passengers and crew barely escaping with their lives,—a fair sample of what occurs every year in the Coral Sea.

The next Australian city at which we stopped was Rockhampton, situated on the Fitzroy River, and nearly on the Tropic of Capricorn. It is built in the hills, and, notwithstanding the heat, has a singularly fine climate. It is a gateway to a great pastoral country, and a port of export for wool. The hills in this vicinity are rich in minerals. From Rockhampton westward a railroad has been built into the interior. Our next stopping place was Townsville, on Cleveland Bay. Here a narrow-gauge railway fifty miles long runs to Charter Tower, and will eventually be extended farther into the interior country. The scenery in the mountains is often beautiful, but not grand. The shore and the islands along the coast are clothed with palms and other tropical trees. Flowers are numerous, and have a powerful fragrance. Over 300 useful woods grow in Queensland, including satin-wood, sandalwood, teak, mahogany, the red cedar and tulip-wood. Beautiful ferns abound, and include many different varieties. In the northeast particularly, the tree fern attains magnificent proportions, often rising from twenty to thirty feet. The sea along this coast abounds in fish, and the fishery of the trepang, bêche-de-mer, or sea slug, employs a considerable number of boats along the coral reefs. These fish are boiled, smoked, dried, or packed in bags for exportation to China. They make an agreeable and nourishing soup, which is much relished by Australian invalids. The dugong, or sea cow, has a delicate flesh of the flavor of veal, and furnishes an oil with the qualities of cod-liver oil. The Chinese are the best fishermen in Australian waters. The climate on the northern coast is dry and salubrious, the highest temperature being 110 degrees in the shade in December, and the lowest 75 degrees in June. The heat on this shore is modified by the gentle breeze of the southeastern monsoon, which blows almost constantly for about seven months in the year.

The next point of interest which came under my observation was Cape Tribulation, which was discovered by Captain Cook on his first visit to Australia. His vessel had to put in here for repairs, as it had sustained more or less injury in penetrating the coral reefs. Captain Cook was one of the greatest navigators of his day. He discovered New Zealand in 1769; but his attempts to penetrate the interior were frustrated by the hostility of the natives, and he had to content himself with a six-months voyage around the coast. He discovered the existence of the channel which divides New Zealand into two large islands. From New

Zealand he went to Australia, and, on April 28th, came in sight of Botany Bay. His discoveries here were also confined to the coasts, as the natives were hostile. However, he formally took possession of the country in the name of Great Britain. From Australia he went to New Guinea, and from there to Batavia, where, his boat being disabled, he had to put in for repairs. He returned to England, June 11, 1771, having circumnavigated the globe in less than three years. He afterward lost his life on the Sandwich Islands, in February, 1779.

Near Cape Tribulation stands Cooktown, one of the most important ports on the Northern Australian coast. It lies at the foot of a towering mountain, and is washed by the waters of the Coral Sea. Back of this town lies Cook's district, which is rich in natural resources, and is said to contain the most extensive gold fields in Queensland. At the time I visited the town, there was a great mining boom, due to the discovery of new and rich mines. Cooktown has a fine climate, and tropical fruits of all kinds grow in profusion. Here can be seen orange trees, cocoanut, tamarind, guava, papaw, banana and pine-apple, in addition to fruits and vegetables of all kinds. This is also a good sugar country.

A great drawback to the settlement of the interior country surrounding Cooktown is the character of the natives, who are said to be very ferocious, many of them being cannibals. I heard of several instances where white men had been murdered, robbed and eaten by these savages. While I claim to have had a considerable experience, and a good opportunity of studying the characteristics of the different human races during the last thirty years, a sense of the fitness of things prevents me from dilating on the results of those observations here. I have no hesitation, however, in saying, that, from the information I derived in regard to these Australian aborigines, and from what I saw of the dusky, greasy features of the half-tamed ones who idle around the towns, and whose only pursuit seems to be begging from and murdering white men, they certainly seem to be the most worthless species of humanity. They have no industry whatever, and have an insatiable thirst for human blood. The majority of them are as wild and savage as the wolves of the forest.

Occasionally, however, the least harmful of them are permitted to approach the seaport towns. For instance, in Cooktown I saw them lurking around the streets, both sexes as nearly destitute of clothing as the law would allow them to appear in civilization. As they wear no costume worthy of mention, I am relieved from description in that line. The men all wear large rings in their noses. You often see women with their naked babies strapped upon their bare, brown backs. They are kept warm by the heat of the tropical sun, and do not seem to feel the need of clothing. It seemed strange to me that the British Government permitted these savages to roam at large, instead of confining them to reservations. I heard a great deal of complaint from European residents on this score. The natives are much better protected from being killed or persecuted by the whites than are our American Indians. I also discovered that the Mongolian is much better protected in British possessions than in the United States, although I heard the same complaint all over Australia that I had constantly heard at home; namely, that the Chinese were the ruination of the country, insomuch that they supplanted white labor in every branch of industry, swarming into the mines, and in all the cities and towns.

As we steamed out of Cooktown, I discovered that our live cargo had been augmented by 200 Chinamen picked up at the different coast towns. These were all bound for the Celestial Empire, intent on enjoying the Chinese New Year among their moon-eyed brethren. The majority of these pig-tail passengers had a return ticket, and expected to go back and make another drain on the Australian resources. We were so heavily laden, both with freight and live cargo, that, had we struck on a reef, the iron vessel would have sunk

like lead. The white passengers would probably
have had to share the fate of the vessel, as the
Chinese were largely in the majority and would
have captured all the life-boats.

All along the coast are numerous lighthouses
and light-ships, with revolving lights, which have
been stationed in different places to aid the mariner
on his way. In the more dangerous portions of
the channel, vessels are required to anchor over
night, in order to avoid the risk of running on hidden rocks and reefs. At last, after a safe but slow
passage, we entered the Albany Pass, and the
Great Barrier Reefs gradually faded from sight.
Many of the islands in the Coral Sea are as bare
as a bone of vegetation, and are partially covered with drifting sand; others are covered with
shrubs. Pieces of wrecks are scattered along the
shores of these islands, and various other objects
which have drifted in from the sea. Albany Pass
is situated between the Coral Sea and Torres
Strait. It is a narrow opening about two miles
long, and half a mile wide, lined with picturesque
points and projecting rocks, and the greater part of
the shore is clothed in luxuriant evergreens, which
add much to the beauty of the scene. Every object
of interest is appreciated by the tourist, as he soon
wearies of the monotony of ocean travel.

The first place of importance in Torres Strait is
Thursday Island, the chief seat of the pearl-fishing

industry on the Australian coast. It is three miles long and two miles broad. Its inhabitants and those of the neighboring groups are principally European divers, who come here solely to engage in pearl fishing, and with the expectation of accumulating a fortune in this enterprise. Pearl fishing in these waters is a growing and prosperous industry. The shells are procured by diving, and bring from $600 to $1,000 a ton. Mother of pearl and tortoise shells abound. This industry is said to be very hard on the lungs, and often causes untimely death.

After crossing Torres Strait, we entered the Gulf of Carpentaria, and skirted the western shore of New Guinea. I was unable to gain much information in regard to the resources of this island, as only a small portion of it has ever been explored or colonized, on account of the hostility of the native inhabitants. Both the English and Dutch have made repeated attempts to explore the interior, but so far have met with very poor success. The sea-coast in the vicinity of Port Mosby and the Fly River, is sparsely settled by Europeans, who are principally engaged in shell-gathering and pearl fishing.

Sailing in the Gulf of Carpentaria, we were fast approaching the Equatorial line. The heat of the tropical sun became terrific, and the passengers had all they could do to keep from melting. The first

half of this passage the heat was the most intense
I had experienced since crossing the Red Sea, and,
if anything, it was hotter than then. In my state-
room in the coolest part of the night, with the door
and port-holes wide open, the heat was suffocating.
I generally beat a hasty retreat to the open deck,
where I could get an occasional breath of fresh
air, more to be appreciated than diamonds in this
latitude. Many of the passengers could be seen at
all hours of the night stretched out on the quarter
deck trying to get a few hours' rest and repose after
enduring the severe heat of the day. The captain
and officers were reduced to the same expedient.
As for myself, I began to ponder, and wonder whether
this was the lovely Australian coast or a temporary
hell on sea.

One phenomenon in this part of the globe is
that the sun is apparently traveling in the northern
heavens, and that the compass points south instead
of north, which seems odd to a traveler from the
other side of the globe.

After two days' sailing over the memorable Gulf
of Carpentaria, we steamed into Port Darwin,
where we anchored for two days, discharging a
large amount of cargo and a considerable number
of passengers, many of whom were bound for the
new gold fields at Ord River, in Western Australia.
I was told that new gold fields are always being
discovered in this country, and that there is gener-

ally more or less excitement in regard to mines.
Port Darwin is the last and most northern point
on the Australian coast. It lies in latitude five,
and is 2,500 miles from Melbourne, and about the
same distance from Hong-Kong. Owing to its
nearness to the Equator, it is extremely hot there.

This port is quite a commercial centre, and has
the advantage of having a spacious and secure
harbor. This harbor is almost encircled by a low
peninsula, extending into the Bay of Carpentaria,
and is considered, next to the one at Sydney, the
best harbor in Australia. The main feature of
interest at this port is the long wharves, which are
being built far out into the harbor. When these
are completed, the cargo can be unloaded directly
from the ship to the cars, instead of being transferred in barges from the ship to the shore, as at
present. The town has no imposing buildings, and
the houses are low and square, with broad verandas built all around them to keep out, as much as
possible, the heat of the tropical sun. The thermometer often rises as high as 130 degrees in the
shade, and I found the heat more intense than at
Fort Yuma or Panama.

The vicinity of Port Darwin is inhabited by savage tribes. Many of these natives haunt the town,
and you often see them rambling around the streets,
the women almost invariably with a baby strapped
to their backs. While several gentlemen and my-

18

self were sitting on the veranda to our hotel, we were approached by one of these brown beauties, who offered to sell us her baby for the sum of ten shillings, as it was the only baby she had. She failed, however, to make a sale, even at this low figure, as we were all afraid to invest in this kind of a curiosity, thinking that it might prove an annoying and perhaps expensive investment in the long run. This only goes to illustrate how far from being civilized these people are, as any one of them will sell their children for a mere song.

CHAPTER XV.

PHILIPPINE ISLANDS AND CHINA SEA TO
HONG-KONG.

On leaving Port Darwin, we set sail for China,
traveling by way of the Philippine Islands, Java
and Singapore. As we steamed out of the harbor,
I had my last glimpse of Australia, a country to
which I had given more time and attention in investigating its various resources than to any other
on my whole tour. As I have said before, Australia
lies thousands of miles out of the beaten line of
travel between India and China, and on that account has not been visited by the greater proportion of tourists. My journeyings in Australia, both
by land and water, amounted to 6,000 miles, nearly
5,000 miles of that distance being devoted to sailing along the sea-coast. I visited all the principal
cities and seaports, and traveled nearly two-thirds
of the entire distance around this mammoth island.
I sailed from Cape Leeuwin, in the Indian Ocean,
to Port Darwin, in the Gulf of Carpentaria. I
also traveled 1,200 miles by rail, which gave me an
opportunity of viewing the principal inland sights,
and forming an estimate of the resources of the

country.　From the Gulf of Carpentaria we sailed into the Arafura Sea, sighting the Island of Sermattan.　This is a small island of no particular importance, twelve miles long and six miles broad, its only visible vegetation being a few tropical plants.　For two days the heat was almost intolerable, and every one donned their white suits, about the only suits worn by passengers, captain and officers in these latitudes.　As they are inexpensive, and much cooler and more comfortable than woolen clothing, travelers in this part of the world usually carry a number of these suits with them.　It is necessary, however, to take woolen clothing too; as, the average speed of the steamer being twelve knots an hour, or 300 miles per day, one travels over quite a number of degrees of latitude in a week, and the temperature varies accordingly.

We had been distributing European passengers all along the coast at the various Australian ports at which we touched, and in turn had picked up Chinese, so that now the Celestials numbered at least 300, and my white companions had dwindled down to a mere handful.　This was anything but pleasant to reflect upon, and I would have much preferred to have the order of things reversed. Life on board of the steamer Airlie, among the coolies, was busy and full of interest, not only to the Chinese themselves, but to the other passengers, who found amusement in watching how the

Chinese conducted themselves. An artist would have found material for at least one day's work, and the illustrated papers could have gleaned some striking views.

Probably the most interesting sight was their gambling games, which they generally kept up from dawn until midnight. They were divided up into squads, seated on the open deck, engaged in various games; were almost stripped of clothing, and would sit in the blazing sun with a fan in one hand and their gambling blocks in the other, apparently trying to fleece each other. Those that were not gambling were lying on their backs smoking opium, or quarreling, and some were even fighting. The liveliest time, however, was at meal time, when a grand rush was made for the table, and they seized their chop-sticks, and shoveled the rice into their mouths as fast as if their lives depended on the rapidity with which they ate. The meal finished, they left the table as unceremoniously as they came, and went to gambling with renewed vigor. Money changed hands rapidly; the poor became rich, and the rich became poor, in a few hours of play. The Chinese have a decided passion for gambling, and I was fully convinced, from what I saw, that they would much sooner gamble than eat.

These Celestials are not the most miserable race in existence, by any means. The deck hands, consisting of a mixture of several Oriental races, were a much more degraded set, even dispensing with chop-sticks while eating, conveying the food to their mouths with their hands, and reminding one of so many dusky pigs gathered around a dough pile. At night their only bed was the open deck, on which they lay down destitute of any covering but their scanty clothing, and, with their faces to the tropical sky, slept much more soundly than do many of their civilized brethren when surrounded by all the comforts and luxuries that man's ingenuity can devise. The engine in the steamer Airlie had a capacity of 314 horse-power, and the ship itself was of 3,000 tons burthen. The officers, consisting of the captain, four mates and four engineers, and the goodly staff of smiling waiters, were all Europeans. The men before the mast, and the balance of the crew, were a mixture of native Portuguese, Maoris, Hindus, Arabs and Malays. They received a sixpence, or twelve cents, a day for their services. They certainly work cheap enough, as they do good work, and have very poor fare, and a white man would hardly be able to do the work they do and endure the heat.

The same rules for bills of fare and hours for serving meals seem to prevail on all steamships which sail in Asiatic and Australian waters. Each passenger has his own particular place at the table, which is always, especially for dinner, bountifully

spread. The few European fellow-passengers I
had on this voyage were a jolly lot, composed of
several London and Australian merchants, and a
Hong-Kong sea captain, who thoroughly understood the navigation of these waters. As the com-
mander of our ship, Captain Ellis, was a fine navigator, we were abundantly blessed in that respect.
Both captains kept me well posted as to the latitude and longitude we were in, and also informed
me in regard to the various objects and islands we
passed, the direction in which we were moving,
and the governments to which the different islands
we sighted, belonged.

We traveled as nearly as possible in a northerly
direction, although a direct course was often prevented by the numerous islands of the Indian
Archipelago. Progress was necessarily slow, on
account of the roundabout way in which we had
to travel, and the many obstructions which occur
in these waters. Our average speed was not over
ten miles, or ten knots, an hour ; while in free and
open ocean, with the monsoon in our favor, we
would average twelve knots an hour. Three hundred miles is considered a day's journey at sea.

Seventy miles from Sermattan, we approached
Damma Island, where we were treated to a change
of scene in the shape of witnessing the eruption of
a large volcano, which appeared at a distance like
a burning mountain. Leaving this grand sight

behind, we passed through Sunda Strait into the Banda Sea. Here the sea was calm, but the temperature of the atmosphere extremely hot, which, of course, we expected, being so near the Equator. After sailing 150 miles in the Banda Sea, we entered the Strait of Manipa, and found ourselves skirting the Island of Amboyna, which is thirty miles long and thirty broad. The elevation of its highest peak is 4,008 feet; it belongs to the Dutch, has a resident governor, and presents the appearance of being a fertile island. Between the islands of Manipa and Borneo is a passage fifteen miles in width, whose waters are said to be 500 fathoms deep. We next passed through Baka Strait. The islands on either side of this passage belong to the Dutch. They are clothed with the luxuriant vegetation of the tropics, and present a very beautiful appearance.

After sailing through the Basline Passage into the Celebes Sea, we found ourselves rapidly nearing the Philippine Islands. We skirted the shore so closely for many miles that a girl could throw a stone from the ship to the mainland. This gave us a fine opportunity of viewing these famous islands. The coast was lined with cocoanut trees, and all sorts of tropical plants were growing in profusion. The sloping hillsides were covered with green crops, and the entire landscape looked doubly beautiful to the eye wearied of the waste of waters.

We passed island after island, each clothed in lovely green, the luxuriant vegetation growing clear down to the water's edge. These islands seem to be favored by nature in every respect; the soil is fertile; the climate mild, salubrious and healthful. I felt as if I had arrived at the Mecca of the South Pacific Ocean.

These islands belong to Spain, and are chiefly colonized by that nationality. The Spanish Government keeps a resident governor here, and at all the seaports men-of-war are stationed to protect the interests of the government and her subjects in this quarter of the globe. Notwithstanding the fact that these islands are so well favored by nature, and so jealously guarded by the Spanish Government, by far the larger proportion of the land is uncultivated and unsettled. The government is determined that the people of no other nation shall be allowed to come in and get a foothold in her Asiatic possessions; consequently, immigration is not encouraged, and these beautiful and fertile islands will probably be sparsely settled for many years to come. Mindanao Island is the most southern of the group.

Leaving the Celebes Sea, we sailed through the Sulu Sea, and were journeying in a roundabout way to Singapore. The ocean in this part of the world is full of islands, capes, peninsulas and straits. Want of space, however, will prevent me

from mentioning more than a few of the principal
ones. As we journeyed leisurely along, many times
sailing close to the shore, I had a bird's-eye view
from the steamer of a number of these islands. It
was a matter of regret to me that I was unable to
have more than a passing glance of the Philippine
Islands, Borneo and New Guinea. I would have
liked very much to pay a visit to each of these
countries to gain an insight into the manners and
customs of the people, and learn something of the
resources of each country. As it was, I had to
content myself with such information as I derived
from Captain Ellis, of the steamship Airlie.

Going from the Philippine Islands to Singapore,
we crossed a portion of the China Sea. The passage was very rough, and sea-sickness prevailed with
the majority of the passengers. I was no longer
troubled with this disagreeable malady, and was
able to sit back and laugh at my less fortunate
companions. I had had, however, the advantage
of an almost continuous sea voyage of 25,000
miles ; and, if there is anything in the old maxim
that practice makes perfect, I ought by this time
to have become a pretty good sailor. The rock-
ing of the steamer in the heaviest gale produced
no more impression on me than being carried by
two coolies in a sedan chair. On this particular
trip the sea was so heavy and the waves ran so
high that the water dashed clear over the hurri-

cane deck. On the way to Singapore we passed near Anger Point, on the coast of Java, where a terrible earthquake occurred five years ago, when the island of Anger Point, including a town of 30,000 inhabitants, was swallowed up in the sea.

Singapore is situated on the south side of the Island of Singapore, and is in the British colony of the Straits Settlements. The port of Singapore is capacious, and the water deep enough for the largest vessels. The harbor is provided with every facility for an extensive commerce, and for fitting out and repairing vessels. In consequence of its geographical position, it is one of the most important ports of Asia, and is resorted to by the vessels of all nations. The city is situated on a low plain fronting the harbor, with hills in the rear, which are occupied by country houses. The principal points of interest are the fortifications, the Government House; the Botanical Gardens, which have a magnificent collection of tropical plants; the Chinese temple, and the Mohammedan mosques.

The Island of Singapore lies at the extreme southern end of the Malay Peninsula, from which it is separated by a strait about forty miles long by from one-half mile to two miles wide. This island is about twenty-five miles long from east to west, and about twelve miles wide. Near the coast are swamp tracts, covered with mangrove trees; but inland there are many small hills from 100 to 500 feet high. The climate is healthful ; but, owing to its nearness to the Equator, very warm. Rain falls in abundance. Wild animals abound, and tigers are said to cross the strait to the island, and carry off, on an average, a Chinaman a day.

The population of Singapore numbers about 125,000. It consists of Europeans, who are largely in the majority, and a mixture of Asiatic races. The natives are indolent, seem to be entirely lacking in ambition, wear very little clothing of any kind, and the highest remuneration they receive for work of any description is a sixpence a day.

After staying two days in Singapore, we steamed out of the harbor, bound for Hong-Kong, a distance of 900 miles. In crossing the China Sea, we were treated to some boisterous gales, and a storm, which lasted twenty-four hours, and carried away two of our life-boats. Once, while the storm was at its height, I waded knee-deep in water on the quarter deck. Even the hurricane deck was washed by the sea from stem to stern. However, the powerful iron steamer plowed its way through the raging billows, and landed us safely on the shores of China. For sixty miles before arriving at Hong-Kong, we were skirting the Chinese shore. The sea in this vicinity was dotted with fishing boats. The waters of the Chinese rivers and seas are teeming with fish ; and fishing is the principal industry of the people who live along the coast.

CHAPTER XVI.

CHINA, FROM HONG-KONG TO CANTON.

HONG-KONG is situated on the southeastern coast of China. This island was ceded to Great Britain, and is considered an important British possession. It is one of a small cluster of islands called by the Portuguese " Ladrones," or " Thieves," on account of the notorious habits of the old inhabitants. This island has an area of twenty-nine square miles ; the extreme length, from northeast to southeast, is ten miles and a half ; and the breadth varies from two to five miles. It is separated from the mainland by a narrow channel, which is a mile wide in some places, and in others it is not over a quarter of a mile to the opposite shore. The capital, which is called Victoria, is situated on the northwestern extremity of the island. The streets are wide and well kept, and the buildings are mostly of brick and stone, and are greatly superior to those of a Chinese city.

Hong-Kong owes its present importance principally to its financial prominence as the headquarters of the banking interest, and to its magnificent harbor, which appeared to me to be almost completely landlocked. Next to the one at Sydney, this harbor is probably the most commodious and secure, and here vessels are anchored from almost every part of the world. Prominent among the forest of masts were those flying the American flag, to me a most pleasant sight, as it brought anew to my mind memories of the home I had left behind, and which was still 7,000 miles away. My first object in arriving at a foreign port was to get a glimpse of the American flag. There are a few American residents in Hong-Kong.

The harbor presented an extremely lively appearance, and the Chinese sampans were swarming in every direction. These boats, from twelve to fifteen feet long, form the only home of quite a number of families who live on the Canton River, and every child large enough to toddle must help pull an oar. As soon as our steamer cast anchor, we were surrounded by hundreds of these sampans, the occupants screaming and yelling, each trying to get the largest number of passengers to convey to the shore. The boat in which I happened to get was manned by a family of ten, varying in age from four to fifty. The old man was occupied in guiding the rudder and the sail, and the rest of the family, from the wife down to the baby, were rowing, each provided with an oar suited to their size and strength.

From this novel experience in traveling on

water, I was to meet with a still more novel one in traveling on land. On coming on shore, I was immediately surrounded by a lot of half-naked coolies with their sedan chairs, and was soon being carried through the streets of Hong-Kong by two Celestials, who took me to the leading hotel of the city for ten cents. This was called the Hong-Kong Hotel, and I was charged the moderate price of five dollars per day for accommodations. The "tone" of the place seemed to be in the price, and in nothing else. Evidently the Europeans do not intend to reside in the Orient for nothing, and are anxious to accumulate fortunes rapidly.

The town, including the Chinese quarter, extends for about three miles along the shores of the bay, and has a steep range of mountains for a background. The climate is a little warmer than that of San Francisco, a little cooler than that of Naples, and, with the exception of certain seasons of the year, is considered healthful. There are several handsome government buildings, a large exchange, a cathedral, the bishop's palace, and extensive barracks. There are also ten large banking houses in Hong-Kong. The houses of the merchants are, as a rule, large and elegant, with broad verandas built all around, and surrounded by tasteful gardens.

Opium is imported more largely at Hong-Kong

than at any other port. It is also the centre of an extensive trade in silk, chinaware, nut oil, amber, ivory, sugar and many other tropical productions. You find in circulation here the silver of almost every nation, and I experienced more swindling in making exchanges, and saw more counterfeit coin, than in any other port. If the natives are behind other countries in point of civilization, they are certainly not behind any other people in the art of fleecing the unwary stranger. The British fleet is stationed in the harbor. Vessels come and go almost daily from this port to Bombay, Calcutta, Singapore, Canton, Yokohama, Sydney and San Francisco.

Immediately southwest of the Capitol is Victoria Peak, 1,825 feet in height, which is used as a station for signaling the approach of vessels. After investigating the leading features of interest in the city, I decided to make the ascent of this hill. So I procured a sedan chair, the two coolies who furnished the motive power of the vehicle agreeing to carry me to the top and back at the rate of ten cents an hour, which I considered much cheaper and better than walking. The ascent was steep and rocky, and I found being carried in this manner pleasant, and more comfortable than traveling on foot. Arriving at the summit, I had a fine view of the Chinese coast and the neighboring islands. The waters of the sea are dotted with fishing boats, Chinese sailing vessels, and craft of every description. Looking inland, the prospect is wild and monotonous. The hills are bare, and entirely devoid of trees, and nowhere can there be seen evidences of cultivation or fertility. Patches of land along the coast have been planted to rice, sweet potatoes and yams ; but the island is hardly able to raise vegetables enough to supply the home consumption.

The streets are guarded by a strong force of Indian Sepoys, and the natives are not allowed to go abroad after eight o'clock without a pass. The most common mode of street conveyance is by sedan chairs, which are carried by coolies. The passage across the Strait of Kan-lung to the main shore is usually effected by means of sampans.

After doing Hong-Kong, I made a short visit to Macao, thirty-eight miles distant. The intercourse between Europe and China began in 1517, when the King of Portugal sent an ambassador accompanied by a fleet of eight ships to Peking. On this occasion the Portuguese ambassador managed to gain the friendship of the Viceroy of Canton, and made an advantageous treaty with him. This was the commencement of the relations of China with Europe. Subsequently the Portuguese rendered the Chinese a signal service by capturing a famous pirate who had long ravaged their coasts. In gratitude for this service, the Emperor permitted

19

them to establish themselves on a peninsula formed by some sterile rocks.

On this spot arose the city of Macao, long the mart of the commerce of Europeans with the Celestial Empire. The establishment of the English at Hong-Kong did much to divest it of its former commercial importance. By the exclusive policy of both the Chinese and Portuguese, Macao was prevented from becoming a free port until 1845 and 1846, and consequently it was long ago outstripped by its more liberal rivals. The trade of this city, however, is still of very considerable extent, its principal commercial intercourse being with Hong-Kong, Canton, Batavia and Zoa. The preparation and packing of tea is the principal industry of the town. The most of the land is under garden cultivation; but the majority of the people, are more or less dependent upon commercial pursuits. This is a notorious gambling resort, and the colonial revenue is largely recruited by a tax on the gaming tables. The sports and young bloods from Hong-Kong come over here on Sunday excursions, and generally manage to leave the larger proportion of their cash behind when they return home. With its flat-roofed houses painted blue, red and green, Macao presents a very picturesque appearance. About one-tenth of the population are of European birth and extraction; the balance, Chinese and half-castes.

I now returned to Hong-Kong, and took a river steamboat for Canton. There were four Europeans on board besides myself, and 800 Chinese. The four Europeans were managers of the English passenger steamer, which appeared to do a rushing business. This steamboat ride proved one of the most interesting experiences in my inland travel. There are rugged ranges of hills on either side of the bay, clothed in dark green foliage from their summits down to the water's edge. Steep acclivities and lofty peaks add to the picturesqueness of the scene.

The Chinese, on this seven-hours trip, occupied themselves in smoking opium, drinking tea and gambling. Gaming is prohibited in China, but is nevertheless carried on everywhere, and is indulged in by old and young with a passion which in some instances almost amounts to madness. All legislation on this subject has been overpowered by the habits of the people, and China is, in fact, one vast gaming house. The Chinese are industrious and economical, but are possessed of an immoderate love of gain and a taste for speculation, which easily tempts them to gambling when not engaged in business. The habit once formed, they seldom recover from it. They cast aside every obligation of duty and family, and live only for cards and dice. When they have lost all their money, they will play for their homes, their lands, their wives, and some-

times even for the clothes they have on. This
passion for gambling has invaded all classes of society, and men, women and children all play. The
lower classes, however, are the most inveterate and
determined gamblers. In almost every street of
the large towns, you meet little ambulating gaming
tables, with a pair of dice placed in a cup upon a
stool, which prove an almost irresistible attraction
to the workman returning from his daily labor.
Once yielding to this temptation, he ever afterward
finds it more difficult to withstand it, and often
loses the whole of his hard earnings in a few hours.

Twelve miles before arriving at Canton, we
touched at Whampoa. Only steamers are allowed
to go up to Canton ; sailing vessels are restricted
to anchorage here. Owing to the rise of the tide
and the nature of the ground, it was found advantageous to construct docks at this place. Taking
advantage of these facilities, large numbers of foreign vessels enter here, and their cargoes are generally transported to Canton in small boats. On
arriving at Whampoa a lively scene ensued. The
river from bank to bank was lined with water craft
containing Chinese boatmen and boatwomen, all
yelling and screaming to attract the attention of
the passengers toward their respective boats. The
scene was a noisy but amusing one.

According to the Chinese, Canton has existed as
a city for forty centuries, and traces are found of

the existence of a city on this site twelve hundred years before our era. Although in the same parallel of latitude as Calcutta, the climate is much cooler, and is considered superior to that of most places in the tropics. Canton is situated on the Canton or Pearl River, about eighty miles from its mouth and ninety miles from Hong-Kong. This river is navigable 300 miles further into the interior. The part of Canton enclosed by walls is about six miles in circumference, and a partition wall runs through the city from east to west, dividing it into two unequal parts. The northern and larger division is called the old city, and the southern the new city. The walls of the city are of brick, and are about twenty-five feet high and twenty feet thick. There are twelve gates, four of which are in the partition wall. The gates are shut all night : in the day a guard is stationed at each to preserve order. For four or five miles opposite Canton, boats are ranged parallel to each other in such close order that they resemble a floating city. These boats are occupied by families, who remain almost constantly on the water.

The Chinese Government has never favored foreign commerce, and Canton was for a long time the only seat of British trade with China. It was no doubt fixed upon by the Chinese Government as the seat for European trade, on account of its distance from Peking. Formerly only a limited number of Chinese merchants were allowed to trade with foreigners, and they were usually men of large property, and famed for the integrity of their transactions. All foreign cargoes passed through the hands of these merchants, and return cargoes were furnished by them. They became security for custom-house duties, and it was criminal for any other merchant to engage in the trade with foreigners. The foreign trade with Canton was naturally damaged by the opening of Shanghai and the ports on the Yang-tse; but still it remains of considerable importance.

Probably one reason why the Chinese care so little for foreign commerce is that their internal trade is so extensive. It employs vessels of all kinds and sizes, which are constantly traversing the rivers and canals, by which the empire is watered throughout its whole extent. This trade consists principally in the exchange of grain, salt, metal, and the productions of the various provinces. China is such a vast country, and its resources are so-varied, that its internal trade alone is abundantly sufficient to occupy that part of the nation which is devoted to mercantile pursuits. The channels of communication, though oftentimes inconvenient, are always thronged with merchandise, which is carried in boats, on carts, on the backs of men and on beasts of burden.

The European settlement in Shamein is con-

nected with Canton by two bridges. On the conclusion of peace, in 1861, it became necessary to
provide a foreign settlement for merchants whose
factories had been destroyed, and it was finally decided to appropriate as the British settlement an
extensive mud-flat, known as the Shamein. This
site having been leased, it was converted into an
artificial island by building around it a massive
embankment of granite. Between the northern
side of the site and the Chinese suburbs, a canal
100 feet wide was constructed, thus forming an
island 12,850 feet long by 950 wide. The Shamein
settlement possesses many advantages. It is close
to the western suburbs of Canton, where all the
wholesale dealers and the principal merchants
reside. It faces a broad channel, known as the
Macao Passage, up which blows a cool breeze in
summer; and the river opposite it affords a safe
and commodious anchorage for steamers of 1,000
tons burthen.

As I have mentioned before, some months prior
to my visit to China the French and Chinese had
had a difficulty, in which Admiral Courbet sank
eleven Chinese ships, and at the present time it
was unsafe for any Frenchman to enter the interior
of China. As the Chinese are always more or less
hostile to foreigners, I was warned that it was not
considered wise for tourists to try to visit the interior until the bad feeling against the French had

in a measure subsided. When I found myself the
only tourist traveling between Hong-Kong and
Canton, I began to think that probably the appre-
hensions of danger were not entirely groundless.
However, I had come to China with the intention
of visiting the country, and had no idea of con-
tenting myself with a view of the outskirts of this
great empire. Having seen Canton outside the
wall, I was possessed with an overwhelming desire
to see the city inside the wall, so thought I would
risk being mistaken for a Frenchman, rather than
go away without seeing some of the country. I
consequently procured a Chinese guide, and sallied
forth. As this coolie said he was an extra good
guide, I agreed to give him extra wages, and we
both decided that seventy-five cents per day would
be a fair valuation for his services.

The preliminaries settled, I followed my Celestial
guide through the nearest gate, and found myself
inside the walls of a city which is said to contain a
million and a half of people. I found my guide
able to speak fairly good pigeon English. I
watched his every movement very closely, as I did
not want to lose him, fearing I might not be able
to find him again. The people all looked as much
alike to me as the two wheels to a wagon ; but my
guide guarded me very closely, as I represented
seventy-five cents a day to him ; and, as he was to
pilot me for two days, he seemed to consider his

position a money-making one. So we both watched each other,—he anxious not to lose me on account of the money, and I fearful that, if I lost him, I would never get out alive.

Before we had fairly begun our sight-seeing, I was approached by some dignified Celestials who demanded my passport, which was readily shown. They desired to know my nationality, what I was there for, etc. I informed them that I was an American citizen traveling for pleasure, to which they replied that America and China were like two brothers, and that I could go where I pleased. I made little comment on this polite speech, but at the same time thought that I would be willing to be a brother to almost anything until I got on the outside of the city. As I was a stranger rambling through the city, without any white companions, I was desirous of keeping on the good side of everybody.

The streets of Canton are very narrow, varying from seven to ten feet in width, and are paved with flat granite blocks. The houses are generally small, seldom consisting of more than two stories, and often only one story in height. They are generally built of adobe or brick, are without verandas, and entirely open in front, closed only by suspended bamboo screens. The windows are small, and rarely of glass,—paper, mica, or some other transparent substance being used. The roofing consists of thin tiles laid in rows, alternately concave and convex, the latter overlapping the former. The roofs are of unequal height, as there is a Chinese superstition to the effect that ill-luck follows eaves which connect with each other. The houses generally contain from three to six rooms. The dwellings of the poorer classes are seldom more than mud hovels containing but a single room.

In the busy part of the city every house is a shop, and here we found the productions of every part of the globe. The Chinese are remarkably expert men of business. After passing miles of shops, I came to the conclusion that Canton must be one of the wealthiest cities in the world, as well as one of the most interesting. There is a striking contrast between the poverty-stricken coolies and the better classes. The former have the appearance of having a hard time to eke out an existence. They live in miserable hovels, and amble through the streets about three-fourths naked, carrying heavily loaded baskets filled with bones, rags, and truck of every description. These baskets are carried by the means of a pole stretched across the shoulders. The streets are so narrow that they are impassable for carriages, the only vehicles used being sedan chairs carried by the coolies. These are found in immense numbers, and offer their services at very low rates. The city is divided into quarters for the various kinds of business, almost

PAGODA.

every trade or occupation having its own separate quarter. Provisions of all kinds are abundant and cheap.

Few large cities can compare with Canton in point of salubrity of climate. The temples and public buildings are numerous; but few of them present features worthy of special remark. The temples are much more attractive inside than out, as they are not stately and imposing like those of Japan and India. In fact, there are not many imposing buildings in Canton. Chinese taste does not seem to move in that direction. The space in front of the temples is generally occupied by beggars, hucksters and idlers, many of them most pitiful-looking specimens of humanity. By the way they stared at me and followed me around, I must have been almost as much of a curiosity to them as they were to me.

The first objects that would probably attract the attention of a stranger on entering Canton are the two pagodas which are situated near the western gate of the old city. One of these, called the plain pagoda, is about 1,000 years old, and rises in an angular, tapering tower to the height of 160 feet. The other, an octagonal pagoda, has nine stories, is 170 feet in height, and was erected 1,300 years ago.

There are 125 temples, pavilions, and other religious edifices in the city. I believe that I derived more satisfaction from visiting the temples than from anything else. The most important one was the Temple of Five Hundred Gods, or "Flowery Forest," as it is called, remarkable for the great number of colossal wooden figures of all colors, with grotesque or hideous faces, which are arranged in close order around the walls of the room. These are the guardian genii of China.

The Hall of Worship is sixty feet square, and in the centre is a gigantic carved statue, in a sitting posture, representing Buddha. It was quite a sight to see the numerous idols, it being on a grander scale than anything that I had seen in the Orient.

In this temple I also saw a statue of Marco Polo, whose father and uncle were the first Europeans to reach China, of whom we have any knowledge. They visited it in 1260, meeting with great favor from Kublai, the reigning Emperor, who decided to send them back as his envoys to the Pope, with letters requesting him to send a large body of educated men to instruct his people in Christianity. The brothers returned home in 1269, and found that Pope Clement IV. had died the year before, and no new pope had been chosen. After a delay of two years, they started, not with the hundred teachers, as requested by Kublai, but with two Dominicans, who lost heart and turned back in the very beginning of the journey. On this trip they took young Marco with them, who, at the time they arrived at Shangtu, in the spring of 1275, was twenty-one years old. Upon his arrival, Marco Polo applied himself diligently to the acquisition of the language; and Kublai, finding him both clever and discreet, employed him in the public service, and sent him on many distant missions. As the years rolled by, the Polos were anxious to return home; but Kublai was unwilling to let them. go. They finally, however, effected their departure, and returned to Venice at the end of the year 1295.

The Temple of Longevity is next in importance to that of the 500 gods. It contains three pavilions, which are well filled with statues and images, about eighty in number; and also a colossal statue in wood, representing an obese old man. Here is kept a family of storks, which are daily fed by the attendants. The other temples are much smaller affairs, and attract little attention after a visit to the large ones which I have just described, with the exception of the Buddhist Temple at Honan. It is called, in Chinese, Hai-chwang-eze, or the Temple of the Ocean Banner. Its grounds cover about seven acres, are surrounded by a wall, and are divided into courts, gardens and burial grounds, in which are deposited the ashes of the priests, whose bodies are burned. There are about 175 priests connected with this establishment. Near this temple are undertaking establishments, a furnace for the cremation of the dead, and a mausoleum in which to deposit their ashes. The Temple of Trade is an interesting place to visit during the Chinese New Year, when one can witness all the pomp and ceremony attendant upon that occasion. All sorts of relics can be seen, from a bronze monkey to a sacred pig.

Another interesting temple is the Temple of the Sages, which contains seventy bronze images of Confucius, and wax candles and incense are kept burning constantly. Certain days of each year are set apart as a time in which to do honor to the memory of Confucius. The Temple of Confucius is of great size. The Chinese have some extraordinary ideas or superstitions in regard to their gods. For instance, they sometimes worship two Joshes, a good Josh and a bad Josh; and they will do more honor, and make more sacrifices, to the bad than to the good,—and why? They will tell you that it is because the good one will do no harm anyway, while it is necessary to placate the bad one, and keep him from sending you to destruction; so they worship him with a great deal of pomp and ceremony.

Statues of the most famous personages in the history of China are seen in the temples. Theatrical performances are sometimes given in the front part of the temples, the charge for admission being ten cash, or one cent. The music at one of these theatres is of the silliest and most monotonous sort, and there are seldom over two or three performers. To me the most ludicrous feature of the entertainment was the loud and frequent laughter and applause, when there seemed nothing to laugh at. Another peculiarity is, that the performances seemed to be all alike. However, I have never regretted the ten cash invested in Chinese theatres.

The narrow thoroughfares are all more or less dark and gloomy, owing to the fact that the streets are so narrow, and the houses so close together. In some instances, the upper stories of the houses are built out over the street, and this excludes the light almost altogether.

There is generally a thorough understanding between merchants and guides, to the effect that the latter are to aid the former all they can in the way of bringing tourists to their shops. As European and American travelers generally invest largely in costly articles and numerous curiosities, as mementoes of their journey, and as presents for the friends at home, it is quite an item to secure this patronage. The shops are all filled with costly wares, such as silks, lacquered goods, porcelain, ivory and curios of all kinds and descriptions. I noticed that my guide, in taking me around the city, never missed an opportunity of dragging me into one of his favorite shops to make purchases.

The guide is always supposed to make his own commissions in the shape of an extra squeeze of the traveler's pocket. Even the coolies who carried my sedan chair would occasionally stop in front of some imposing shop to gladden the heart of their merchant friend with a sight of the traveler, thinking, perhaps, he could be induced to buy some of the beautiful wares that are displayed ; but I turned out to be a visitor in search of strange sights, instead of a purchaser of curiosities; so, after a brief glance at the tempting display, I would invite my coolie team to move on.

The majority of the people of China seem to have less enjoyment and pleasure than the people of any other country I have visited. You seldom see them idle their time away, or indulge in any pastime except that of gambling. They rather seem to drag out a dreary, monotonous existence, which mainly consists in working, paying taxes and dying. I verily believe, from what I saw of them, that the Chinese are the most industrious race under the sun. It is work, work, work, on land or on water ; no rest, no recreation, no play,—always work.

Prominent among the industries of Canton are the weaving of silks and other stuffs ; the manufacture of porcelain, screens, umbrellas, ivory fans and many articles too numerous to mention. These employ thousands of hands, and the products are

20

sold at the lowest prices. There are no large manufacturing establishments, the workmen either working at home or in small companies. The compensation they receive generally varies from twelve to twenty-five cents per day.

The rich in China make little display of their wealth. In fact, they rather try to conceal it ; for the government has never favored the accumulation of money or power in the hands of the people. The legal rate of interest has been fixed by the government at thirty per cent. per annum. There are many reasons assigned for this by Chinese economists, one of which is that, since money has borne this high rate of interest, no one thinks of hoarding it, and the circulation of it has been more general and continual. Another is that the purpose was to prevent the value of land from increasing and that of money from diminishing ; and that, in fixing it at a high rate, it has endeavored to render the distribution of land proportional to the number of families, and the circulation of money more active and uniform.

The cultivators of the soil in China are extremely poor, never accumulating capital. This may be owing to the land laws, although they correspond to some of the advanced ideas of modern agrarian theorists. All waste lands belong to the crown ; but any one who brings them under cultivation acquires a clear title, and can freely dispose of the property. The property of a deceased person passes to his male children in equal shares, and can not be bequeathed away from them. The greater part of the soil is owned in small tracts varying from five acres down to one-sixth of an acre. The possession of ten acres is considered well to do, and the owner of an estate of 1,000 acres is considered a millionaire. Over two-thirds of the land is cultivated by tenants on the half-profit system, the landlord providing the houses and paying the taxes; and the cultivator or renter, the simple implements and his labor. One bad season reduces these tenants to beggary. In the vast territory of the Chinese Empire, some district is stricken by famine nearly every year, either by drouths, floods, locusts, or in consequence of an insurrection.

My guide was very talkative, and seemed to delight in my questions about the manners, customs, habits and beliefs of his people. He informed me, with a great deal of pride, that the Chinese were the greatest and oldest nation on earth, and seemed to consider their religion a great improvement on ours. He thought their gods, made with their own hands, much better and purer than our unseen God. Their superstitions and religion, or rather want of religion, is the outgrowth of centuries of unbelief and idolatrous worship. Missionary work in China has not been attended with the same success that it has experienced in Japan and India; for the

Chinese are not so receptive as these nations, and, as a matter of fact, are completely indifferent to religious matters. The government does not favor Christianity; they look with suspicion upon the missionaries and their teachings, and imagine that, under a pretense of religion, they are really manœuvring to overthrow the empire.

The Chinese are about as far behind civilization and scientific research as they are in matters of religion, are perfectly satisfied with things as they are, and have no desire for improvement or advancement. They have no railroads, and do not want any, saying that, if the time ever comes that they should want them, they will build them themselves without any advice, assistance or interference from Europeans. They think that the introduction of modern inventions would work hardship on the laboring classes, as it would deprive them of employment.

My guide would have done for a Mormon, had he lived in Utah, as he told me he had three wives, and that, as soon as he could earn eighty dollars, he would buy another. A wife, he said, cost anywhere from eighty to one hundred and forty dollars, according to her age and beauty; and a man is privileged to have as many wives as he can afford to keep. The first wife, however, is always the mistress of the house, and the others are subordinate to her.

My guide took me for a promenade on the high wall, from which I could look out over the city, with its masses of low, flat houses ; could see the bustle and hear the yelling and screaming of the people who thronged the streets. It seemed a veritable Babylon.

The execution ground is an interesting place to visit. Here sometimes twenty-five or thirty criminals are executed at once, and the average number of criminals beheaded yearly is said to be 350. The worst class of criminals are cut to pieces upon the cross. Shops where idols are made and repaired, are also places of interest. The Arsenal, where they have a large number of breech-loading guns, presents a lively scene, for 400 Celestials are kept constantly employed here.

Last, but not least, I was taken to a Chinese restaurant, where everything was served in regular Chinese style. The bill of fare consisted of dainty dishes, such as bird's-nest soup, sweetmeats, roast cat, shark's fins, raw fish, roast frog, rice and tea, for which we had neither sugar nor milk. I partook freely of the tea, and sparingly of the roast cat. This is a fair sample of the edibles at a Chinese restaurant or hotel. There are no European hotels inside the wall in Canton.

Another great industry in Canton, which I had almost forgotten to mention, is the tea-drying establishments, where teas are cured and colored. The

tea production is one of the most important of the
resources of China, and a million and a half tons
of tea are produced annually.   This gives employment to thousands of people, as the tea goes through
a number of processes from the time it is gathered
until it is ready for the market.   The cultivation
of rice probably ranks next in importance to that
of tea, and these two products form the chief staple
of food of the Chinese.   The cultivation of rice
is similar to that of grain, although, unless grown
on damp, marshy ground, it has to be irrigated.

Canton is situated in the Province of Kwang-tung,
which is one of the most productive in the empire.
In addition to the cultivation of tea and rice, silk
is produced in the district forming the river delta,
which extends from Canton to Macao.   Sugar is
grown on the banks of all the rivers, and at Lo-
ting, 150 miles east of Canton, matting, fire-crackers,
sugar and palm-leaf fans are annually exported to
the number of four or five million to New York
alone.   Three large coal fields exist in this province.

The highest official in Canton is the Tsoung-tow,
or Governor-General, called Viceroy by the Europeans.   He is appointed by the Emperor for a
term of three years, and his jurisdiction extends
over the Province of Kwang-tung and Kwang-se.
There is also a Fou-youen, or Sub-Governor.   The
Tsoung-tow has the general control of all the civil
and military affairs.   The Fou-youen exercises a

similar kind of authority, but is more especially charged with the civil administration.

A peculiar custom in China is that the aristocracy keep their women in seclusion. They rarely leave their residences, and are seldom seen in the shops. When it becomes necessary for them to go from one place to another, they are transported through the streets in a sedan chair, or jinrikishia, with their faces entirely concealed from view by a heavy veil. You will hardly ever see a woman on foot in the streets of a Chinese city, unless she belongs to the coolie order. One of the strangest and most usual customs which prevail, among the upper classes is the habit of compressing the feet of the women, a fashion dating, it is said, from the highest antiquity. From the time a little girl is born, her feet are compressed with tight bandages, which hinder their growth. Girls whose feet have not been properly tortured by bandages in infancy find it no easy matter to get married, especially if they are ambitious to marry a person of high rank. It is looked upon as a disgrace in China to be an old maid. The women of the lower class are not so particular about the size of their feet, and there are probably many coolie women who have never had shoes on their feet.

Women are considered inferior beings in China, and have to endure all kinds of privation, contempt and degradation. When a son is born, there is

great rejoicing ; but the birth of a daughter is often
regarded as a humiliation and disgrace to the family.
A man is everything ; a woman, nothing. A young
Chinese girl lives shut up in the house where she
was born, and is treated by everybody as a menial.
She is not taught to read or to write, her sole education consisting in learning how to use the needle.
When she is old enough to be married, her husband
is selected for her by her parents. She is never
consulted, oftentimes does not even know the name
of the man she is to marry. A young girl is simply
an object of traffic, a piece of merchandise, to be
sold to the highest bidder.

In many parts of China, female children are
drowned or suffocated soon after they are born.
There are numerous reasons for this ; but the
principal cause is the poverty of the parents. The
birth of a male child is looked upon as a blessing,
as a boy is soon able to work and help his parents,
who rely upon him as a main support in their old
age. A girl, on the contrary, is regarded as a mere
burden. In certain localities, where the cultivation
of cotton and the silk-worm industry furnish young
girls with suitable occupation, they are allowed to
live, and their parents are even unwilling to see
them marry. Self-interest is the supreme motive
of all Chinese.

After spending several days in Canton, in which
time I devoted myself to seeing the strange sights,

and finding out what I could in regard to the manners, customs and social usages of this peculiar
people, I made arrangements to visit the rural districts, as I wished to see something of the interior
of China, outside of the great cities. The first
step in this direction was to hire a couple of coolies
and a sedan chair, and I was soon carried out
among the rice fields and tea plantations. I also
visited the silk districts. This is a peculiarly productive and fruitful region, and the whole country
looks like a garden. The land is under the highest
state of cultivation, and every nook and corner is
well fertilized, irrigated, and covered with a vigorous growth of vegetation. Tropical fruits attain
the highest perfection. The oranges, for example,
though smaller than the Los Angeles orange, were
the sweetest and best flavored of any I have ever
eaten. Everywhere could be seen instances of the
untiring industry and energy of the Chinese. All
manual labor is done by hand, and no machinery is
used, either in planting or gathering their crops.
Much of the land is so fertile, and cultivated with
so much care and skill, that three harvests a year
are regularly gathered.

Next to rice, silk and tea, probably the most
valuable production of China is the bamboo, which
yields a large revenue. The uses to which it is
applied are many and important. There are sixty-
three varieties of bamboo in the Chinese Empire,

and a bamboo forest will yield a considerable revenue if the owner understands how to regulate the cutting. The cultivation of useful vegetables is an industry to which the Chinese have always been especially devoted, and has always attracted the attention and received the encouragement of the government.

Of all my journeyings in China, I found traveling on the rivers the liveliest and most amusing. The bays and rivers are all whitened with water craft of every kind and description, and the water, if anything, seems to be more populous than the towns. The boats are built in all sorts of fantastic shapes, —some like houses, others shaped like a fish ; and all sorts of extraordinary figures have been chosen for models. Some are of the rudest construction, and others fitted up with considerable pretensions to elegance. These boats cruise around incessantly, without ever coming into collision with each other, and their skill in this respect is really wonderful ; but, then, they are born, live and die upon the water.

Everything necessary for subsistence can be found upon these boats. Some are nothing more nor less than provision shops ; others are small bazaars ; and the occupants of others are busily engaged in selling fruit, flowers, fresh fish, soup, rice, cakes, and many articles too numerous to mention. To add to the confusion of the scene at

night, they were incessantly beating the tom-tom
and letting off fire-crackers. This river population,
however, does not enjoy a very enviable reputation
for intelligence, honesty or morality. It was a
matter of wonder to me, at first, how they managed to keep their little children from being
drowned; but I soon discovered how they did it.
They would tie a rope to the child's arm or body,
and fasten the other end to the boat, or else they
would tie an empty bottle, or some other hollow
vessel that would answer in place of a life-
preserver, to the child's body. Accidents to these
children are almost unknown; they are apparently
not born to be drowned.

As another illustration of how poorly labor is
remunerated in China, I will state that on one
occasion I had a dozen shirts washed and ironed
on one of these river craft, for which they charged
me the small sum of thirty cents. The Chinese
have reduced the cost of living to the lowest possible figure, and an entire family can subsist
comfortably, and have fish, rice, tea and vegetables for ten cents per day. In the southern
provinces the climate is warm and balmy, and very
little clothing is needed for comfort, even in the
winter months, and very little is worn by the lower
classes. In mid-winter you will see people almost
destitute of clothing.

In the interior of China there are extensive

timber regions; but no effort has ever been made
to protect these forests, and they are fast disappearing. That is not to be wondered at, however,
when civilized people in our own country are de-
nuding our mountains of their magnificent growths
of timber in the most reckless manner, and no
effort is made to stop this vandalism. In swampy
lands grow willow and bamboo, which are extensively used in the manufacture of furniture. China
is also rich in mineral deposits; but for many
reasons this resource has never been developed.
They have not the requisite facilities, and transportation, except along the lines of the rivers and
canals, is exceedingly slow and tedious. There
are vast pastoral regions in China; but very little
attention is paid to stock-raising, and the horses
are small, and not so valuable as those found in
other countries.

It will thus be seen that the resources of China
are vast and various, and, in addition to the variety of its natural productions, it possesses an
inestimable boon in the industry of its inhabitants.
The Chinese Government does not know how to
turn to account the immense resources of the empire. Should the day ever come that this land
shall have a wise and judicious ruler, one who is
animated by a zeal for the public good, and has
patience enough to guide this industrious people
into new and untried fields of labor, the condi-

tion of the lower classes will be considerably ameliorated.

In the interior of China, off from the line of the water-courses and canals, and especially in the mountainous districts, the roads are very rough and narrow, and in the remoter regions are more like trails than roads. On bad roads, the sedan chair, or palanquin, is much used, and is the most comfortable conveyance. A team of four coolies can travel at the rate of six miles an hour. On good roads the two-wheeled jinrikisha is the preferable conveyance, the motive power generally being a tandem team of two coolies, although occasionally in some districts a horse is used.

The following was written from Canton to the Modesto, Cal., *Herald:*

LETTER FROM CANTON.

CANTON, China, Dec. 24, 1885.

EDITOR HERALD:—Since the last notes I sent you from India, I have traveled some 15,000 miles more on the Orient side of the globe. I came over the Indian Ocean, around to Australia. This was a pleasant journey with a calm sea. In Australia I traveled about 6,000 miles by land and water. In the interior I went by railway 1,200 miles, including the principal portions of her farming and mineral districts, and in many respects I found Australia to be a poor country, especially in the line of agriculture. The last four years have been a succession of drouths, and have been severely felt by sheep and stock men, as well as teamsters. Harvest had just commenced when I was there, but it will only be small strips of grain that will be cut. The best I saw was in Adelaide and Melbourne valleys and in Victoria; but these had poor impression on my mind favorable to an agricultural country. New South Wales and Queensland, in many parts, were dry as a bone, and destitute of vegetation. Water-courses had run dry, and a great number of stock had perished, and the balance was on the brink of starvation.

Australia will have to import wheat largely this year from New Zealand or other places; but the rise and fall in wheat does not trouble my mind. Enjoying sights and the customs and manners among the different nations on the globe, is at present the height of my ambition.

From Australia I embarked for China by way of Torres Strait, Manila, and the Philippine Islands. Here the tropical fruits and foliage were growing in profusion. The green hillsides had the appearance of beautiful landscapes. The first half of the passage was the hottest since I crossed the Red Sea. While we were sailing in the tropics, over the Gulf of Carpentaria, near the Equator, it was 108 degrees in the cabin saloon. This seems warm for December; but it had to be endured. The last part of this voyage has been a stormy one over the China Sea. The rolling waves have washed the hurricane decks from stem to stern. However, the faithful iron steamer has plunged through the swell of the sea, and anchored us safely in the Flowery Kingdom.

After I had done the principal sights of Hong-Kong, I took a steamer up the Pearl River ninety miles to Canton, the Paris of China, and here I expect to eat my bird's-nest soup to-morrow for Christmas dinner. I have seen many curious sights in Canton, including the largest temple, with its 500 Joshes. Here I had to ride in the sedan chairs in the narrow streets, carried by two Chinamen, but found it cheaper to make use of the coolies' legs than to wear out my own. Here you see the style for the ladies to pinch their feet instead of Modestoans who pinch their waists.

After I have visited all the leading points of interest in the Celestial Empire, I will extend my tour to Japan, and, after sight-seeing in that country to my satisfaction, I will embark for San Francisco by way of Honolulu, and my trip around the world will be about 50,000 miles, or long enough to have earned the right to be in fellowship with other "Globe Trotters." Truly yours, OSMUN JOHNSON.

CHAPTER XVII.

CHINESE COAST AND SHANGHAI.

HAVING finished my tour in the interior of China, I returned to Hong-Kong, where I embarked for Shanghai on the steamer Thibet, belonging to the P. and O. Steamship Company, Captain Moody commanding. The greater part of the voyage we were in sight of the China shore. Along this coast is a range of mountains, or hills, apparently destitute of vegetation, and here and there a peak towering high above the level of the others adds to the picturesqueness of the scene. It was now the typhoon season, and we met with a heavy gale which sent one of our life-boats into the boisterous sea. This storm, however, was of short duration, and we did not feel its effects so much as if we had been in the open ocean, instead of being so near the coast. Four hundred miles from Shanghai is a place called Turnabout, which is a diverging place for steamers.

The principal objects of interest on this route were the Chinese fishing fleets, and we would often see as many as fifty of these boats in a group. They are divided off into pairs, and drift leisurely

along until their boats are filled, when they take
their cargo to one of the principal ports and dispose
of it.   The fish are usually either dried or salted.
As the Chinese waters are teeming with all kinds
of fish, this industry forms one of the principal resources of the people along the coast, and they
carry it on the year around, regardless of typhoons,
monsoons, or any of the perils of the deep.

The principal ports at which we touched on this
voyage were Swatow, Foochow, Ningpo and Amoy.
These are regular coaling stations for the different
lines of steamers that ply along the Chinese coast.
Boats often take refuge in these harbors to avoid
being shipwrecked by the fearful gales which prevail during the typhoon season.   Swatow is a seaport town in the Province of Kwang-tung.   It has
a good harbor, and carries on quite an extensive
commerce.

Amoy is in the Province of Fokien.   It is situated on the slope of a hill on the southern coast of
a small and barren island ; is a large and exceedingly dirty place, about nine miles in circumference,
and is estimated to have a population of 250,000.
Both its foreign and coast trade are extensive and
valuable, and its native merchants are considered
to be among the wealthiest and most enterprising
in China.   Amoy was captured by the British in
1841, and was one of the five ports opened by the
commerce of Great Britain by the treaty of 1842.

Foochow is the capital of Fokien, and is situated 150 miles north of Amoy. *Fou* signifies, in China, a town of the first order; *tcheou*, a town of the second order; and *tsien*, a town of the third order. These three orders of towns are always enclosed by ramparts. Foochow is surrounded by a wall seven miles in extent, and from twenty to twenty-five feet high. There are seven gates in this wall, over each of which are high towers. Outside of each gate are large suburbs, the most extensive being those on the south side of the city, which are called Nanti. These extend southward four miles along both sides of the river, and communicate, by two bridges, with a small, densely populated island called Chungchow. The northern bridge is called the Bridge of Ten Thousand Ages, and is said to be over 800 years old.

The city is irregularly built, and the houses are of wood, and usually one story high. The streets are paved with granite, and in many instances planted with trees; but they are exceedingly filthy and narrow, and are infested with beggars, whose appearance is loathsome in the extreme. A great number of the inhabitants live in boats on the river. Some of the residences of the civil and military officers of the province are handsome buildings, and the temples are numerous. A singular feature of Foochow is the great number of towers erected in all parts of the city,—on the

21

walls, over the streets, and even on the house-
tops,— some of which are covered with grotesque
ornaments. There are several cotton, paper and
hardware manufactories here, also several hundred
furnaces for making porcelain. There are lead
mines near by, and great tea-growing districts
within seventy miles. The commerce of this city
is chiefly with Japan and the maritime provinces of
China. This port is much frequented. The channel of the river, and a sheet of water called Lihu,
or West Lake, on the western side of the city, is
crowded with all kinds of vessels and floating habi-
tations.

Ningpo, the principal city of the Province of
Cheh-kiang, is situated on the Takia or Ningpo
River, about sixteen miles from its mouth. It
stands in a fertile plain, and is surrounded by a
fine old wall twenty-five feet high, sixteen feet
broad, and from four to five miles in circumference.
There are six gates and two passages for ships, in
this wall. Ningpo contains a population of about
a half a million. In ascending the river the huge
ice-houses, with high thatched roofs, and a large
white tower, which rises to the height of 160 feet,
and has fourteen stories, will attract the eye of the
stranger. This place has long been celebrated for
its religious and educational pre-eminence, and contains a large number of temples, monasteries and
colleges, few of them of any architectural preten-

sions. In the centre of the city is a striking structure called the Drum Tower, which dates from before the fifteenth century. Brick is the ordinary building material, and the dwelling houses are mostly one story. Large salt works are carried on in the vicinity of Ningpo. Between the months of April and July, thousands of fishermen are engaged in catching cuttle-fish.

Shanghai is situated on the western bank of Hwang-pu River, about twelve miles from the point where the river empties into the estuary of the Yang-tse-kiang. It seems more like a part of the ocean than a river, however, as it is so wide at its mouth that both banks can not be seen at the same time. The walls which surround the city are about three and one-half miles in circumference, and are pierced by seven gates. The old or native portion of the town may be said to illustrate all of the worst features of Chinese cities. The streets are narrow and dirty, and there is an entire absence of all sanitary arrangements; in fact, the native town has nothing but its geographical position to recommend it. However, as it possesses a good and commodious anchorage, and is easy of access to the ocean, it forms the principal port of Central China. From the western wall of the city, there stretches a rich alluvial plain which extends over an area of 45,000 square miles, and is intersected by numerous waterways and great chains of lakes.

Old and New Shanghai are said to have a combined population of 500,000 inhabitants, including
the boat population, which numbers over 11,000.

On anchoring at Shanghai, we were, as is usual
in Chinese ports, surrounded by the moon-eyed
runners of both sexes, in their rickety sampans,
who seemed considerably more anxious that the
passengers should be conveyed from the ship to
the shore than the passengers themselves were. A
landing being effected, we found the wharf lined
with traveling chairs and jinrikishias.   After selecting my sedan chair, I was carried along by the
two coolies at a lively rate, and proceeded at once
to take observations on the Oriental and Occidental sights which I passed, finding them to be
many and interesting, especially in the Chinese
quarters.

Both portions of the town are situated on nearly
level ground, the part occupied by the foreign
population stretching along the banks of the River
Hwang-pu, and there are many handsome dwellings
and extensive warehouses.   The public buildings,
especially in the British settlement, are large and
fine, and what was once a reed-covered swamp is
now one of the finest cities in the East.   In strolling
with my guide from the European to the native
town, I found the contrast to be most striking.
On one hand were lofty mansions, and broad, clean
streets, where occasionally one would get a glimpse

of some fair European damsel, which, here let me remark, are exceedingly scarce in Asia. To my mind, they will always outshine the native beauties, no matter how high the rank or how small the feet. In the Chinese city were narrow streets or lanes, which seemed to run in every direction but the right one.

The commerce of Shanghai is said to be more extensive than that of any other port in the Eastern world, not excepting Calcutta or Bombay. In the European settlement, Great Britain, America, Germany and France are represented. The native city presents a strange conglomeration of wealth and poverty. By the side of the merchant clothed in a costly silken robe, could be seen the professional beggar, or the poor coolie, whose only covering was filthy rags, and who was loaded down like a pack animal with his heavy bamboo baskets. Here was the child of the Orient, and there the traveler from foreign lands. The streets were filled with people, some riding comfortably along in their traveling chairs, others peddling curios and simple wares. It was certainly a strange conglomeration.

I had now come to the conclusion that all of the large Chinese cities bear a close resemblance to each other, and, when you have seen one, with the exception of a few variations, you have seen them all. I found the saying, "that, when you have seen Canton, you have seen the best and worst of China," to be true.   There is the same life, the same bustle, the same confusion, the same idolatrous worship of Brahma, Buddha or Confucius, as the case may be,—the same everything.

As my visit to China occurred in mid-winter, my tour did not extend to Peking, and I thereby missed getting even a glimpse of the youthful Emperor's palace.   The principal visitors to Peking are diplomates.   As it is in the extreme northern portion of the empire, it is not generally visited by many travelers; and I was frequently told, that, when I had seen Shanghai and Canton, I had seen the best of China.

While there was much, of course, that I left unseen, I had traveled over a considerable area in the Chinese Empire, and had spent some little time among this strange people, with whose habits and customs I had already become to some extent familiar from my observations among them in California, where they have become quite numerous since the discovery of gold in 1849, but whose coming is now restricted by acts of Congress and treaty stipulations.   Much more knowledge, however, was to be gained of them in their own country, and the time passed among them was pleasantly and profitably spent.

I must now bid adieu to the Flowery Kingdom, and resume my journey eastward.

CHAPTER XVIII.

THE YELLOW SEA, AND COAST AND COAST TOWNS OF JAPAN.

On the 15th of February I embarked at Shanghai on the steamer Costa Rica for Nagasaki, in Japan, and we were soon drifting into the Yellow Sea, with the last objects of the Celestial Empire gradually fading from our view. With a stiff monsoon breeze in our favor, we soon crossed the Yang-tsi bar, and in forty-eight hours the beautiful coast of Japan appeared before us. The Yellow Sea, whose waters mingle with those of the China Sea, is noted for being very boisterous. Typhoon gales, causing shipwrecks, are of frequent occurrence; but fortunately our voyage was brief and pleasant, and without accident or incident worthy of note. Nagasaki, the first seaport city in Japan, is of considerable commercial importance, and is also a great coaling station for several large steamship lines. Coal is the staple export.

The first feature of interest noticed in sailing into this port is the long, narrow harbor, which appeared to be rim-bound by lofty and uniform ranges of hills. This harbor, next to Sydney and

Hong-Kong, is the most beautiful in the world.
The sloping, picturesque hills in the background,
cultivated, as they are, to perfection by terrace
farming, present, from their tops to the water's
edge, a variety of tropical plants, and add greatly
to the beauty of the city's surroundings. The
highest of these hills is called Hicockson, from
which I obtained a most excellent view of the city,
its harbor, and the surrounding country. Many
vessels lay at anchor, among others two American
ships, with the stars and stripes flying to the breeze,
and serving as a reminder that every day was now
bringing me nearer home.

The population of Nagasaki is about 15,000,
consisting principally of Japanese, with about 300
Europeans. The principal points of interest in
the city are the pagodas, public bath houses, tea
houses and fifteen temples for worshipers of
Buddha. Buddhism is the religion of the country.
Foreign missionaries of various denominations
have done much to convert the people to Christianity, and both Catholics and Protestants have
houses of worship here, where they have met with
better success in their work than in other parts of
Asia.

Japan, however, has few missionaries compared
to the extent of the field before them; and it will
require more than a mere handful of Christian
men to remove the superstitious faith of 37,000,000

heathens imbued with the idolatrous practice and teaching of Buddhism. But the work done so far has been well done ; and, however slow the good work may be going on, the natives are gradually abandoning the old faith for the new, and there are marked evidences everywhere, that the Japanese are a more progressive race, with a higher civilization, than their celestial neighbors across the Yellow Sea. They are fast imitating Europeans in all the arts and sciences, and a large number of their young men are sent to Europe and America to be educated in the best institutions of learning. The Japanese officials and people of rank are imitating Europeans in dress and customs to a small extent ; but the people of the lower orders do not seem to have either means or desire to imitate anything, and the men and women among them dress much the same.

One of the sights which most attracted my attention in Nagasaki was the women stevedores. I saw fifty Japanese women loading our vessel with coal. They were strung out in a line, standing six feet apart on planks, the line reaching from the coal barge to the steamer ; and in this manner the coal was transferred in little bags by being tossed from one woman to another along the line until its destination was reached. Another gang, consisting of small girls, were similarly engaged in tossing back the empty bags to be refilled, and in

JAPANESE WOMAN SPINNING SILK.

(330)

this way 400 tons of coal was transferred from the
barge to the steamer within four hours. These
little Japanese coolie women, dressed in rags, were
as active as cats until their task was finished ; and
their weather-beaten complexions were in no wise
beautified by handling the coal. This novel piece
of drudgery was my first sight of women acting as
stevedores ; but, while it might be a novel one in
San Francisco or New York, it was not along the
shores of Japan.

I visited with much interest the tea houses and
the various temples, through which I was piloted
by my guide. Before entering these sacred pre-
cincts, my shoes had to be removed, and I walked
over the floors in my stocking feet while viewing
the glittering bronze images representing their
idolatrous religion. These temples are as sacred
to these heathens as St. Peter's is to the Romans.
Christianity is to-day protected in Japan, and
Nagasaki is now, as it has been in former years,
the nursery of the Christian religion on the island.
At present there are about 50,000 of various
denominations in this vicinity who are devotees of
the Christian faith.

After taking in all the sights at this place, I
embarked for Yokohama by way of the " Inland
Sea," visiting several seaports along the coast.
After leaving the harbor of Nagasaki, we passed
through a narrow entrance guarded by fortifica-

tions, and the next object that came in sight was Papenberg Island, from which many thousand Christians were hurled into the sea over 200 years ago, in an attempt to forever abolish Christianity from the Island of Japan.

From Shimonoseki to Kobe, the entire length of the Inland Sea is 275 miles. This is, without doubt, the loveliest sheet of water in the world. Neither Lake Tahoe, Lake Como, Lake Luzern or Christiania Fjorden, in Norway, compares with this beautiful blue sheet of water dotted with its 3,000 picturesque islands. In whatever direction the eye turns, a panoramic view meets it that baffles description. Every nook along the shore presented to view clusters of villages, and the hillsides were dotted with cozy homes of terrace farms, with every acre cultivated to perfection by the industrious Japanese. The foliage of trees on the islands casting shadows in the sea, and the swarms of Japanese fishing boats of every description, added to the attractiveness of the scene. This sea being difficult to navigate, on account of the narrow and crooked passages between the clusters of islands, lighthouses and signals are stationed all along the coast, and steamers are all required by law to carry pilots. Never before in my life can I record having seen so many beautiful attractions in so short a voyage as that over this Inland Sea,—scenes which will never be forgotten.

Kobe is situated half way between Nagasaki and Yokohama. It is the only city in Japan in which the Europeans have control of the municipal government, and is the second seaport in size and importance in Japan. Kobe has a deep harbor; and we were here saved the trouble and annoyance of having to be transported from the ship to the shore in the boats of noisy runners, who infest many of the seaports of these islands; for here we were moored to the wharf, and could step ashore without danger to life or limb. The European colony is built on the water front, and has many attractive public and private buildings. Enterprising merchants and ship-owners here do a large commercial business with Chinese and Japanese ports.

The streets in Japanese cities are much broader than those in China; but the houses are light frame structures of light boards, and generally two stories in height. The windows have paper lights instead of glass. In fact, glass is not used in Japan, either in windows or doors. The latter are worked on slides, on which they are easily moved, being almost as light as a feather. The houses have little furniture of any description, as it is not considered necessary to comfort in Japan; but a white straw carpet covers the floors. Their quaint little houses are kept as neat as a pin, and the whole family sit on the floor in a group when eating their meals.

The kitchen is the main room, though strangers are always entertained up-stairs.

A stranger entering one of these houses, is generally met at the entrance by two of the inmates, who make salutations by bowing three times, each succeeding bow being lower than the preceding one; when, for the last one they get down on their knees, and bow nearly to the floor with their heads. The stranger is then invited to remove his shoes, and is escorted up-stairs in his stocking feet. His shoes must be left at the door under all circumstances. The reason of this rule being enforced is to preserve the carpet from being soiled. The kitchen floor is not generally carpeted, nor painted; but it is varnished, and kept as bright as a mirror. They do not propose to have it scratched by the foreigner's shoes. All Japanese wear wooden shoes, with a strap over the toes. These shoes are so simple that it takes but a second to remove them at the door before entering. The bath is taken in a large vat adjoining the kitchen. Bathing in Japan is considered as necessary as eating.

Hiogo is separated from Kobe by a small stream, and is densely populated. The sights of interest in this city were its temples, theatres, shops and tea houses. The tea houses of Japan are classed as the moral and immoral. A vulgar dance house is often called a tea house. The native restaurants, road stations, or wayside inns, where refreshments of sweets with tea and saki are served, are also called tea houses.

The theatre in Japan begins in the morning, and continues all through the day, and the audience carry their lunch with them. To a stranger the performances appear to be of the simplest and silliest nature, not over three performers appearing on the stage at a time ; and in many instances the performance is similar to those of the Chinese. The music is poor and uninteresting ; it sounded like *chink-chink-chink*. To be compelled to remain in a Japanese theatre all day would prove extremely monotonous to a foreigner. On entering a Japanese theatre, you are compelled to ascend a flight of stairs, the performance being on the upper floor, where there are no seats, except small mats, which are placed on the floor for each person who enters ; and no other alternative is left but to sit flat on the floor. A box with hot charcoal is placed by the side of each auditor, from which he can light his pipe or warm his hands and feet during the performance. The admission to a Japanese theatre is four cens, or two cents, which is very reasonable compared to prices charged in European and American cities. This admission entitles the visitor to remain all day and witness all the various plays. Stoves are not used in Japan, but in their stead braziers or small wooden

boxes with a charcoal fire made in the centre.
This fire is usually kept in the kitchen, where the
family sit, surrounding it as we do a stove or fire-
place.

From Kobe I visited two of the most important
cities in Japan, Osaka and Kioto. It is twenty
miles by rail from Kobe to Osaka, and the route is
over the most fertile and level section of country in
Japan. We passed through, on this journey, a
continuous line of well-cultivated gardens planted
into "paddy fields," each divided into half-acre
lots, and levied for irrigation. These fields were
clothed with the most luxuriant vegetation, even
though it was winter.

Osaka is situated on a level plain, is one of the
three imperial cities of Japan, and is the second
city in size in the empire, having a population of
nearly half a million inhabitants. The city is built
on both sides of the headwaters of the Yodagawa,
and steamers can enter from the port of Hiogo and
Kobe; but the large bulk of freight is carried by
rail via Kobe. A great many small canals are cut
through the city, and the bridges of Osaka can be
counted by the hundreds, reminding one of Venice
or Stockholm.

I visited while here many places of interest, and
was entertained by many interesting sights.
Among these was the castle on the banks of one of
the many streams which intersect the city. Its wall,

sloping from the water's edge, and built of immense blocks of granite, is sixty feet high. Near the castle are two forts, and a garrison of 15,000 men. The Imperial Mint, also located here, covers an area of forty acres.

The Buddhist temples of Osaka number about 1,400, many of which I visited, where I found great numbers of devoted natives on their knees clapping their hands in devotional prayer to their idols. The Temple Tennoji, situated in the outskirts of the city, is the largest and most imposing. I paid a priest here two cents to inspect all the bronze idols contained within this temple, and for the same price was permitted to climb to the top, from which I obtained an admirable view of this interesting city, the surrounding country and ocean for many miles.

In riding through this strange city with my coolie team in a two-wheeled jinrikishia, I was greatly confused with strange sights and customs. My tour through the city was made all the more interesting, on account of it being a holiday. It was a New Year's, or tenth day of rest. On this occasion I had an opportunity of seeing people of every rank and grade, of both sexes, and representing ages from one to eighty ' years, who thronged the streets in their holiday attire, celebrating with the greatest pomp and ceremony at their sacred shrines. Thousands of women carried

22

their babies lashed to their backs, Indian fashion.
The lips of the young women were painted blood
red, and their cheeks were smeared with white lead.
The ugliest among the married women had their
teeth blackened.

Every one was bareheaded, without exception,
from an officer of the highest rank to a coolie of
the lowest order; and many who were too dignified
to walk were pushed and pulled along in the jinrikishia, or carried in a palanquin (or traveling
chair used by the better classes) by the half-naked
coolies. Adding to all this the loud gibbering and
bawling in the native tongue, and the continuous
clattering from their wooden shoes, and there was
a combination of noises and sights which were
hard on the ears, but exceedingly interesting to the
eye. For variety and confusion, this exceeded
anything I have witnessed in China. Such scenes
were quite a novelty to me at first; but, after five
weeks' rambling through the empire, I became
better acquainted with the native customs, and the
novelty of the thing soon disappeared.

I was soon able to handle the chop-sticks in
eating the soaked rice and other native foods. A
good appetite created the necessity for learning
this art, and forced me to take advantage of the
opportunity. Raw fish is a dish relished by many
of the native population; but this was more than
my appetite could relish, and I afterward discov-

ered that it was more a matter of taste than
practice in Japan.

The male population of Japan are small and
slender, and the greater number are also bow-
legged, and very unattractive in appearance. The
females are very small, short waisted, have a
healthy complexion, small black eyes, and are
much better looking than the men. The female
beauties exhibit great taste in ornamenting their
hair according to the custom of the country. I do
not suppose that there is another nation in the
world whose women take more pains, or exhibit
more pride in dressing and ornamenting the hair
than the Japanese. As a rule, women barbers go
from house to house, where they spend two or
three hours on a single head. After banging and
combing, the polishing touch is put on with a good
supply of sticky grease, which gives the hair an
exceedingly glossy appearance. The hair is
dressed in this manner generally once a week, but
never oftener than twice. After the hair is "done
up" in this slow and expensive manner, they take
the greatest precaution to preserve it intact as long
as possible, which is more easily done, as wooden
blocks, lined with velvet and cut to fit the neck,
are used instead of pillows, and sleeping in this
manner enables them to preserve the ornamentation of their hair for days at a time.

The women wear loose-fitting costumes, except

around the feet, where the fit is so close as to impede
the motion of the limbs, so that, at first sight, one
would hardly believe they could walk at all.   Over
the upper portion of the body a loose over-blouse
is worn, with the sleeves a foot or so longer than
the arms ; and at a hasty glance the body has more
the appearance of being wrapped in loose cloth
than in a dress suit.   The men wear black clothes
wrapped tightly around their legs as a substitute
for pants, a loose blouse over the upper portion of
the body, and an overskirt reaching nearly to the
feet.   Without regard to rank or sex, they all
wear flat, high wooden shoes, with snow-white
stockings.   Everybody goes bareheaded, from the
infant to the aged; and, no matter whether you
meet them on the highway, in the remotest part of
the country, in the densely crowded city, or
whether they are exposed to the blazing sun or the
bracing frost, they are bareheaded, this being the
custom on their lovely island.

The marriage customs are similar to those of the
Chinese,—the contract being made by the parents
or middle-men instead of by the parties themselves,
and it is of frequent occurrence that the groom
and his intended bride have never seen each other
before the day of marriage.   The wedding ceremony consists in coming forward, and, in the pres-
ence of the mediators, taking each other by the
hand, and drinking saki, the native wine.   It is

JAPANESE WOMEN ORNAMENTING THE HAIR.

the custom for the newly married couple to go and live with the bridegroom's parents; and, after three or four years of married life, the man is allowed to buy another wife, so that a man frequently has two or more wives, according to his means. The price of a wife varies from $80 to $300, and even higher, according to her rank and beauty. While visiting a friend in Yokohama, I learned the following facts, illustrative of the hold this peculiar custom has upon the people. In his employ was a female Japanese servant who had been married two years, and who was now working to earn enough to enable her husband to procure a second wife. I talked with the woman, and discovered her reason for so doing. She said she thought it was all right, as the money would be spent in a good cause,— an opinion in which our American and European wives would hardly be found to concur.

The husband here has a right to divorce himself at any time from any or all of his wives, after they have been living together a sufficient length of time, provided they have no children. The husband has more privileges than the wife under all circumstances, he being the lord and master of the household, and the wife the slave.

Girl babies are not considered desirable by the Japanese, and, when a girl is born into the world, it is regarded as a misfortune by the family;

whereas, on the birth of a boy, the reverse is the case, and there is great rejoicing, it being looked upon as a profitable increase. The peculiar custom is practiced of exhibiting fish on every house where a boy has been born within a year.

An agreeable feature of travel among the Japanese is their extreme politeness, it being as natural for them to be polite to each other as it is for them to eat. Politeness is a part of their religious teaching, impressed upon their minds from infancy ; and, wherever and whenever they meet, they make salutations by bowing several times, each apparently endeavoring to bow lower than the other.

It was amusing to see children of every age, in the cities or villages, swarming in the roads and streets, which they use for a playground, and those that were too small to walk were fastened to the backs of their older and larger sisters, papoose fashion. I have sometimes counted twenty or thirty of these little girls, from six years upward, in groups, where they played for hours, each with a little one on her back. All were bareheaded, most of the small children had their heads closely shaved, and many were clothed only in rags padded over each other, presenting quite a comical appearance. I was informed that they were thus sent out into the streets to play, with the younger ones strapped upon the backs of the older ones, in order that the mothers might be relieved of the care and trouble of looking after them. The absence of street-cars, carriages, and other vehicles with horses attached, rendered it perfectly safe for them to be in the streets.

The Japanese dancing and singing girls also afforded considerable amusement. There are organized groups of these maidens who travel around and sing and play for pay. They are generally girls of respectability, and sing in singing halls, while the dancing girls are generally of a low order, and find their audiences among the tea houses. Owing to the peculiar inharmonious sounds from the odd-looking musical instruments used by the singers, one not accustomed to or unacquainted with Japanese music would have no desire to attend one of these exhibitions more than once. I witnessed a dance by three of these dancing girls given at one of the tea houses; and, from the manner in which they exhibited their persons, and from the motions of their bodies, together with the constant manœuvres with their fans while dancing, I would judge the whole affair to be of an immoral nature. In one corner of the room sat an elderly woman playing a guitar, or three-stringed banjo, and heartily laughing, to attract the attention of the audience. One attendance at a place like this was enough for me. The dance was called Jon Keno, a name well befitting it.

I now turned my eyes toward Kioto, twenty
miles by rail from Osaka. Kioto is called the City
of Temples. It was the capital of Japan for over
a thousand years; but within the last fifteen years
the seat of government has been moved to
Yeddo, or Tokio, a more central location in the
empire. At one time Kioto had over a million
inhabitants; but the population in 1870 was estimated at 370,000. This city and its environs is
one of the most interesting places in Japan. It is
situated in a valley between the ridges Hujsizan
and Higushiyama on the east, and of Tennosan on
the west. The hills surrounding the city are
covered with temples, pagodas and shrines cf the
Shinto and Buddha sects. A visitor can have
access to every department of these by paying two
cents to the attending priest, who, with shaven
head and in stocking feet, shows visitors through
these temples, groaning slightly as he gives the
history of the sacred idol. Glittering decorations
of bronze bedeck the sacred images.

I was informed that Kioto had 300 temples of
the Shinto sect, and probably as many more of the
Buddhist persuasion. At the festivals, the followers of Buddha, while pleading to the bronze images,
clap their hands, while the priest beats a tom-tom.
They believe that the souls of the dead visit their
families every year, on the 13th day of August,
and remain three days before they return to the

tomb.   The Shinto temples are similar to those of
the Buddhists on the exterior; but at the altar, on
the inside, they make a display of looking-glasses,
or mirrors, before which they perform their rites.
These looking-glasses, or mirrors, serve as a substitute for the sun, which was worshiped in ancient
times by these people, and is still the great object
of religious veneration among the followers of the
Shinto doctrine.   These temples contain numerous
pictures of horses, and I was led to believe that
this animal held a sacred place in their hearts,
which I afterward discovered to be the fact.   This
sect have a kind of spirit worship, the word *sinto*
in fact meaning spirit worship; and they believe
that great numbers of spirits exercise an influence
over the world, the sun being the greatest of all,
and the elements after him.   These are called Dai
Zin, meaning " Great Spirit."   There are a large
number of inferior spirits also,—heroes, in the
main, who have been canonized for their worthy
deeds or good qualities.   Among the latter there
is one called Fatsman, the God of War.

The Sinto was the ancient faith of Japan; but
Buddhism has taken its place to a great extent.
The two religions, however, are badly mixed up,
Buddhism having appropriated many of the Sinto
doctrines, and the Sinto sects having taken up
many modes of worship, and images, from Bud-
hism.   I was told that many rejected both of these

religions, and •the idol worship attending them. Among these were some of the best-educated people who were the followers of Confucius and his teachings, and belonged to a school of philosophers called Sinto. The latter have no temples or external forms of worship, but follow, as a rule of life, the precepts of the great Chinese sage.

I was very much impressed with the total absence of hostility between the different sects. The greatest toleration prevails, and all classes believe in a spiritual Emperor called Dairi, whose proper title is the Mikado. He is supposed to be the vicegerent of God on earth, absolute in power and of divine commission. He claims descent from Sin Mu, who was the first to establish a regular government in Japan, about 600 B. C. The person of this being is considered so sacred, and he is considered so holy, that it would be desecration for him to be exposed to the open air, or to touch his feet upon the ground. Many other silly notions concerning him are entertained, and all bow to him as the one great Superior. They also have a sacred dance before their idols.

One of the most imposing sights in Kioto is the old Imperial Palace building and square, containing about thirty acres, surrounded by a high wall. On entering, we passed through a large iron gate. I was more impressed with the quaintness of its architecture than with its beauty. Since the

MR. JOHNSON RIDING IN A SEDAN CHAIR IN THE INTERIOR OF JAPAN.

removal of the Mikado to Tokio, little attention
has been given to its repairs by the Viceroy.

One of the greatest attractions in the city is an
image of Buddha, which contains many tons of
bronze. Kioto contains many ruins which mark a
period of calamity from earthquake and fire. I
found it the most interesting city in Japan on
account of its ancient and modern wonders. Besides her numerous temples and shrines, there are
many theatres, tea houses and amusements of every
kind, a detailed description of which can not be
given in these pages, as time and space will permit
a brief mention only of the principal objects of
interest. The shops are filled with curious and
costly wares, silk factories are numerous, and tea-
curing establishments, where many hundreds of
women are constantly employed.

I obtained a commanding view of the city and
surrounding country from the top of the mountain
called Shogan Zuka, to which I was carried in a
traveling chair by coolies. From this height I
was enabled to study the topography of the district
in every direction. The manner in which this
broken region is cultivated by terrace farming
from the hill-tops to the bottom of the deepest
ravines, a system of cultivation which I observed
in all parts of Japan, impressed upon my mind the
reason why 37,000,000 people were enabled to
subsist in a country smaller than California.

There is a similarity in many respects between Japan and California in regard to climate and soil, though California is far ahead of Japan and of every other country under the sun, in climate and in resources, and in the favors which nature has extended; and yet California now supports only one million of people, while Japan supports thirty-seven millions. While California, up to the present time, has depended mainly on her great fields of wheat, requiring the labor of but few, who are sparsely settled over her vast and fertile valleys, Japan is tilling every foot of her fertile soil to perfection in small farms, bringing into cultivation every inch of available space, and producing every variety of crops instead of one, so that, in case of over-production of certain cereals, they have others in reserve, and are not dependent upon one alone. By this system of farming, with an inferior climate and inferior resources, they are enabled to support a population thirty-seven times greater than that of California.

The principal crops raised are tea and silk. I noticed a tea plantation on the hilliest and rockiest ground in the neighborhood. The tea bushes resemble grape-vines of the same age, and are planted similarly to our vineyards. In every direction, all over Japan, we find these little fields, in which men and women can be seen in groups tilling and toiling from morning until night, except on

FROM PHOTOGRAPH OF MR. JOHNSON IN JAPANESE COSTUME,
WITH FUSIYAMA FOR A BACKGROUND.

every tenth day, which is set apart for rest. Japan, though favored by nature in many ways, is not a fruit country, and what little is raised there is of an inferior quality. Nor is it a good sheep country, there being a species of herb growing in the vegetation which keeps those animals from thriving.

After spending some time in seeing the sights and investigating the resources of the country in and around the cities of Osaka and Kioto, I returned to Kobe, and embarked on the coast mail steamer for Yokohama, a distance of 350 miles, or a thirty-five hours voyage. Shortly after leaving Kobe, we quickly sailed out of the Inland Sea into the open Pacific Ocean, keeping near the shores and stopping at all the ports. From the immense cargoes coming into and going from them, and the numerous steamer lines plying along this coast, a stranger would naturally judge the resources and commerce of Japan to be something enormous.

As we sailed along the coast, the main point of interest in view was the Fusiyama Mountain, said to be the most graceful mountain in form of any in the world. Its towering peak, covered with perpetual snow, and 14,000 feet above the level of the sea, can be seen above every other object for 100 miles out in the Pacific Ocean. This volcanic mountain has a crater two miles in circumference; but there has been no eruption for several years. It is a famous resort for tourists and visitors, and the natives formerly made pilgrimages here for the purpose of idolatrous worship; but the custom which necessitated such a hazardous climb is nearly abandoned, their worship being confined to the temples nearer home, where perhaps the same reward is meted out to them.

CHAPTER XIX.

THE INTERIOR OF JAPAN.

As we steamed into Yokohama, we found that spacious harbor full of anchored vessels. Our steamer was soon surrounded by row craft, from a canoe to a sampan, all being propelled scull fashion and with great speed by the noisy boatmen and boatwomen. On this occasion I was transported in the Club Hotel's steam tender, and landed with comfort, thereby avoiding the tedious bargaining about tariff, as well as the danger of being drenched and half drowned by the natives before reaching shore, which experience I had met with in other Asiatic ports.

The word Yokohama signifies "opposite shore," this city lying opposite to Kanagawa. The latter place was for many years the residence of foreigners; but of late years they have been permitted to remove their business quarters to Yokohama, which is the leading treaty seaport in Japan. It is a city of 50,000 inhabitants, including 4,000 foreigners, is built principally on level ground, and is surrounded on three sides by ranges of hills. Several canals are cut through the city, and these are crossed by bridges in every direction.

The European settlement extends along the water front a long distance, and is called the Bund. It contains some large commercial houses, steamship offices, numerous banks, three churches and a few good hotels. Among the latter the leading ones are the Windsor, the Grand, and Club Hotels, at all of which the rate is three dollars per day. This locality was formerly a swamp ; but, since its cession to Europeans, it has been reclaimed, and it is now the most beautiful part of the city.

The more prominent among the European residents, the consuls, merchants and missionaries, have their private residences on a lofty eminence called the " Bluff," from which I had a fine view of the city and bay. This elevation reminded me of Nob Hill, in San Francisco, only it is of much less importance. I made many acquaintances living here, and used to make frequent visits to the " Bluff," and, in the society of my newly found friend, Mr. Jensen, and his estimable wife, passed many pleasant hours.

The principal business portion of the city is confined to Main street, which, from its width and the architecture of its buildings, bears evidence of European civilization and enterprise. Porcelain factories, silk establishments and tea warehouses, where by a certain process the moisture is extracted from the tea, and the leaves are cured and prepared for the foreign market, are among the enterprises started by foreign capitalists. A stroll through the principal tea establishments, where hundreds of native women are engaged in taking the tea through these various processes until the finishing touch was reached, was very interesting and instructive.

The various nations of the world are well represented at this port, and the flags flying from the different consulates designate the different countries represented. The American Consul, Mr. Green, was the only one I had occasion to call on, as it was necessary to procure a passport from him, which document I afterward found to be as useful as coin, in my travels from Yokohama through the interior, whenever I crossed the treaty limits.

The native portion of Yokohama is full of strange and interesting sights, and the principal streets are illuminated with Japanese paper lanterns. One noticeable feature on the streets is the low-story booths, tea houses and the public bathing houses. The principal streets in this quarter are Bentondora and Hanchdora, the shops along which are crowded with native wares and curios of every description, either in porcelain, silk or lacquer cabinets, any of which can be purchased at astonishingly low prices.

It is here where tourists generally make large purchases of presents, souvenirs and curios for their friends at home. The duty I paid at San Francisco on my collections amounted to more

than the original purchase price in Yokohama.
Some of the merchants display their goods and
wares on the open streets ; and, in the little booths
fronting the streets, whole families can be seen
sitting in groups, flat on the floor, around a brazier
of hot coals, smoking their pipes. There are
numerous theatres where the same silly performance heretofore described can be witnessed for two
cents. The tea houses and dance houses are of
the same character as I found in other Japanese
cities, and a stranger has no desire to visit one a
second time.

The most singular custom which attracts the
attention of the visitor is the manner in which
public bathing is conducted. The public bathing
houses are free for inspection from the sidewalks,
and you can sometimes see thirty or forty women
bathing at the same time, and oftentimes as many
as 150 may be seen bathing in the same water.
On disrobing, they plunge into a large wooden
vat, where the process of scrubbing and washing is
kept up for nearly an hour, and they are constantly
going and coming, dressing and undressing. These
bathing establishments, being public institutions,
sanctioned by the government, any passer-by has a
right to look in and witness the performance ; and,
this being an old custom among the people, these
women are perfectly indifferent whether Europeans
or natives watch their plunging and splashing. At

JAPANESE LADIES BATHING.

(358)

the entrance is a gate-keeper, who allows none but females of respectability to enter. Up to within the last few years it was the custom for males and females to bathe together ; but now they have a railing which separates the sexes. Bathing is indulged in daily by the Japanese, and, if cleanliness is akin to godliness, surely the Japanese can claim the kinship. In this and in many other customs the Japanese are behind the civilization of the age.

The common mode of travel in Japan is by means of the two-wheeled jinrikishia, shaped something like a small gig, and generally drawn by a single coolie, except for rapid traveling, when two are employed. It is quite a comfortable and convenient means of travel, enabling a sight-seer to ride over the streets of a city and its surroundings almost as rapidly as he could with a team of horses. A large number of these coolies have picked up sufficient English to enable them to explain the various objects of interest as they travel along, and in this manner the tourist is saved the expense of employing an interpreter.

From Yokohama and Tokio, I made many excursions to the interior in this kind of a rig, the motive power being two coolies, who would haul me along at the rate of fifty miles a day, for which valuable service they charged me sixty cents a day, furnishing their own food, which consisted chiefly

of rice, tea and brandy, or at least a substitute for
the latter,—a kind of innocent liquor made of rice.
One would think that very little could be made at
such low wages ; but everything in Japan is correspondingly low. I have seen these coolies, when
on the way, stop for refreshments and rest, as they
usually did at stations every fifteen miles, and pay
one cent for a glass of brandy, one cent for a cup
of tea, and two cents for a mess of rice, while raw
fish and other luxuries would be correspondingly
low.

Another mode of travel, in which I also had
some experience, was by means of the sedan chair,
or, as it is sometimes called, the traveling chair, in
which I was carried by two half-naked coolies, with
a bamboo pole resting upon their shoulders. This
mode of travel, used in the hilly districts, and over
rough and broken sections, is fast going out of use ;
but, in the narrow streets in China, it is the principal means of conveyance.

Wagons of any kind are almost unknown in
Japan, the only vehicle used as a substitute being
the large two-wheeled carts which are pushed and
pulled by a number of coolies, according to the
size of the load. I have often seen a half-dozen of
these coolies moving one of these carts loaded with
produce, to market, a distance of twenty miles.
Everything seemed to be operated with man power,
and this power was certainly utilized for everything

for which it could be made available, which is but natural among a poverty-stricken people, and in an over-populated country.

Horses are few in number and of an inferior breed. Chubby ponies, smaller than the California mustang, are used principally in the mountainous districts as pack animals. I have seen a long string of these animals with lumber and poles thirty feet long packed lengthwise on a saddle frame as long as their backs. The only advantage I could see to the horse by this arrangement of the load was that he was enabled to walk in the shade of his burden, which projected twelve feet beyond his head and tail.

From Yokohama to Tokio was a pleasant railway ride of eighteen miles, the Pacific Ocean being in full view nearly the whole distance. The route ran through a level and prosperous country, every acre of which was cultivated; and it seemed like riding through continuous gardens of rice, tea and vegetables.

Wheat is also raised, though on a very small scale, and generally as a second crop after the rice and other crops have been removed. It is planted in rows, and the crops raised amount to comparatively nothing for such a large population. What small quantity is raised is converted into a coarse meal, and made into sweet-cakes, which are served as refreshments. The European population of the empire import their flour from India and San Francisco.

Tokio, the seat of government, or the new and eastern capital, covers a greater area than New York City. It has a population of nearly one million, is intersected by numerous canals and bridges, and contains a greater variety of sights of interest than any other city in the Orient. Here I also found many temples, shrines and every idolatrous object appertaining to heathendom. The most imposing sights were the Shibba Temples and surroundings, from which a beautiful view can be obtained of the city and surrounding country in different directions, a distance of eight or ten miles.

The Osaka temples, in the Osaka district, were also objects of special interest. The Temple of Kin Kin Zan is an enormous structure, with a costly ornamented exterior, and with its altar ornamented with bronze and gold. The walks to this temple were thronged with worshipers who were hastening to perform religious rites to their imaginary gods. To hear and see how devotional they were while pleading to these glaring images for mercy was a touching scene. They bow and clap their hands repeatedly, calling to their idols in most imploring tones, and cluster around these inanimate figures with offerings. In the performance of these superstitious rites, they often work themselves into a state of unconsciousness, like the negroes of the South in their religious fervor.

As usual, a priest with shaven head was on hand to take the small admission fee, and do the honors to visitors. Inside of the temple grounds, there were tea booths, bazaars, art galleries, theatrical performances and other attractions. This temple and its surroundings, so closely mixed up with idolatries, business life and pleasure resorts, makes the Osaka district one of the most important and curious places to visit in the city. Near this temple stands the statue of the Goddess Emma, encircled by a cluster of children.

I also visited while here the Mikado's Palace, which was in course of construction in place of the one burned down a few years ago. It will be a magnificent building when finished. The Citadel, the Castle and fortifications were also inspected by me with much interest. The Imperial buildings correspond with the architecture of other important buildings throughout the city, and are all built low, in all probability on account of the frequency of earthquakes. Tokio and its environs contain many dilapidated temples, the wreck and ruin of which were caused by earthquakes, fire, war and other destructive agencies.

While here I visited Veno, three miles from the centre of the city, where, among many other objects of interest, can be seen the main museum, which I

found filled with all kinds of ancient wares, implements, tools, coins, swords, etc., revealing to a certain extent the character and customs of the early
inhabitants of the island. Every kind of wild animal peculiar to the country was well represented in
the collection of skins deposited here. In point of
interest and display, I found the museum and art
gallery a fair sample of many I saw in Europe.

In Veno I found many elegant gardens and
ornamental residences belonging to the more opulent citizens of Tokio. Here also are many
imposing tombs of the Shoguns, the former rulers
of Japan, among them being one who concluded a
treaty with the United States a few years ago. I
regret that space will not permit a more complete
and interesting description of all of these wonderful sights ; but I must journey on.

Leaving Tokio, I visited Nikko, situated seventy-
five miles in the interior, and amidst the grandest
mountain scenery in the empire. This journey
included a ride by rail to Utsonomaya, fifty miles
from Tokio, and through a moist, level country,
planted largely in tropical fruits.

At Utsonomaya myself and guide put up at the
Yama Hotel, the most important in the town,
where I was served, in pure native style, with all
the luxuries of the land, and I might add that the
enjoyment afforded by the native customs was more
palatable than the articles on the bill of fare. I

have already mentioned the remarkable politeness of the Japanese, and, as usual, I was entertained with it here. On entering the hotel, I was met at the door by the host, hostess and a servant, each of whom made salutations by bowing three times, at the last bow falling down on their knees, and almost touching the floor with their heads.

According to custom, my shoes were removed, and I was politely invited up-stairs in my stocking feet into the parlor, which I found to be kept as neat as a pin, but as bare of furniture as a barn, except a straw carpet laid on a springy bamboo floor. Here I was invited to be seated on a mat placed in the middle of the floor, and a little brazier of hot coals was left near my feet, while the servant girl brought me a cup of tea, without a saucer, with some native refreshments. The only objection I had to the tea was that the cup was too small, containing not more than four thimblefuls of the beverage.

Supper was served in half an hour. Half-boiled rice was brought in a wooden tub the size of a peck measure, and the other dainty dishes were raw fish, native brandy warmed, shark's fins, and a mixture of vegetables, soy and sea weed. Two chop-sticks were furnished me to gather in the food with, and within two feet of this sumptuous repast were two blushing maidens watching and attending to my wants.

One of these, kneeling on the floor, held in her
hands a wooden tray, from which I received my
rice in a tiny cup, which, as soon as emptied, was
to be replaced on the tray to be refilled by her
from the smoking rice tub. This was to be filled
and refilled as often as I should desire it. This
maiden served the meal, while the other stood
upright in her white stocking feet, ready for extra
service, such as keeping the paper-light or fire-box
in proper order ; or, if anything else should be
wanted from the kitchen, such as raw fish or
warm brandy, for instance, she would glide after it
as noiselessly as a ghost. They watched me
amusedly in my awkward efforts to eat with the
chop-sticks, with which, though difficult to handle,
I managed to catch all the rice my appetite
required. I did not indulge in the rest of the
luxuries (?), on account of the offensive flavor, which
I found to be most disagreeable to both taste and
smell.

Some little time after this dining and wining had
concluded, and when the hour was growing late, I
was invited to take a bath before retiring for the
night, which I was obliged to consent to, owing to
the strict custom of the country to indulge in the
luxury of the bath every night. If I had deviated
from this custom or declined, it would have lowered
me in the estimation of the household, and doomed
me as an unclean person, much lower in their esti-

Mr. Johnson Dining in Native Style.

mation than one who should decline to wash his
face and hands before going to breakfast, would be
with us.

I was escorted to the bath-room by the two
female servants and my guide. The room contained a large oblong vat, with warm and cold
water, and I was informed by my guide that it was
the custom for the two maid servants to wait on
me while at the bath ; that they were there for the
purpose of rubbing and scrubbing me with brushes
and towels until I was perfectly clean.

Truly, I had been convinced and struck with the
politeness, kindness and hospitality of the Japanese;
but I now began to think they were going to kill
me with these qualities, and, for the first time in
my life, I thought I had too much of a good thing.
As a few hours before they had tried to overfeed
me, now they were going to try to overwash me ;
so I declined their service, and told them that,
according to our American custom, we rubbed and
scrubbed ourselves while bathing, and that I must
stick to that rule or not bathe at all, upon which
they gracefully withdrew, and I was left alone to
take the plunge. The only objection I found to
the bath was that everybody bathed in the same
vat and in the same water, the water being changed
only once a day.

However, I came from that bath a wiser and a
cleaner man, and, returning to my bare parlor,

entered into speculations as to how I should sleep during the night, as neither bedstead nor bed-clothes were in sight. But a few moments elapsed, however, before two heavy quilts were brought in, one of which was spread in the centre of the floor to lie on, and the other had long sleeves in it like an overcoat. After the two maids had assisted me in getting my arms into its sleeves, and a hollow wooden block to fit my neck for a pillow had been furnished, I was invited to lie down, which I did. Near my wooden pillow was placed a brazier of hot coals to keep me warm during the night, and a kind of grease-light, in a paper lantern, was left on the floor near my feet, and kept burning all night.

My guide was put to bed in the same manner at the door, as a body guard. He was a guardian to be most feared, as he had the best opportunity of robbing me. In the slide door stood the two little black-eyed beauties watching my awkward movements as long as my eyes remained open. They could not have been married, for their teeth were not blackened. I was to all appearances more of a curiosity to them than their strange customs were to me. I was treated to a shock of earthquake during the night, a frequent visitor in Japan ; but it must have been a light one, as neither the bamboo walls nor the paper windows were affected by it. Morning came, and, finding myself not robbed, I at once placed more confidence in my guide ; and

24

here let me say, that I was never robbed out of a farthing, either in Japan or on any other part of my journey, except in the extra tips I had to pay waiters and guides, which many tourists style "highway robbery."

For this interesting night's accommodation the rates were as reasonable as could be expected, taking into consideration the various extras and attention furnished. Forty cents paid my entire bill, including the bath, hot coals, light, etc. I was charged half-price for my guide, as he was considered of much less dignity, and had to be contented with common fare and attention. I almost forgot to mention that my passport was examined here by an officer, and, on my identification as an American citizen, all was well, as the citizens of this country are held in higher regard than those of any other. This is a fair description of the customs, fare, etc., of the interior hotels in Japan, and every foreign tourist in search of pleasure will be likely to share the same comforts, and be served with like fare and attentions, as I have here related.

There are no European settlers in the rural districts of Japan, and no hotels kept on the European plan. The Japanese in these districts do not want to sell or rent land to foreigners, and do not allow them to become interested in any public enterprise, or get a foothold or controlling interest in anything;

and these restrictions are especially enforced against the British. The Japanese, being a wide-awake nation, want to manage their own affairs, and are aiming to place themselves on a level with other civilized countries.

At Utsonomaya I hired a pair of coolies and two two-wheeled jinrikishias to convey myself and guide to Nikko, a distance of twenty-two miles. The road was a steady incline until we reached Nikko, at an altitude of 2,000 feet above the level of the sea. The route was very attractive, both sides of the road being regularly lined with shade trees, which, on account of their age, were of enormous size. They must have been planted by former rulers over 1,000 years ago, and the shade from them proved a boon to the weary traveler.

We soon arrived at Nikko, the headquarters of the Buddha and Shinto sects. This place contains many imposing temples, and some of the grandest mountain scenery in Japan, including cascades, rushing waterfalls, lofty mountains, rugged cliffs and crags, and arches of the most curious formation.

I found here a group of forty-seven temples of most stately structure, and of grand architectural design, carved and engraved on the exterior, and with ornamental altars in gold and bronze in the interior. Thousands of tons of bronze must have been used in their construction, and, since leaving Rome, I had seen no such imposing splendors to

MR. JOHNSON IN THE JINRIKISHA, THE COMMON MODE OF TRAVEL IN JAPAN.

excite my admiration as I found here in Nikko, which has been truly styled the Rome of Japan.

This is the burial place of Toku Iyyani, the founder of the Shogun dynasty, and one of the most celebrated warriors in Japanese history. The sacred ground containing the ashes of this distinguished ruler is on a sloping hill, to which I gained access by following my guide up a long flight of granite steps, through temples filled with glittering objects in gold and bronze, and guarded by shaven-headed priests. My guide was kept busy explaining to me the wonderful sights met with on this journey, and my memorandum book seemed fast filling with descriptions of temples, shrines, tombs and statues, much of which, I regret, for want of space must be omitted from this narrative.

After a few days of sight-seeing in this wonderful city, I returned to Yokohama via Tokio. My next expedition was to Enoshima, a little island, twenty-two miles from Yokohama, a lovely resort, and one of the first places visited by tourists after they have done the sights of Yokohama. One of the curious features of this island is a natural cave, 400 feet long, which penetrates the bluff near the level of the sea. This cave contains many sacred relics, idols guarded by priests, who charge a small fee of admission to view the secrets contained within its long and crooked recesses.

This island is full of native shops, well stocked

with shells, beads and other curios gathered from the sea, and many of the natives make a living in this way, depending on visitors for customers. From this island I obtained a beautiful view in every direction. The ocean seemed alive with its

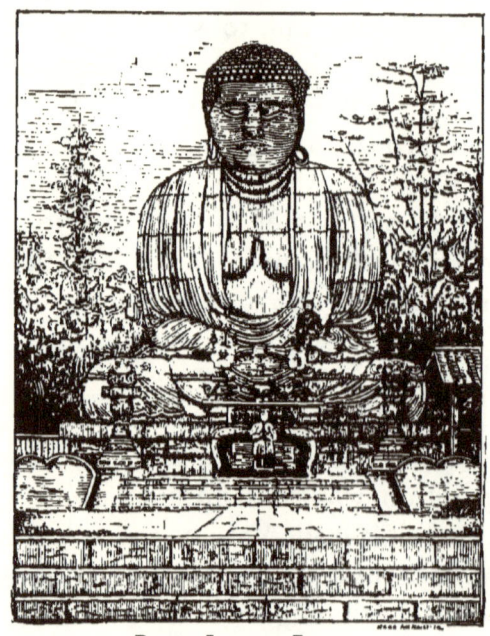

BRONZE IMAGE OF BUDDHA.

clusters of fishing boats, and other drifting objects, which added to the attractiveness of the scene.

Returning to Yokohama, which had now become the central point of all of my movements, I started with my jinrikishia and coolie team for Kamakura, where Diebutsi, the great bronze image or statue of Buddha, is located. It was cast over 600 years ago ; is fifty-three feet high, and ninety-six feet in circumference, and the face is eight and a half feet long and sixteen feet wide. I found the inside hollow, and the space within used as a temple. This image is in every respect a most wonderful piece of workmanship. According to the usual custom among tourists, I had my photograph taken, with the image as a background, being placed in a sitting posture on one of its thumbs, from which my figure appears insignificant when compared with the enormous proportions of the statue.

Kamakura is eighteen miles from Yokohama. It was the capital of Japan from 1190, during a period of about 400 years ; and the military headquarters of Toriton, a famous Prince in Japanese history, were established here. Kamakura contains several grand temples, the most imposing of which is the Tsurugoaka Hill, a temple of Shinto origin, which I entered by climbing a flight of fifty-eight steps. Here I was shown many old relics, swords, curious designs of bows and arrows, pieces of blades, and many other weapons used by a warlike people. These silent monitors were representatives of stormy and warlike periods in the nation's history, and, while preserved as objects of curiosity by the natives, they are of equal interest to the foreign visitor.

While here I visited the tomb of Bill Adams, an English pilot, and the first white man who died in Japan.

Leaving this tomb with my coolie outfit, I was soon hurried into the streets of Yokaski, a favorite seaside resort, frequented by many visitors from Yokohama. This place, according to its size, was the most stirring place I visited in the empire. The government Navy Yard, dry docks and Arsenal are located here. I saw many new ships in course of construction, and many old ones launched for repairs. Some of the largest machine shops in the East are located here, and 2,000 mechanics of various grades are employed, at wages ranging from twenty to fifty cents a day, without board. A visit to this busy city can not fail to impress the visitor with the enterprise of the Japanese.

I returned to Yokohama, twelve miles away, on a little steamer, which made four regular trips a day. The picturesque scenery along the coast served to remind me that Nature had bestowed her favors upon Japan with a lavish hand. What food for an artist these lovely islands, picturesque shores and inland attractions would afford ! The next place visited was the favorite health and pleasure resort called Miya-Notta, which contains several mineral springs of a sulphurous nature, visited by many natives and tourists, who drink and bathe in the waters. It is situated in the midst of beautiful mountain scenery, to reach which I traveled via Odawara in the usual tandem style.

From Odawara the road was over a rough and broken trail, and I was obliged to change my mode of conveyance to the sedan chair, which has been described before. After traveling extensively over China and Japan, I had become accustomed to the different modes of travel, and was now equal to any emergency.

The district traversed by us appeared to be occupied chiefly by peasants, who lived in dilapidated huts, situated in the centre of their patchfields, which were cultivated chiefly to rice, vegetables and tea. Their lot seemed to be to live poor and die poor. Japan, though ground down with taxation and over-population, has less paupers, I am informed, than any other nation, according to population.

Before leaving Yokohama to resume my travels, I visited several Japanese Christian churches and schools. Many of these heathen have been converted to Christianity through these influences. English is taught in these schools, and the teachers and missionaries of both English and American nationalities work harmoniously together in christianizing and educating the people. I conversed with Mr. Bennett and Mr. Jewel, missionaries, and with Mr. Baker, a teacher, who informed me that much good had been accomplished through their labor and influence. These schools were well attended by many nations, who rapidly learn the English language. Several young Japs acted as assistant teachers. I noticed that many Europeans had mastered the Japanese language and spoke it with perfect ease. Notwithstanding that their language has forty-seven letters, it is an easy language to learn.

I found the churches filled with people of every age, who seemed very devoted to their new-found religion. To see these natives in a Christian church, on their knees, in white stocking feet, and especially the chubby children, was a novel scene. You can always correctly estimate the number of people in a Japanese church before you enter, by counting the number of shoes left outside the door.

The author sent the following communication from Yokohama to the Modesto, Cal., *Herald:*

LETTER FROM JAPAN.

YOKOHAMA, Japan, Jan. 28, 1886.

EDITOR HERALD :— Since my last letter, sent you from Canton, China, I am now 1,800 miles nearer home. For several weeks I have traveled extensively in Japan, and I find it the most beautiful and interesting of any country I have seen during my whole journey around the world. I find the people here nearer up to the scale of our advanced civilization than in China or India, and, as a rule, they are gentlemanly and polite. If a stranger enters a Japanese house, he is cordially met in the doorway, and salutations are made by bowing the head twice near to the floor. In the seaboard cities they are largely imitating the Europeans, both in customs and costumes; but in the interior I had to use chop-sticks, the same as in China.

I have visited all the leading places of interest in Japan,—temples, tea plantations, navy yards, arsenals, tea-drying establishments, silk works, porcelain factories, bazaars, public bathing houses, tea houses, theatres, castles, rice fields and the depositories of relics all over the country. The grandest place for sight-seeing is Nikko. It is called the Rome of Japan. This point I have just been visiting. It is ninety-five miles from Yokohama, located in the midst of a group of picturesque mountains. Here are forty-seven stately temples, many of which are ornamented with costly, glittering bronze. Nikko is the ancient headquarters for the two prevailing religions of the country, the Shinto and the Buddhist. The latter is the principal one and the most pious. Among other attractions are waterfalls that continually flow near the temples from the snow-clad mountains. Here are large pagodas, images of many descriptions, representing the Japan gods, and other curious relics and scenes to attract the eyes of a tourist and arrest his attention.

The interesting places which I have visited, aside from those mentioned, are Tokio, the capital ; Osaka ; Kioto, the old capital ; Nagasaki, Kobe, Kamakura, and Yokaski, the government Navy Yard of Japan. Near by here I saw the grave of Bill Adams, an English pilot, and the first white man ever buried in Japan. Near by is also the great image of Dibutsi, the Japanese god, where I had my photograph taken on the thumb of the image. The Inland Sea of Japan, over which I traveled for 240 miles, is the most beautiful sheet of water I have sailed on in my whole journey. This coast has the most beautiful and picturesque landscape scenery from the shores to the hill-tops, which surround it in every direction, and the water of the sea is dotted with fishing boats, which add beauty to the sight all along the coast. The ride I had over this silvery sea, with its thousands of attractions, will never grow dim in my memory.

In a few days I will embark for the Sandwich Islands, the last country I will have to visit before I have accomplished my tour around the world.

Yours truly,   OSMUN JOHNSON.

In a week's travel through Japan, I had witnessed many wonderful sights, and visited many famous places ; I had studied her resources and the customs and industries of her people; I had seen more of her temples, shrines and idols than I ever care to see again ; I had viewed her many attractions with interest and pleasure, had experienced the kindness and courtly demeanor of her people, and been treated with the highest consideration and respect, according to their custom. An unknown white man traveling through her interior for hundreds of miles, and left to the mercy of the natives, instead of being robbed and plundered, I had been treated as a nobleman of high birth ; my passport as a citizen of the United States entitled me to the highest consideration; and, in conclusion, I will say of Japan, that, with her mountains of picturesque scenery and inexhaustible mineral wealth, with her extensive timber regions, with her valleys and hills cultivated to all varieties of tropical products, with her beautiful seas and lakes and bays alive with fish of all kinds, with her extensive seaboard and secure harbors, giving her greater commercial advantages than any other country in Asia,—with all these natural advantages, and with a healthy, happy, industrious and ambitious people, she can not fail to soon take her place among the civilized nations of the world.

I found her people to be as honest as the day is long ; courteous, kind, polite and good humored ; fond of joking, great imitators, and anxious to acquire knowledge. I enjoyed my visit among them more than that among any other people on my tour around the world, and it is with many regrets that I am now obliged to bid good-bye to the Mikado's empire.

The following was written at Yokohama by Mr. Johnson to the Stockton, Cal., *Independent:*

LETTER FROM JAPAN.

YOKOHAMA, Japan, Jan. 18, 1886.

For several weeks past I have traveled extensively in the interior and on the sea-coast of Japan. Of all the countries visited in my journey around the world, I have found Japan the most interesting. I have just visited Nikko, about eighty miles north of Tokio, the headquarters of the Buddhist and Shinto sects, the two prevailing religions of Japan. The temples of Nikko have a group of picturesque mountains for background. There are here, in all, forty-seven stately and costly temples, ornamented with bronze and engraved images, and objects representing the Japanese gods. Thousands of tons of bronze must have been used in constructing these imposing temples and pagodas. Among other grand attractions in and around Nikko are seven waterfalls in streams that rush from the snow-clad mountains a short distance from the city. In other places in Japan, like Tokio, Osaka and Kioto, I have seen grand temples, pagodas and castles and interesting curiosities in architecture; but since I left Rome I have never seen so many beautiful relics, temples and tombs as at Nikko. This place is, in fact, called the Rome of Japan.

Nikko is ninety-five miles from Yokohama, and on the trip from the last-named place I first took the cars to Utsonomaya, a distance of seventy-seven miles. There I hired two coolies with "jinrikishias" for myself and guide, to convey us the remaining distance to Nikko. That was a curious turn-out for a Stanislaus farmer to ride in,—a little two-wheeled concern with two half-naked coolies for a tandem team. I have, however, become an expert in the "jinrikishia" and traveling chair in Japan and China. I have sent you by this mail a photograph, taken for me while sitting in the queer two-wheeled vehicle behind my coolie team.

On this tour I was supplied with a passport from the American consul, and I found the document as useful as coin. Whenever I entered a Japanese hotel at night, I was met at the door by the host or hostess, who made salutations by bowing almost to the floor. After my shoes were taken off I was invited up-stairs, and shown to the best room, which was bare of furniture. I was politely invited to squat on the floor on a white mat, and then a small vessel of hot coals was left at my feet. Next came a servant girl with a cup of tea served on a small red wooden tray.   The fault found with the cup of tea was that it was too small, containing not over four thimblefuls. Half an hour later supper was served, consisting of half-boiled rice in a vessel the size of a peck measure, vegetables, warm Japanese brandy and raw fish, with two chop-sticks to gather in the rice.   Two blushing maidens stood opposite the rice dish, and they amused themselves watching my poor headway with chop-sticks.   Fortunately, I had ample time to catch all the rice that my appetite called for, and I have now learned to be quite handy with the sticks.   The smell of the vegetables, raw fish and brandy, was enough for me, and satisfied my appetite without tasting these dainty Japanese dishes.   At bed-time two quilts were placed on the floor, one of them having long sleeves to put one's arms into before lying down flat on the mat. For a pillow a wooden block was furnished, hollowed out to fit the neck, and a vessel with hot coals was left near my head to keep me warm through the night.   In this position I was ready to sleep.

The whole country is cultivated into gardens instead of farms, and I can now understand how 37,000,000 of people live in a country smaller than England.   The Inland Sea of Japan for 240 miles is the most beautiful sheet of water I have seen in my whole tour.

I have now traveled about 45,000 miles, through America, Europe, Africa, Australia, India, China, Japan, and many islands, in the journey; and in a few days I will start for the Sandwich Islands, the last country to visit before I have made my trip around the world.

OSMUN JOHNSON.

CHAPTER XX.

HOMEWARD BOUND ACROSS THE PACIFIC, VIA
HONOLULU, TO SAN FRANCISCO.

ON the 9th day of March I embarked on the
four-masted steamer City of Peking for San Francisco, via Honolulu. This vessel is the largest
American vessel afloat, and is in reality a floating
palace upon the Pacific Ocean. She has a carrying
capacity of 5,500 tons. Her entire length is 425
feet, and her engines are of 800 horse-power, con-
suming forty-five tons of coal every twenty-four
hours. It took a small army of servants to keep
her clean, and in every department they could be
seen scrubbing day and night. The cabin fare was
good, though it was not the custom to serve as
many lunches as they do on the English steamers,
on which eating and s'eeping seem to be the main
occupation through the day and night.

I found this Trans-Pacific steamer as comfortable
and well kept as she looked, and considered myself
very fortunate in being able to secure such accommodations; for, at the outset, my aim had been to
include in my tour of the world as many countries
as possible, even though I should be obliged to go

out of my way, or out of the regular course of travel for hundreds of miles or more, and without regard to the extra time employed or expense incurred.

I started out to see the world, and I wanted to see it. An opportunity now presented itself to visit the Sandwich Islands, — an opportunity rarely afforded the tourist on leaving Asia. It happened in this way : From China to San Francisco, there are two regular mail lines, the Occidental and Oriental, neither of which touch at Honolulu, as the distance would be increased 500 miles ; but on this occasion an arrangement had been made by Claus Spreckles, the Sandwich Island sugar king, with the steamship company, to carry and land for him 900 Japanese emigrants, who were under a three-years contract with him to work on his sugar plantations on the islands.

I rejoiced at this opportunity of visiting, on my homeward journey, another interesting country, and hastily took advantage of it. It seemed to me that Providence had favored me throughout my whole tour, and had allowed me a full share of the world's most wonderful sights. I had been per-mitted to visit two more countries than the average tourist, to wit, Australia and New Zealand, and now the Sandwich Islands were to be added to the list.

Having secured passage, and gone aboard, the

anchor was raised, and we steamed out of the beautiful harbor of Yokohama. The snow-clad peak, Fusiyama, the last visible object in the Mikado's empire, soon faded from our view, and we were fairly on our way across the Pacific.

Besides the 900 emigrants on board, there were passengers of every grade and rank,—lords and millionaires, Oriental diplomates and ministers to Washington; missionaries, worn out, and returning home; students from various parts of Asia going to attend institutions of learning in America,—all of whom contributed their talents and experience toward making the voyage one of interest and pleasure. The cargo consisted of tea, porcelain and silk.

The distance from Yokohama to Honolulu is 3,400 miles. Besides the huge engines of the vessel, every mast carried sails, contributing, with favorable winds, fifty miles a day to her speed, which ordinarily averaged from ten to twelve knots an hour, according to the favors of the breeze. The first half of this voyage was stormy, with prevailing head winds, and we encountered a gale which maintained its fury for twenty-four hours, raging as furiously as any typhoon I had experienced in the China Sea. It is not often that the Pacific belies its name; but on this occasion its waves rolled mountains high, often enveloping the whole ship from stem to stern. The storm did not

25

last long, but abated with the change of latitude, not a great distance from Honolulu. The Pacific again became pacific, and the remainder of the passage was pleasant and agreeable. The route over this portion of the ocean being clear of islands and other objects, as well as of fog, there is less danger of collision than on the Atlantic side, where accidents are of frequent occurrence.

There was much more life aboard this steamer than on any other on which I had sailed, on account of the large number and great diversity of the passengers. The first three days out, the Japanese emigrants were nearly all sea-sick; but, after they had recovered from this unpleasantness, the scenes and occurrences among them were very interesting, especially at meal times, when these 900 half-naked Orients could be seen rushing and scrambling for their places with chop-sticks in hand. Instead of "feeding the fishes," as at the beginning of the voyage, they were now feeding themselves, which change soon began to tell on the rice baskets, as they gathered in basket after basket with their chop-sticks.

Between meals they would amuse themselves by wrestling, in which exercise they proved themselves experts, thoroughly skilled in the art, and displayed great activity and strength. One of the novel features of their mode of wrestling is that, while engaged in the exercise, they are never in an upright position, but squat down on their haunches, in this manner throwing their bodies forward and resting upon their hands and toes when grappling with each other. The tussle ends when one has forced the other outside the ring made by them at the beginning. These happy Japs contributed largely to our amusement during these monotonous days in mid-ocean.

On the thirteenth day out from Yokohama, we sighted the Sandwich Islands, and on the same day cast anchor in Honolulu. This shore presented an agreeable change of scene after being at sea nearly two weeks, with naught but the wide ocean in view and the salt air for a tonic. After the officers of the port had boarded our vessel and gone through the usual formalities according to law, the passengers were put ashore in a steam tender, and the vessel remained in port thirty-eight hours to discharge her cargo and leave the Japanese emigrants. This brief time was occupied to a good advantage in taking in the sights of this tropical city and its nearest surroundings.

Honolulu is the capital of the island group, and the residence of King Kalakaua, the reigning monarch. It has a population of about 15,000, many of whom are foreigners, consisting of Americans, Germans, English and Chinese, and the business is almost entirely carried on by foreign houses. It is a lovely city, the tropical shade trees and the luxuriant foliage in the gardens and climbing about the verandas of the houses, adding much to its beauty and attractiveness. It is built on a gentle incline at the mouth of the Valley of Nuuanu, and has for its background a long range of picturesque hills, of the most peculiar shape.

Though favored by nature in many ways, Honolulu has one of the poorest harbors which I visited. This is on account of the long stretch of barren coral reefs, which prevent heavily laden vessels from entering. They are generally anchored a mile from shore, and the cargo and passengers are transported in barges and tenders. It is a busy and prosperous place, owing its prosperity largely to enterprising Americans, and Claus Spreckles, the sugar king, is looked upon as a power in the land.

The briefest description of these islands would be to designate them as an interesting chain of mountains in the Pacific Ocean. In all there are thirteen, eight of which are inhabited, and the remainder uninhabited. All are mountainous, and chiefly of volcanic formation, occupying an area of 7,628 square miles. The entire population of the group amounts to about 85,000.

Hawaii, the largest of these islands, has an area double that of all the rest combined. It contains four volcanic mountains, the most interesting of which is Mauna Loa, 13,600 feet in height, with a crater 8,000 feet in diameter, and at the present time very active. Lack of time prevented me from visiting it.

These islands were discovered by Captain Cook, in 1778, over 100 years ago. He found the inhabitants a fierce and warlike people, many of them cannibals. He was at first received with a friendly spirit, but afterward met his death at the hands of a native. Much progress has been made by the people since that time through missionaries, and their intercourse with other nations ; and they have become Christianized and civilized. Just newly from Oriental cities and idolatrous scenes and customs, as I was, the first sight of Western civilization afforded a striking contrast ; the very air seemed different, and I breathed freer.

Lying in the tropics, between 18 deg. 54 min. and 22 deg. 2 min. north latitude, and 155 deg. and 161 deg. west longitude, these islands have a most salubrious climate, and the temperature is very even the year around. Frost is unknown, and tropical fruits of all kinds grow in profusion. Many consumptives and invalids from all countries visit these islands, and experience great relief. Honolulu and Naples have similar climates and similar attractions, and my impressions were that these two places would be the loveliest winter resorts in the world, excepting our own coast resorts, such as Monterey, Santa Barbara, San Luis Obispo, Los Angeles and San Diego.

We barely had time to drive to the Sugar Bluff. The Pali and sugar plantations are the first places generally visited by tourists, and the productions of the islands are as sweet as the climate. The following is the last letter of this tour, written for publication. It was mailed at Honolulu to the Modesto *Herald.*

LETTER FROM HONOLULU.

HONOLULU, March, 1886.

EDITOR HERALD:— As I have kept you posted about my movements from all the principal points in the European and Oriental world, I will now send you my last letter of travel, from the Sandwich Islands, which is the last point I will touch in my journey around the world. The Sandwich Islands are 3,400 miles from Yokohama, the last point I visited in Asia, and from that place we brought a cargo of tea, silk and porcelain; also 900 Japanese emigrants, who came under contract to work on the Spreckles sugar plantation for the next three years.

The first half of the trip from Yokohama to Honolulu was a stormy one. It is not often the Pacific belies its name, but our four-masted iron steamer Peking was partly covered up in the swells of the sea, that were moving like rolling mountains; but as we neared Honolulu and made a change of latitude and longitude, the storm abated, and the Pacific was again pacific, and we enjoyed a pleasant passage with a calm sea.

Honolulu is a busy and interesting city, made so by American enterprise, and the Sandwich Islands is one of the smallest countries I have visited in my whole tour; but it is the sweetest one, as the sugar fields extend in every direction.

I have yet to breathe the air of the salt sea for over 2,200 miles before I have accomplished the trip around the world. As I expect to see you in Modesto at an early day, I will not trouble any further with a long letter.

Yours truly,   OSMUN JOHNSON.

After our drive through the country, we returned to Honolulu, and re-embarked on the steamer, which was now getting ready to sail. We had

2,200 miles more between here and San Francisco, and I was becoming anxious to start toward home. Just as we were about to leave the harbor, a sad accident occurred within one hundred yards of where we lay. One of the boilers of the steamer Mariposa, belonging to the Spreckles sugar line, plying between San Francisco and Australia, exploded just as she was steaming out of the harbor, causing the death of three of her passengers, and wounding many more. I was an eyewitness to this sad scene, and almost within speaking distance. This steamer was said to be the fastest running between Australia and San Francisco, and over-crowding with passengers and freight caused the accident.

Shortly after this accident, we steamed out, homeward bound ; the panoramic ranges of mountains along the coast of the islands, covered with tropical foliage, were soon lost to view, and balmy breezes and a calm sea exchanged for blustering winds and a boisterous ocean.

We were now speeding away in the channels of American commerce, and stately ships of modern construction were continually hovering in sight, presenting quite a contrast to the clumsy hulks left behind in the Oriental seas. This voyage was devoid of anything of special interest or worthy of mention. On the 7th of March, after a voyage of eight days, we neared the California shore ;

THE CLIFF HOUSE AND SEAL ROCKS.

(392)

the seal rocks, the Cliff House and other familiar objects came in sight; and we soon entered the Golden Gate, through whose portals I had gone out less than a year before in starting on my journey around the world.

The cheerful thoughts which rushed through my brain, and the peculiar feelings of gladness and joy on this memorable day, can not be described. Suffice it to say, that there were thoughts of congratulation that this perilous circuit of 50,000 miles around the earth had been successfully accomplished, and that in less than one year's time; and there were also thoughts of gratitude to that kind Providence by whose care and favor I had been preserved from all danger and harm, and had thus been safely brought to my journey's end.

Within this short space of time the writer had been constantly in motion on land and water; had traveled on the most important and longest railways in the world, both above ground and underground; had sailed on thirteen of the largest steamers afloat, crossed the stormiest oceans and the calmest seas, sported on the most attractive lakes, rivers, bays and straits; and had been through the longest tunnels, including that under the River Thames and the great St. Gothard: he had traveled by nearly every method of locomotion known to man,—in Norway using the cariole, in Egypt the camel, in India the elephant, in Ceylon the buffalo, in

Venice the gondola, in Australia the two-wheeled hansom, in China the sedan chair, in Japan the two-wheeled jinrikishia : he had visited the largest cities, seen the greatest of the world's wonders, had drank from the cup of Nature, and fed upon the beauties of art ; had seen strange people and strange customs, heard strange voices and strange sounds, and had now returned to his own country and home a wiser and a wealthier man,—wiser because of the great amount of knowledge and experience obtained, and wealthier because wiser.

If, dear reader, the writer has in these pages been able to interest you with a description, brief though it may be, of his experiences and observations in his journey around the world, he will, he assures you, feel duly compensated for the time and expense required in the publication of this volume ; and, if there is therein contained that which may prove of service to the future traveler, the writer will heartily rejoice in that he has been able to contribute something, small though it may be, for the benefit and instruction of his fellow-man.

APPENDIX.

It is deemed appropriate to quote, in an Appendix to this narrative, extracts containing kind remarks and favorable mention of the local press, to the editors of which the writer has been known for over half a score of years, and whose favors he gratefully appreciates and hereby acknowledges.

There will also be added letters, not elsewhere appearing in this book, written by the busy traveler to the home papers from various points abroad.

FROM THE MODESTO, CAL., "HERALD," APRIL, 1886.

Mr. Osmun Johnson, who has been absent from Stanislaus County on a tour through the principal countries on the globe, returned home on Friday evening. His brief letters in the *Herald*, from various points on his travels, show that he is a man of observation, and that he notes things differently from most travelers. His last letter, written at Honolulu, appears in this paper, and now we all welcome him safely on American soil. His travels have been in all countries, England, Ireland, Scotland, France, Germany, Switzerland, Spain, Turkey, Russia, Greece, Sweden, Denmark, Norway, Italy, Egypt, India, Australia, Japan, China, Africa, and the Sandwich Islands. He arrived in San Francisco on Thursday last, and thinks California best of all.

.FROM THE "STANISLAUS NEWS," APRIL 5, 1886.

Mr. Osmun Johnson, a respected citizen of Stanislaus County, returned here last evening from an extended tour around the world, having during the time traveled over 50,000 miles, and visited all the different countries and the principal cities and places of note in each one. Mr. Johnson brings many curiosities with him; and, being a man possessed of excellent memory, he tells many interesting stories of his travels. Among some of the souvenirs that he has in his possession, are the photographs of many of the nobility of the different countries,— Gladstone, Prince of Wales and family, the Czar of Russia, Garibaldi, the King and Queen of Japan, and various others,—the most of whom he had the honor of seeing. He also collected specimens of all the foreign coins, and many other little trinkets too numerous to mention. One can not spend an hour more pleasantly than by listening to Mr. Johnson relate some of the details of his tour.

FROM THE OAKDALE, CAL., "GRAPHIC," MAY 10, 1887.

Among the visitors to Oakdale last Saturday was Mr. Osmun Johnson, a farmer living some eight miles from Modesto. Within the year Mr. Johnson has traveled extensively in the United States, in all the countries of Europe, in Egypt, India, Australia, China, Japan and the Sandwich Islands. He kindly showed a few friends some pictures, coins and other mementoes of his journeyings in far countries. Mr. Johnson is writing an account of his tour around the world, which he will give to the public by and by. We have no doubt it will be original and interesting. Mr. Johnson has a farm of some 2,000 acres, which he cultivates mainly in wheat, and has a number of blooded horses. He is a practical man. His observations abroad will no doubt have a direct bearing upon the every-day life of people, that can be understood and appreciated by his neighbors of Stanislaus and San Joaquin Counties.

FROM THE STOCKTON, CAL., "INDEPENDENT," APRIL, 1886.

Osmun Johnson, of Stanislaus County, who started in July last on a trip around the world, was in Stockton a few days ago. His travels have been in all countries,—England, Ireland, Scotland, France, Germany, Switzerland, Spain, Turkey, Russia, Greece, Sweden, Denmark, Norway, Italy, Egypt, India, Australia, Japan, China, Africa and the Sandwich Islands.

FROM THE MODESTO, CAL., "HERALD."

We give, this week, another letter from our European correspondent, Osmun Johnson. This time he dates his letter from Rome, and gives a lively history of his travels in the German States, Denmark, Sweden, Norway and Austria. He is now doing Italy, and will sail from thence to Turkey and Egypt, where he will again write us. We return thanks to him for a photograph of the Pope, and a little book of photographic scenes of the most attractive buildings and places of interest in the "Eternal City." The people of Stanislaus will read with interest what their representative farmer has to say about the foreign countries over which he travels.

LETTER FROM JAPAN, PUBLISHED IN THE KILBOURN CITY, WIS., "MIRROR-GAZETTE," FEB. 25, 1886.

The following letter was written to L. F. Anderson, near Kilbourn, by Osmun Johnson, now traveling in Japan. Mr. Johnson lived here with his father about twenty-six years ago, going to California, where he has accumulated a fortune in farming. He is now making a tour of the world. Mr. Anderson showed us a large photo of Mr. Johnson seated in a Japanese vehicle, the motive power being two Japs, illustrating the style in which he travels.

YOKOHAMA, Japan, Jan. 20, 1886.

FRIEND LAFAYETTE:—I am now traveling in Japan, the most interesting country on the globe. I am 1,800 miles nearer home than when I wrote you the last letter from China. In Japan I have been sight-seeing extensively from the mountains to the sea. From here I will sail in a few days to Honolulu and to the Sandwich Islands, the last country I will visit before I have accomplished the tour around the world. I expect to anchor in San Francisco the 25th of February, which will make my travels about 50,000 miles in all, including America, Europe, Asia and Africa, and Australia. And I have found the trip to be interesting as well as long. I have seen the largest mountains, the largest rivers and waterfalls, the largest oceans and inland seas on the globe, and have been visiting all the ancient images representing the heathen gods. I have seen, in India, China and Japan, thousands of ancient ruins, relics and religious curiosities. Being a stranger in strange lands, I have enjoyed the tour to the greatest satisfaction among the heathen as well as the Christian nations, and the information I have gained in this tour among all the different people on the earth, of their manners, customs and costumes, could not be exchanged for land or coin. I have just been visiting Nikko, one hundred miles north of Japan, the most interesting point in the whole country. There are forty-seven temples, stately and costly, ornamented with glittering bronze and brass, and immensely large images representing the heathen gods. In China and India I have been traveling largely in the sedan chair carried along by two heathens; but on this occasion I came in a little two-wheeled concern called "jinrikishia," which was drawn by two half-naked natives, bowling me along in good style at the rate of six miles an hour. In the night at the hotels there are no furniture nor seats; but I had to sit flat on the floor to eat my rice with two chop-sticks, and sleep accordingly. Together with this I will send you my photograph in the jinrikishia, a fair sample of how I have been traveling in Japan and China. When I get to Sandwich Islands, which will be the next country I will sail to from Yokohama, on the steamer "City of Peking," you may hear from me again. My best respects to all relatives and acquaintances. From your wandering friend,

OSMUN JOHNSON.

LETTER FROM HAMBURG TO THE MODESTO "REPUBLICAN."

EDITOR REPUBLICAN:—Since I landed in Europe I have traveled through Ireland, England and on the Continent, about 2,000 miles ; including France, Bavaria, Austria, Bohemia, Russia, the whole German Empire and Switzerland. I will only have time to name a few of the leading points of interest. In Ireland I found no snakes, but the Pats appeared to be numerous. In London, after paying my respects to John Bull, Esq., I rode under its five million of inhabitants on the underground railway, including the River Thames. I inspected some of the most important public buildings of London, among which were the Exhibition of Inventions, the finest in the world ; the Queen's Palace, the Tower of London, the statue of the Duke of Wellington, St. Paul's Church (one of the largest in the world), the Parliament House, Crystal Palace and Mark Lane Grain Exchange. In Paris, I visited the tomb of Napoleon Bonaparte, Place de la Concorde, the Grand Opera House (the largest theatre in the world) and the Louvre. The men and women of Paris have the strange custom of sitting at tables placed on the sidewalks, and unconcernedly sipping their wine, while thousands of people are surging around them on every side.

The main attraction in Switzerland is the lofty mountains and the huge glaciers. Berne is not a large city; but its ancient buildings and its high mountains make the place interesting to tourists. From Switzerland to Bavaria was but a step, as these little kingdoms and states are not much larger than Stanislaus County. From Bavaria I crossed the Alps into Austria. For about 100 miles these great mountain ranges surpass anything I ever saw in the way of grand scenery. Vienna is the finest city I have yet seen in Europe. It is located on both sides of the Danube, contains over a million of inhabitants, and is a great manufacturing centre. I inspected several factories here, including the extensive fan factory belonging to Mr. Grunbaum, a brother of our Modesto Grunbaum. He employs 300 operatives, men and women. He exports his faus to all parts of the world. Mr. Grunbaum very kindly showed me over the city, and pointed out to me the sights of Vienna. From Vienna I journeyed to Bohemia, thence to Saxony. Dresden, the capital of Saxony, has a population of about 100,000, and is the finest pleasure resort in Europe. It is like Monterey, in California, or Saratoga, in New York. There I met with people from every part of Europe and America, from an English lord to a plain, scientific American. The largest church in Dresden belongs to the English and American residents.

From Dresden to Berlin is only a few hours' ride. Berlin is about the size of Vienna, but built more in the American style than any city I have seen in Europe. The streets are wide and airy, the architecture is modern, and the mansions of the opulent citizens are stately and tasty, more than in any other city on this side of the Atlantic. There is a marked contrast between the broad streets of Berlin and the narrow, uncomfortable streets of London and Paris. A noticeable feature of this country is the small farms. They appear like door-yards when compared with California farms. Women can be seen all over the country, working in the fields. No farm machinery is to be seen anywhere in this country. Main strength and stupidity seem to be the motto in this realm. The largest team I have seen in the country was a spike team of three oxen pulling a plow. In one instance I saw a woman plowing with a team of oxen, also another woman hauling a load of hay with two oxen.

Since I have been traveling in Europe neither my body nor brain finds time to rest. I am continually in motion. In cities I am either traveling on tramways under ground, or on elevated railways above ground, and from one motion to another. I have to study new coins and new languages. In England it was shillings and pence; in France it was francs and centimes; in Austria it was gulden and kreutzers; in Germany it is marks and pfennigs. What is to come remains to be seen. When I get to the dykes of Holland and the Nile of Egypt, I may give you some items on irrigation, as I know you are so deeply interested in that subject. I will soon leave Hamburg for Northern Europe, thence across Russia to Constantinople.

Your well-wisher,
OSMUN JOHNSON.

LETTER FROM EGYPT TO THE MODESTO "HERALD."

In my last letter, sent you from Rome, I had scarcely space or time to give more than a faint description of my route and the sights which presented themselves in Europe, and, as I have been in all the leading cities in Europe, and the extreme length of sunny Italy, I must not omit giving a brief account of Naples, the most beautiful city in the world, with its fine climate and picturesque views, both from land and water. Naples, with its 600,000 inhabitants, is situated on the Mediterranean Sea, or Bay of Naples, and it is the most attractive city I have approached in my travels either in Europe or America. It has the most interesting surroundings. Around it are Mount Vesuvius—"the burning mountain," Capri, Mount Angelo, the Grotto and Pompeii. Mount Vesuvius was in volcanic eruption, with the appearance of red fire and of sulphurous vapors, and a noise underground. The ashes, stones and lava thrown out through this vapor were the grandest sight I ever saw. The leading attraction in the city is the National Museum, consisting of large statues of ancient heroes, sculpture, paintings, specimens of ancient coins, in gold and silver, and house utensils made of Pompeii material since seventy-nine years after the birth of Christ. In the gallery were many rooms in which were oil and landscape paintings, and pictures and inscriptions of every kind and in every style. There are also other museums in the city, large churches, fine public buildings, with flowing fountains, large statues on horseback, and sculptures. In fact, the city is crowded with curiosities of the past ages.

Life in the narrow streets of Naples is interesting to sight-seers. A large portion of the small trade and shop-work is done out-doors on the sidewalks, such as shoemaking and tailoring. They have many small boys in their employ who learn trades, and the streets are thronged with venders of wares. Dealers in produce of all kinds call out at the top of their voices the articles they have for sale, which makes the streets of Naples lively in appearance and produces a scene of confusion.

From Naples I resumed my journey to Brindisi, sixteen hours' run over a level and interesting country. There I embarked on a large Mediterranean steamer for Egypt. On this coast the sea was calm as a mill-pond, and the trip was more enjoyable than on the stormy Atlantic, the Baltic or the North Sea. On this ship were tourists from many parts of the globe, from an English nobleman to a Stanislaus farmer. The first country we approached was Greece. We passed the cities of Navarino, Zante, Candia and Ghazzi, and this was the last glimpse of Europe. I am now in the land of the Pharaohs. Here I have seen many interesting objects for a tourist to rest his eyes on. I am now about half-way around the earth. I have yet three more great divisions to visit—Africa, Asia and Australia—before I have accomplished my journey around the world.

I will write you again, from Hong-Kong.   Osmun Johnson.